SALLY

J. SCHLENKER

Bieke Publishing, LLC

To my husband, Chris, who encouraged me to write, and drove me around on weekends to research Sally.

To Sally Ann Barnes, 1858 to 1969.

Is the world constructed of atoms or stories? I think stories, but if it's constructed of atoms, then the atoms surely weave themselves into stories. There are so many stories, with lights still flickering that won't be dampened.

I embark upon a pilgrimage of sorts, not a pilgrimage to distant places to find answers, but on a pilgrimage exploring my own soil. As Dorothy tapped her ruby slippers and said, "There is no place like home," I too awaken to the realization that our roots provide our greatest and wisest vantage point.

Sally walked through these same woods that I now walk through. The most satisfying pilgrimage is finding those sacred places in our own back yard. This is a quest to awaken the spirits who once toiled, shed tears, laughed and loved here and to connect with them.

— J. SCHLENKER

INTRODUCTION

Sally was an enigma—not only to me, but to the people I heard talking about her while growing up. I met Sally only once, and it was brief. I was eight years old. The encounter, which is described in the Afterword, left a lasting impression on me.

Nigger Sal is what I first heard her called. I also heard the name *Nigger Nell* used in conjunction with Sally. I was told they were sisters. Decades later I found sisters was a polite way of hiding a birth of less than desirable circumstances.

Depending on who you asked, her name was Nigger Sal, Aunt Sally, Sally Erwin, Sally Bunzo or Sally Bonzo. Her first name was Sally or Sallie, possibly Sarah in the census. Her last name turned out to be Barnes.

And as for Nell—well, she *is* a mystery. I have a theory. However, I can't prove it because I know of no one left alive who knows the actual truth.

I spent three years off and on researching Sally's centenarian life. There was little, if any, paper trail. The further back I tried to go in time, the more the reports about her conflicted. Sally's existence, especially the first half, was shrouded in mystery. My investigation led me down a road—or rather a fork in the road—that said there were two Sallys. It was a challenge, on some days frustrating and on other days rewarding.

I have wanted to write Sally's story for years, but have struggled with the truth of what I was writing. I concluded the only way I could write it would be as fiction. I have kept a lot of the names the same, but the account stems from my imagination and the few tidbits of information I could obtain.

I've tried to keep Sally's dialect as it might have been. More than likely, most everyone's dialect would have been similar, but it would have made the story difficult to read. I've used some actual names and real documents. The letter written by John Brandon Erwin is copied exactly as it was written as are other pieces from the Knisely report, an Erwin family history I obtained from the Kentucky Historical Society. Also, obituaries from the Lewis County Herald are copied as is.

"*M*iss Sally, why are you sitting out here? Did you get lost?" the young nurse asked, shaking her head and scowling. She released the brake, gripped the handles and turned the wheelchair around, wheeling her to the opposite side of the room. The harshness in her manner reverberated through the metal of the chair. "Now, now. I thought I told you about this yesterday. You'll be just fine in this spot. This is where you're supposed to be sitting. It's for your *kind*."

The old woman slumped over by the weight of time, stiffened in the wheelchair, and raised her blood-flecked eyes. "Alice brought me out here. She went to get me a blanket. And then, she's gonna help me into my chair, the one with the purty pink flowers." She smiled as if temporarily forgetting her anger. "Pink's my favorit' color."

"Now, dear, you know that's not your chair. *That* chair is in the white folk's section," the young nurse said in a patronizing tone, sprinkled with disgust.

"So? I's lived with white folks all my life," Sally said with a strength that hardly seemed plausible for a one-hundred-

and-nine-year-old woman. She finished her statement with a smack of her gums.

"Sheila, it's all right. I moved her out here, and I'll take care of it," Alice said, rushing over, blanket in hand. Alice wedged the blanket under her arm and put one of her hands on the wheelchair handle next to Sheila's hand. She squeezed it so hard that her knuckles turned white. She bit her lip and counted to ten under her breath. God knows Sally didn't need a scene. Nor did she, as tomorrow was her last day at the care center. Sheila was her replacement. What in the world were they thinking? Sheila had the bedside manner of a fiery dragon, and sometimes the breath of one.

The two women glared at each other in a momentary standoff. Alice had no intention of backing down. She was older and more experienced and had nothing to lose. She was sure, although young, Sheila had been around the block enough to know she wasn't bluffing. Alice felt the tension releasing down her spine as Sheila loosened her grip and let go of the handle. She grabbed hold of the other handle before Sheila could reconsider.

Alice took a calming breath and mustered a smile. She motioned Sheila aside and said in a tranquil, quiet voice, so that Sally wouldn't hear, "The last time we tried to take her to the back, she became agitated and disoriented, and her blood pressure shot through the roof." Alice turned back toward Sally and smiled. Alice's voice returned to the louder than normal pitch she and the rest of the staff used when speaking to the residents, almost all of whom were hard of hearing. "Said, *If Rosa Parks wasn't gonna move from her seat to the back of the bus, she would not be segregated to the back of the nursing home. Said, She lived with white folks all her life. Shouldn't be any different now.* Isn't that right, Miss Sally? You have as much right to this chair as anyone."

"Yes'm," Sally said, smugly, smacking her gums. She had

no teeth left and refused to wear her false ones. They stayed in the cup on the nightstand by her bed.

The young nurse stepped back a distance, looking indignant, her arms crossed, her eyes narrowed. "Well, I guess. Just hope no one complains."

"No one has yet. And besides, it was white folks that brought her in," the older nurse said. The younger nurse stepped several paces back but continued to observe the situation. Daggers were no longer shooting from her eyes, but her arms remained crossed.

Sally moved a little in her wheelchair. "That be Ben. He be like a son to me. No, Ted. I forgot. Ben died. I outlived 'em all," Sally said, shaking her head and looking down at her lap the whole time. "Yes'm, it was Ted brought me here. I couldn't take care of him no longer. I didn't wanna come here, but he said it was fer the best." A tear rolled down Sally's cheek. "I took care of all of 'em since they was young'uns." Sally tried to raise her head but only managed a slight upward tilt of her reddened eyes, now permanently sagging with age.

"Go on," the senior nurse said to the young nurse. "I'll see that she's taken care of."

Still, Sheila stood there, unbudging, until Mac tapped her on the shoulder. "Sheila, could you go check on Mrs. Alberts?" the young orderly asked. "I tried to help her, but she needs your expertise."

Sheila's whole demeanor changed when she heard Mac's voice and saw his smile with those white sparkling teeth that glittered against the perpetual tan he kept year round. "Sure, Mac. I'll get right on it," she replied, her voice dropping to a Marilyn Monroe whisper. She walked away with a sway to her hips. Mac followed. He turned and winked at Alice.

"Mac to the rescue. No woman around here can resist Mac. He's a heart throb to all the young gals—and some of the old ones," Alice said, taking Sally's hand and resting her fingers on her pulse. "I hope you didn't let Sheila get to you. I think she gets to a lot of people. Anyway, she's new, and she's not used to colored folks, at least being treated like regular folks. It's ignorance, Sally. I hope you'll forgive her." Sally gave a barely noticeable nod, and Alice gave Sally's hand a soft pat before releasing it. "Your pulse is fine. You're doing great, sweetheart. You'd think me being older, I'd be the prejudiced one, but it's all in how we're taught. My husband's family was part of the abolitionist movement—something both he and I are proud of."

"I reckon."

"I looked at your chart. Saw the year of your birth listed as 1858. I bet you've seen a lot in your day."

"Yes'm."

"Are you cold?"

"A little," Sally said. The nurse put the blanket on Sally's lap. "Been through a lot worse than her."

"Yes, I'm sure you have. Here, let's wheel you over by the window and get you settled in that big chair of yours."

Alice looked at the empty chair. All the other seats were occupied. She wondered if the other residents were reserving it for Sally or whether they didn't want to sit there because it had been tainted by Sally. Ethel had told her the other day that one woman refused to sit in it because a nigger had sat there. She'd said, "I don't know. I guess when Sally dies we are going to have to fumigate that chair." Alice had always liked Ethel, but that statement set every nerve of her body on fire. She didn't want to believe Ethel had that kind of bent to her.

"Here we are, Sally." Alice set the blanket aside and lifted Sally out of the wheelchair, being careful of the thin, veiny skin of a woman of one-hundred-and-nine, settling her into her special chair. Even though the chair was bigger than normal, Sally's frail, hunched over body made it appear humongous. She reminded Alice of one of those little apple dolls, shriveled and bent, sitting there. Alice placed the blanket on Sally's lap. "You'll be in the sunlight. You should be warm enough." She paused and tucked the blanket into the edges of the chair. "Miss Sally, I was wondering. Last Sunday, a lady came to see you? She looked to be around my age."

"Why you wonderin' so much? You writin' a book?"

The nurse laughed. "You're still feisty for your age. I heard that about you. No, I wish I could write a book, but I'll leave that to my daughter. She's an English and literature teacher. It's her first year of teaching."

"Some says I's tough. Maybe so. I's had to be or wouldn't have made it this far. At least I got that way the more older I got." Sally paused. "That be Nell. She's my grand young'un. And, even if you was writin' a book, I couldn't read it. Ne'er learnt." Sally perked up. "Nell could read it to me. She always been a smart girl. I's so proud of her."

"No, I guess a lot of colored folks, even white folks your age, can't read. But I notice that you keep a Bible by your bed."

"Yes'm. Nell reads it to me when she comes. She don't come too often. She lives a far piece away. Has her own family to take care of, now. I got lots of the verses memorized. Ne'er went to school. But Nell, she be the educated one of the family." Sally said the word *educated* with both reverence and pride. "She's a school teacher, too, like your daughter, and a *Sunday School* teacher." Sally's whole manner took on a radiant glow when she talked about her granddaughter. She displayed a toothless grin and lost some of her slump. It was as if she gained a good inch in that chair.

"Sounds like someone to be proud of."

"Yes'm, named her after my grandmama. She be the first

Nell, the one who came to Kentucky with the Erwins." Alice's heart took a leap at the mention of the Erwins. "Nell, she kinda famous in her day. Known as the woman with six fingers on each hand and six toes on each foot."

"Oh, that is unique," Alice said, trying not to blow her cool while uttering a silent prayer, *Please, please, Sally, tell me more.*

"Yes'm."

"Some of the Erwins come to see you from time to time. Can't be the same ones. Must be some of their children?"

"Yes'm, their grand young'uns. And, they's all gettin' old." Sally laughed. "Like me."

"We are all getting old, Miss Sally. Did I tell you I'm retiring?"

"Yes'm."

"But, I'll be back to check on you. I promise."

"I's used to promises bein' broken," Sally said, losing the inch she had previously gained.

"Miss Sally, I mean it. I want to hear your stories. I would love to hear about you and your life with the Erwins and Ben and Ted," Alice said. Alice remembered a man—not the one who had brought Sally in, but another white man who came by and pumped Sally with all kinds of questions. Said he was a relative. Sally kept telling him she didn't remember. Alice had to pull the man out into the hall and ask him to leave. She asked Sally who he was after he left.

"Oh, he be the one Ben ran off a time back. He come 'round ax'n questions then, too," she had said.

Sally's attention drifted to the window. The snowflakes grew large and gained momentum. "Massa Erwin, he died durin' the Civil War. Was a heavy snow fell then, too."

"Did he fight in the war?"

"No, too old. One of his sons died in the war. Fought for the Union. John Brandon, like his papa, didn't think slavery was right. My own mama and papa died when I was just a young thing."

"I'd love to hear about your life, Sally."

"Not much to tell 'bout me."

"Now Miss Sally, I know that's not true," Alice said.

"I mostly looked after the young'uns. I took care of their child'ns and their child'n's child'n. I took care of a lot of young'uns durin' my lifetime. It's my favorit' thing to do. *Was* my favorit' thing to do. I love child'n. They so innocent. Why if I did become educated, that is if I's born in a different time, I'd probably be a nurse like you and take care of babies. I helped deliver 'em. I bet I delivered o'er one hund'erd babies or more in my lifetime. Can't count, either. But I know it was a mighty big number. Why if I close my eyes and imagine, I can still feel those babies in my arms and smell the sweetness of their little bodies."

"I think you would make a good nurse," Alice said and smiled.

"And I could tell if it gonna be a boy or a girl. There was signs. I could feel the mama's bellies. If the sweat had a sweet odor, I know it was gonna be a girl, but if'n the sweat had a salty feel and smell, I knew 'twas gonna be a boy. And there was other ways of tellin', but mostly I's just felt it in my gut. Hardly ever was wrong, except'n one time. It was twins—a boy and a girl." Sally gave a raspy chuckle. "My mama..." Sally's voice trailed off. "My mama, I remember she told me she know I was gonna be a girl. Maybe it was a gift—somethin' I got from her. I know my own baby gonna be a girl."

"So, you ended up with the Erwins after your parents died?" Alice asked, steering Sally in the direction of talking about her earlier life, hoping the Barnes connection might reveal itself.

"Nell and Ib and the Erwins was the only family I know after my mama and papa gone. As of late all those memories

7

from long ago start floodin' in. Sometimes they make me happy. Sometimes they make me sad. I close my eyes and see all they's faces as plain as day. And I 'member it like'n it was yesterday."

Sally closed her eyes and became still. Alice's heart leaped as she automatically reached for Sally's pulse. She was sleeping.

JOHN ROLLED over in bed and kissed his wife on the cheek. "Today's the big day. How does it feel?"

"Getting old? It sucks," she said. She tried to open her eyes all the way but could only manage a squint. "Did the alarm go off already?"

"Yes," he said. "You didn't hear it? You're getting the hang of retirement early. You slept right through it. And, by the end of this year, I can retire, and we can throw that damn clock out the window." Alice managed to open one eye all the way and groaned.

She sat up in bed and shuffled her feet around, feeling for her slippers. "I'll put on the coffee and pop some bread in the toaster, but come Monday, I'll be sleeping in, and you're on your own."

"I would have never dreamed you could be so cruel in retirement. I was expecting pancakes every morning after you retired," he teased.

"I thought we had this discussion," she said, sitting on the side of the bed. "You weren't going to be demanding when I retire. This is my time. You'll get your time soon enough." John laughed while his wife rolled out of bed and headed for the bathroom.

"I'm hopping in the shower," he yelled as his wife walked

down the hall on her way toward the kitchen. "Keep the coffee and my measly piece of toast hot."

Alice set the juice glasses down on the breakfast table just as John came back in from retrieving the newspaper off the porch step. "I'm worried about what will happen when I'm no longer there to look out for her."

"Sally?" he asked, looking over the top of his newspaper while putting the nub of his cigarette out in the ashtray.

"Yes, the new girl—she treats Sally like she's dirt." Alice took a sip of her coffee, warming her hands against the sides of the cup. She peered out the window. The snowflakes that were so pretty coming down were now sticking to the ground, making up for what had melted off yesterday.

"What's the new girl's name again?" He reached for another cigarette.

"Sheila," she said, while still gazing out the window. She turned her eyes back to her husband. "John, you said you would quit."

"I am, sweetheart. When I retire. I promise."

"You've promised before."

"I mean it this time. I really do."

"Those things will kill you," she said, with a steely eyed stare and pucker of her lips.

"Nothing's been proven. Besides, my doctor smokes the same brand."

"Do you mean the doctor you never go to?" Alice raised an eyebrow. John ignored her and looked back down at his newspaper. Alice let out a sigh and looked back out the window. "Do you think it will be a bad winter?"

"I don't know. Looks like it might be," John said, taking a peek out the window over his newspaper.

"I don't know if she can make it through a hard winter," Alice said, staring dismally out the window at the snow coming down.

"How old is she again?"

"One-hundred-and-nine."

"I can't even imagine being that old. In fact, I'm not sure if I want to even make it to that age. No offense, sweetheart, but I wouldn't want to spend the last of my life in a rest home."

"I feel old now, and none taken."

"Sweetheart, you don't look it." He laid his paper on the table and spread the margarine on his toast. "I hope you are not going to let retirement get you down. You have time now to work on that genealogy you've talked about for ages."

"Yes, I'm sure I'll be spending most of the winter in the library. But, from time to time I'm returning to the care center to check on Sally. How can I not, now? Besides, I promised her."

"I thought you might." John smiled. "You've taken such an interest in her. But that's you, Alice. One of the many reasons I married you. You care about people, the downtrodden people of the world. Why else would you be working at the care center instead of in a doctor's office or at the hospital where you would still be helping people but would be making more money doing it?

"You would be concerned even if you hadn't found out about the connection. Speaking of which, did you find out any more about the Erwins or why her last name is Barnes? Has she said anything?"

"She talked about them yesterday. I got so excited. Then she fell asleep. On the day I talked to the Erwin lady who came in to see Sally, I got shivers up my spine. I hounded her —no hounded isn't the right word—I discreetly persuaded her to talk about her family, trying not to seem too eager or give myself away."

"Oh, I'm sure you were casual." John laughed.

Alice furled her eyebrows. "Of course I was. You know

me. If anything, I was too much so. Maybe I should have been more aggressive, coming down on the woman, hard, like you do on the witnesses in the court room. I was laid-back about it. I didn't want to arouse any suspicions. Didn't want her to think I was prying into her family affairs."

"Yes, I know you. I think I know you *well* after thirty years of marriage," John said with a grin. "I know how you can get over enthusiastic about things and at the same time worry too much—such as worrying that people might think you are prying. I wouldn't call it prying at all."

"I worry about *you* and all that smoking you do. Not to mention how it stinks up the house."

"Sweetheart, give it a rest. I'll quit come retirement. Promise."

"Okay, okay. I *will* hold you to that."

"Oh, I have no doubts. Besides being a compassionate woman, you're also a persistent woman."

"I did get the Erwin lady's name and phone number. I told her I'd be glad to call her if there were any change in Sally."

"Sweetheart, she might not mind telling you about her family. You never know unless you ask. These things have to be approached right. You don't have to go about it in a roundabout or devious way. You should give her a call after you retire."

"I don't know. I'm afraid I'll say something to make her think something is up. When we walked out together that day, all she said was that Sally had always been a part of the Erwin family. A lot of people don't like talking about their family's past, especially when it involves owning slaves. I have no idea what the Barnes connection is. I wanted to tell her my maiden name was Barnes and ask her where Sally got the last name of Barnes, but thought, no, the timing wasn't right. I think I was more afraid of my deep dark secrets being exposed, more so than any the Erwins might have.

11

"Doesn't matter now. And for all I know, she might not have known the family history that far back. She looked to be somewhere in her late fifties or early sixties. Sally was born in 1858. That's what her file says. Just has the year. It's sad, isn't it? Not to even know your own birthdate? I wonder if Sally ever celebrated birthdays?

"Anyway, I won't see the Erwin lady again. How could I, as today's my last day? That is unless she just happens to come in sometime when I go in to visit Sally. And, of course at her age, who knows how many days Sally may have left?" Alice took a drink of juice.

"At least you got the Erwin woman's number. You didn't tell her you'd be retiring soon, did you?"

"No. That *wouldn't* have been smart, now would it?"

John laughed. "Give retirement a few days and when you feel comfortable with it and brave enough, call her. What can she do? Hang up on you? But, I doubt if that happens."

"I might. You know, Sally loves that big stuffed chair that sits in the main room. I moved it over by the window so she can look out. Sheila told her she shouldn't be sitting there. Can you imagine? Telling a one-hundred-and-nine-year-old woman she shouldn't be sitting in a chair because it's in the area where the white folks sit?"

"Too bad Sheila's not a man. It being your last day, I think I might come down there and punch her out for you, I mean *him* out for you."

"Well, I wish you would. Doesn't bother me she's a woman. She is kind of burly looking. Mac came along and saved the day."

"Is Mac the guy who works out? The one with the bedroom eyes?" Alice snorted a laugh.

"Yes. That's the one. All he had to do was brush up next to Sheila, and she melted like a schoolgirl with a crush."

"Ha."

"I think he's part Latino. But that doesn't bother Sheila. But, Sally being colored—that's a different story. I don't understand the way people think. Things have got to change in this country."

"Things are changing. It's January 1968. We're at the dawning of a new age. Look at all Dr. King is doing. Things are starting to get better. You'll see."

"You always were the optimist of the family, which is hard to believe after all you see in the courtroom. There is still so much resistance. People have such attitudes about color. Sheila's not the only one there that acts like that. She's just the most blatant about it."

"Change always takes time."

"Too much time. The Civil War was a little over a hundred years ago. You would think it hadn't ended."

He looked at his watch. "Speaking of time, I've got to get a move on. Sweetheart, you've got to quit worrying about Sally." John reached over the table, placing his hand over his wife's.

"I feel like I owe her."

"Sweetheart, you don't owe her anything but kindness. I know you didn't tell the Erwin woman your maiden name, but have you told Sally?"

"No, I don't want to spook her. She's too old and frail for that. On the other hand, she's got a will and determination that's as tough as all get out."

"I guess you would have to be willful and determined to have lived through what she has and to have lived as long as she has," he said. He gave his wife's hand a firm embrace before pulling away. "I've got to head to the office. I have a meeting at nine and need to get some work done before it. And, you better get ready. Don't want to be late on your last day." He finished up his juice, grabbed his last bite of toast and kissed his wife. "Bring me home a piece of cake since you won't be making me pancakes every morning."

"Why would you think there would be cake to bring home?"

"You've worked there for thirty years. I'm sure they'll send you off with a big bang."

"Don't forget to grab your umbrella by the door. The weather man said this snow may turn to sleet."

"Ah, you do care. It may not be pancakes. We'll work on that. I look forward to you looking after me in your retirement." He kissed his wife fully on the mouth.

"What was that for?"

"For being you. Because you care so much. Enjoy your last day and don't let Sheila get to you."

Alice set the dishes in the sink and climbed the stairs toward the shower. She paused and looked in the spare bedroom and said out loud, "Yes, this room will make a dandy office for working on family history."

2

"*O*h, there you are," the night nurse said as Alice entered Sally's room. "Big day for you today. Wish it were me that was retiring.

"First thing Sally asked this morning, before even getting her breakfast, was *where's Alice*. Said she had to tell you. What —I don't know. You wouldn't tell me, would you, dear," she said, giving Sally a wink. "The most talkative I've seen her since she's been here," she said to Alice as she grabbed her clipboard. "Here, let me take away the breakfast tray, and I'll be off. I'll see you tomorrow night, dear," she said, smiling at Sally. As she turned with the tray, she gave a sad turn of the lips, something common in a nursing home when saying goodbye to a resident that old.

"Guess I won't be seeing you again, Alice. So, I'll wish you good luck, now."

"Thanks, Pat," Alice said as Pat wheeled out the breakfast cart.

Alice touched Sally's frizzy white hair and wiped her chin that was sprinkled with gray wisps of hair where a piece of the egg she had for breakfast had fallen. "What is it you have to tell me, sweetheart?"

"You be wantin' to know 'bout my family. It played heavy on my mind all night. I told you 'bout the massa, how he died when the war was a goin' on. Last night, I dreamt 'bout how it was back then. It was all so real. Realer than this here bed. I miss all of 'em so much." Sally's tired eyes grew moist.

"I's don't know 'bout my own family 'fore the war. Only that they be slaves, and that it be hard. Folks don't like to talk 'bout the hard times. But the mistress come from a grand family and she talk 'bout it plenty.

"I's little when the mistress talk about how it was 'fore the war. The mistress had a fallin' out with her family 'bout marryin' the massa. That why they come to Kentucky. They try to make it work in Virginia, first. The mistress—oh, she be a proud woman. She didn't wanna leave that big plantation and start o'er. She always talkin' 'bout her family's fine plantation. But, the massa, he have a way with her. I seen he had a way with most women, not that he e'er strayed. I's just a young'un, but I know he had good looks and a silver tongue.

"Yes'm, it was 1819 when the mistress married the massa. It was after her mama died. I knows the story by heart. The missus tell it of'en 'nough. Yes'm, she threw out her mournin' clothes and instructed the slaves on that Virginia plantation to clean ever' nook and cranny in the house and make a big ole feast, somethin' befittin' a fine southern weddin'. Her eldest brother gave her away."

"No, I won't marry him. He's ugly and boring."

"It's that lowly clerk who made eyes at you last week isn't it? Don't think I didn't see you smile back at him. Elizabeth, what will people think? Such flirtatious behavior. We have a reputation to uphold."

"Flirtatious? Mother, you're living in the past. In case you haven't noticed we are in the eighteen hundreds, now. And *lowly clerk*? Really, Mother?" she exclaimed with a scowl. "John Leander Erwin is a successful merchant. Just because he works at a trade doesn't mean he's beneath us."

"I'll have you know I'm as fair minded as anyone. I can appreciate anyone who works hard. Our family works hard. We manage this farm and eighteen slaves. But you can certainly do better, Elizabeth. Entering into a marriage with your dear cousin would more than double this family's slave ownership. You would have an easy life."

"John Leander doesn't believe in slavery." The statement rolled off Elizabeth's tongue with pride. There were so many things she admired about John Leander that she found lacking in herself and her own family.

"John Leander, is it? Not Mr. Erwin?" Mrs. Dickenson huffed. "Of course he doesn't believe in slavery. That's because he can't afford to own slaves," her mother said, turning away from her daughter and wiping her finger along some dust highlighted on the table by the sunlight coming through the window. She looked at her finger in disgust. "I must bring this to our house Negro's attention."

"Oh Mother, you think everything is so black and white," Elizabeth said, before breaking into laughter.

"Now, what's so funny about this situation?" Her mother turned and glared at her daughter.

"I made a joke. Don't you think that's funny, Mother? It sounds like something John would say. He's so witty."

"No, I don't. I don't think this situation is funny at all. Your head has been turned by his good looks and charm. Do you think you are the only young girl that he has taken a fancy to? I'm sure there have been others before you. Maybe more than we care to know about. I dare to think of the man's past. After all, he's nearly thirty. Another thing to consider. The man's thirteen years older than you. He's probably left a trail of broken hearts in this wake. And if you're not careful, you're going to be one of them—another conquest. Probably keeps a list in that ledger I've seen him write in." Her mother put her hand up to her forehead. "Oh, God forbid, Elizabeth. Tell me it hasn't gone that far."

"Oh, Mother, you are so melodramatic. John Leander's not like that at all. He has all the respect in the world for me. He's only ever acted like a proper gentleman toward me, and I've never even heard him mention another woman." Elizabeth paused, adjusting the ruffle on her dress while contemplating her next words. "He's only waited to marry because he wants to make something of himself before settling down."

Her mother's eyebrows raised, and she took a step back. "Marriage? Settling down? He has spoken of marriage to you?" Elizabeth's mother shook her head. "This has gone much further than I had even imagined. Oh, Daughter, what have you been up to? That strong head of yours will get you into trouble. I rue the day. You are going to bring shame on this family, yet. And your fine cousin. What will he think?"

"Mother, the only shame this family bears is incest and slavery. Everyone marries a cousin in this family. It's a wonder no one is walking around with two heads and a tail after all the inbreeding." Elizabeth broke out into laughter. "I don't know what's come over me. Why I feel almost giddy today."

"And I feel faint. If there weren't so much to tend to, I might take to my bed," her mother shrieked. "I'll tell you what has come over you. You're a young, foolish girl—one who has had her head turned by the flattering tongue of a man almost twice her age. Now, your cousin, on the other hand…"

"I will not marry my cousin, and that's final," Elizabeth said, storming off.

"Do you want me to go after her?" Elizabeth's brother asked as he entered the drawing room. He let out a chuckle.

"No, no. What good would it do? And, why do you find this amusing? I'm at my wit's end with that girl. You can't talk any sense into her. At least not now. We'll wait until she cools down. She will be the death of me, an early death, mind you."

"Now, Mama. I do incline to agree with Elizabeth. Your mere opposition to her propels her forward in this endeavor. Young girls fall in love. They also fall out of love. Perhaps if you would ignore the situation, give her some time, you and she might be on more friendly terms?"

"In love? Elizabeth doesn't know what love is. And ignore the situation? If only her father hadn't died when she was an infant. Maybe she wouldn't be so strong-willed. I would have had more time to see to her. Managing this farm without him took a toll on this family."

"Now, now, Mama," her son said, resting his hands on his mother's shoulders. "She does have a mind of her own, you know. You should be proud. Willfulness can be a good thing. She takes it after you." He grinned.

"Well," she said, placing a strand of hair that had fallen out of place back into her bun, "it's almost time for dinner. Where's Sarah? Never around when I need her. And look at the dust on this table. Is that girl blind?"

"Could be, Mama. In case you haven't noticed, Sarah isn't a girl any longer. Could be losing her sight. Do you want me to fetch her?"

"No, no, I'll do it. I want to make sure she's preparing the roast right. Last time it was dry. Don't you think?"

"I thought it was fine. You're distraught over Elizabeth. Don't go taking it out on Sarah, or we'll get burnt potatoes to go along with a dry roast," he said with a hearty laugh.

His mother frowned.

"Now, Mama, only trying to elevate the mood a little."

Mrs. Dickenson walked out of the room in a rage, mumbling, "Like I said, that girl is going to be the death of me."

"JOHN, I don't know if we should go through with this."

"Elizabeth," he pleaded, raising her chin with his hand, looking into her eyes and following with a light kiss on her lips. "It will be fine. You will see. You love me, don't you?"

"Yes, of course, I do. But Mother is ill. Last month when she took to her bed, well, I…"

"I know. You blame yourself," he said. Elizabeth let out a heavy sigh. "Darling, it's not your fault."

"But almost a year has passed since we started courting, and still Mother's stance has not changed. And, my cousin keeps hanging around. Even on her death bed, she is pulling strings. I know she is behind him coming by so often."

"You're upset, and no wonder. You can't let your mother get to you. What happened to that strong-willed, want-to-take-charge-of-the-whole-state-of-Virginia girl I first met?"

A tear welled up in Elizabeth's eye as she lowered her head again. "I don't know. Sometimes, I think I've lost her. I might as well surrender to my fate and marry my cousin."

"Elizabeth, what are you saying? I would be forever heart-broken if you did such a thing. You cannot possibly mean this? No, I won't stand for it. I know that girl I first met is still in there." John raised Elizabeth's lowered chin up with his pinkie finger and winked with his blue eyes, one of the first features that turned her head in his direction. The second thing that drew her to him was his calm, reassuring voice.

―――――

"THAT MATERIAL WILL GO NICELY with your hair." Those were the first words he had ever spoken to her. She had been in his store on numerous occasions, but he had only glanced her way. So bold. She had been wavering between a gingham check and a cornflower blue. "And the blue in this material will definitely highlight your eyes," he had said, holding the edge of the material in his hand. He was standing so close she could feel his breath on the back of her bonnet. The whole conversation was quite scandalous for a store clerk. Her mother didn't hear the utterances he made as she was outside instructing their slave on the proper way to load the flour onto the wagon as some of their last purchase had spilled out on the way home.

"Why, Mr. Erwin, aren't you a devil," Elizabeth said, batting her eyelashes, exuding southern charm. He grinned. "My mother said to pick out whatever I want. Next week is my birthday."

"And what specific day might that be if I might ask?"

"February twenty-nine. I was born on a leap year."

"Oh, well you are a rare woman, indeed," he said while writing in his ledger.

"Sir, what are you recording?" Elizabeth stood on her tiptoes, trying to peek in the large, leather-bound book he held close to his chest as he wrote.

"Why Miss Dickenson, I'm recording your birthday. It deserves recording, don't you think? See here." He lowered the book so she might see. "A place of prominence, right

21

beside the entry for the new side saddle I got in only last week." He pointed to the shelf behind him.

Elizabeth looked up. "Oh, it's such a thing of beauty. Have you had any interest?"

"Some. But I have been debating whether or not I should sell it or keep it."

"Why would you keep it, Mr. Erwin? Why on earth would a man need a side saddle?"

"As a wedding present for my bride," he said, winking.

Elizabeth blushed and turned her head toward the door upon hearing her mother's voice. "So, Elizabeth, have you decided?" She looked back at Mr. Erwin to see his smile had become subdued, and his face had turned to all seriousness upon the entrance of her mother.

"Yes, Mother, I think I will go with this blue silk material," she said, once again looking in the direction of Mr. Erwin with a smile. She detected his own suppression of a grin.

"Hmm, good choice. Yes, this will do quite nicely," her mother said, as she picked up the material and inspected it before looking back in their direction.

Elizabeth noticed the double take her mother did upon seeing the expressions on both of their faces and grimaced a bit as her mother said sharply, "Mr. Erwin, I will send my son in to settle up the account."

"Yes, ma'am," he said. How polite, Elizabeth had thought at the time—not the words, themselves, but the way that he had said them. Yes, John Leander Erwin was the rarest of men.

Why was she even thinking about reconsidering? This man would always be an adventure. What would she have to look forward to with that cousin of hers? A humdrum existence. Oh, and the thought of kissing him. Her stomach turned inside out at the thought. On the other hand, the thought of kissing John Leander sent shivers up her spine.

No, there was no way she could end up with her cousin. She would turn into her mother, no less. She cringed. No, she wanted more out of life. Much more.

———

"ELIZABETH?" John pleaded, yet again.

"Yes, John, you are right. I will get her back—that head-strong girl you fell in love with."

"We will wait a bit longer. I know your mother is getting weaker. We won't distress her anymore."

"But, can you wait? She could have many months yet. And, then I must wear black for a year. Can you actually wait that long?"

"You are worth the wait, my dear Elizabeth."

3

"*T*he mistress say she and her mama make things right on her death bed. Her mama make sure that she an' Massa Erwin was gave a piece of property. Nell and Ib was part of that property, a weddin' present to 'em, 'long with Henry and Jacob. Her mama say she is to have four slaves should she and John Leander e'er 'cide to leave. Henry and Jacob took off when the war ended. So's I ne'er got to know 'em. As soon as they's be free, a lot of the slaves left, but Nell and Ib was loyal to the mistress right up till the day she died. That be 1895 when she died.

"After the massa passed, she depended on Ib and Nell more than e'er. Everybody always call him John Leander. The missus say that was what he was called in Virginia so as not to get him confused with another John Erwin in the area. The missus say he weren't a good sort, and it wouldn't be good to get 'em confused."

"Miss Sally, you have a good memory. Why, I sometimes can't remember what I did yesterday," Alice said.

"Sometimes I 'member those times that were so far away like they was yesterday. All the people—they be like ghosts that come to life. 'Specially as of late. I can look up, and one or more of 'em might be in the room with me, beckonin' me to join 'em."

"I hope you won't join them just yet. I, for one, would miss you."

"Aw, honey." Sally mustered the sweetest grin, her gums showing prominently.

Sally closed her eyes for a while before she opened them and spoke again. "John Leander weren't happy at all in Virginia. That's why they up and moved to Kentucky. If they hadn't, I's don't know what might've come of me. Course, they was all there a good bit 'fore I was e'en born.

"They didn't leave the plantation in Virginia till after 'bout ten years. Started a family first. The missus, like a good many women, lost babies, two of 'em. Nell and Ib made the trip with 'em, mostly on foot. All the slaves mostly walk barefoot in the warm months, but the missus sees to it all the slaves has good shoes made fer the trip, special ones for Nell. Nell always have to have special shoes made. Ib and Nell, just girls at the time.

"They loaded up two wagons and had a couple of mules and a horse to pull 'em. And they carried that side saddle from Virginia to Kentucky inside one of the wagons. Accordin' to the missus, John Leander could have sold it many times o'er, but no, he save it for her. She always have a big smile on her face when she talk 'bout that saddle and how she knew she would have it one way or the other that first day she spied it in the store. Massa Erwin say he gonna get the missus a fine horse when they's get to Kentucky. And, he make good on that promise. He buy her a grand white one.

"Took nigh onto three weeks to make the trip. Wasn't that far, but seemed like it at the time. Wouldn't e'en take a day to drive it in a car now. Oh, lawd. So much has changed since back then. An' then some hasn't, the way we's still get treated.

Maybe not so bad 'round here, but I see's the TV with the riots and all. An' I see's Dr. King on the news and how's he gonna make it all right. But, back to my story.

"After they get settled in good, and the child'n all grown, the missus start gettin' homesick fer back home. So, once again, they load up a wagon, and take Ib and Henry with 'em and go back fer a visit. The missus took her finest clothes and the white mare the massa gave her fer her birthday. Sometimes, the missus rode side saddle on that trip alongside the wagon they took. The missus had some fine jewelry, but nothin' she treasured more than that there side saddle. Nell always keep it polished up shiny fer her. The missus say a side saddle was the way of royalty.

"The massa gave her that white horse on her birthday. It was on her real birthday, the one that come on leap year. The missus always liked to brag that unlike other women, she only aged one year fer ever' four." Sally chuckled. "When her birthday did roll 'round ever' four years, we was all in fer a big treat. Ib and Nell worked fer days ahead, bakin' pies and cakes.

"Yes'm, times sure have changed, but I 'member Ib combin' the missus' hair. By the time I knew her, it was as white as mine is now. They say it were yellow back in her young days. The whole time Ib be combin', the missus be tellin' the story of how they crossed the mountains and braved the Indians, and Ib be rollin' her eyes 'hind the mistress's back while she be tellin' the story. Ib tell us when Missus Erwin not 'round there only be two Injuns, and all they's interested in was the deer they be a huntin'.

"But the missus, she tell her version of the story so much, I knows it by heart, just like I was there with 'em, e'en though I hadn't been born yet. And the way she related the Indian part, with arrows flying right by their heads, was much more excitin' than the way Ib related it, 'specially to a young'un, like me."

Sally took a pause and gave a little grunt.

"As I was sayin', one time they went back. Was the only e'er time they went back to Virginia to visit. The missus wanted to show off and prove how well she and John Leander had done. But, it all backfired on her. She ne'er much talked 'bout that visit. Oh, she put on a brave face and said how happy they was to see 'em an' all, but when she weren't 'round, Ib tell a different story. The family all but shunned her. Made her feel 'neath 'em. Maybe that why the missus always had a soft spot in her heart fer me. She knows what it like to be made to feel lowly. Sometimes she say, *we's all out here in this wilderness, together.*"

A smell pervaded the room. It happened often at the nursing home. Sally had talked nonstop, and Alice, so enthralled with what she had to say, had neglected to ask her if she needed to go to the bathroom. "Sally, here, let me help you to the toilet." Sally tried on her own to get out of the chair that was in her room. Alice grabbed hold of her arm, giving her the extra lift she needed. She got her settled on the commode and stood by the partly cracked door, giving her some privacy and dignity. It was a good fifteen minutes before Sally was ready to get up. Alice wiped her like a mother would wipe a baby and helped her with her dress.

Sally only ever wore a dress. Said she never wore pants. Something wasn't proper about it. The nursing home fitted her with a loose smock dress, something comfortable for Sally, as well as for the nurses who worked there and the doctor who visited the patients once a week. Alice washed her own hands and helped Sally with hers, before helping her into her wheelchair. Her head slumped as she closed her eyes. Alice watched Sally slumber for a moment. She instinctively checked her pulse at such moments but could see Sally's chest heaving up and down.

Alice looked up to see Ethel in the doorway. "Aw, there you are. I figured you would be in here. I hope you didn't forget lunchtime?" Ethel had a big grin on her face. "Wanted to make sure you remembered what time it was." Ethel had never announced lunch to Alice before. But, then, today was her last day. More than likely there was a potluck waiting for her in the cafeteria. And a cake. John was right. No one retiring here ever left without a cake. She hoped Sheila wouldn't be there. At the same time, she was both shocked and elated that Sheila had offered to take over her duties today. That gave her the entire day to spend with Sally. Either Sheila wasn't so bad after all, or she made the offer to get out of fooling with Sally, herself.

"Let me find Mac to help Sally with lunch, and I'm on my way," Alice said.

4

"*M*iss Sally, I brought you something," Alice said as she entered Sally's room. Sally sat in her wheelchair facing the window. Alice patted Sally's thinning head of hair that resembled cotton with one hand and held out her offering with her other hand. "Do you like cake?"

"Yes'm. Aw, chocolate," Sally said, smiling. "Chocolate's my favorit'."

"Mine, too."

"Once, Coon brought me a whole box of chocolate-covered cherries. He hear'd I's sick and thought they might cheer me up."

"Did they?"

"Yes'm."

"Who was Coon?" Alice asked, thinking Coon might be one of the Erwins or possibly a Barnes.

"Did I say Coon? No, I meant Blink. Coon was Blink's daddy. Coon's son worked for Ben and Ted when he was a boy. Farm chores. They always stayed close friends. But this was long after he was a man. Ben told him I's in a poor way.

Said he saw those chocolates and just had to get 'em fer me. Said they reminded him of all those cherry cobblers I's used to make."

"That was nice of him. I thought he might be one of the Erwins."

"No," Sally said bluntly. She took hold of the fork and in slow motion put a bite of cake in her mouth.

Alice watched as Sally churned the cake around with her gums. Sally had perfected eating without teeth, although aesthetically it wasn't the most pleasing thing to watch. A lot of the patients had to be spoon fed, but surprisingly, Sally ate most days on her own. Those days were getting fewer, though. After two more slow bites, she pushed the plate aside and looked up at Alice. "I believe I'll save the rest fer later."

"It's a lot of cake," Alice said. "I could hardly finish my own piece. I'll wrap it up and leave it in the refrigerator in the kitchen and put your name on it so no one else will eat it." Sally smiled, spreading her lips wide—lips that were milky white against her pink gums. The sad truth was that upon seeing Sally's name on it, and with several bites missing, Alice knew no one would touch it.

"You were telling me about Elizabeth and John Leander," Alice reminded Sally, hoping she hadn't tired of telling the story.

"Yes'm."

"I'M GOING to end up like my father if I don't do something, Elizabeth," John Leander said. He sat on the edge of the bed, staring down at the floor, his head resting in his hands.

"John, that's not true. You are nothing like your father. You are a hard worker."

"And, what has it got us? We've been on your family's

farm for ten years now, almost eleven. This is not what we planned. We had such big dreams when we first married. Do you remember those dreams, Elizabeth?"

"John, John, we can persevere. I know you have been in a state of melancholy as of late, but it will pass," his wife said, placing her own hands over his. She gazed into his blue eyes. The wrinkles around them showed more than ever, but the sparkle emanating from those eyes still shined through.

"I won't keep living with your family. I feel like I'm getting handouts. I've always been an interloper here, and always will be."

"John, you are a proud man. I admire you for that. But, look what you've accomplished. You have a fine business. What are you suggesting? That we move to town? Close to the store?"

"No, Elizabeth. Not at all."

"Then what, John?"

"Land is for the taking in Kentucky."

"Kentucky? Aren't there Indians?"

"Some, but most are friendly."

"John?" Elizabeth pleaded while rubbing her fingers through his hair.

"I thought this was what we wanted, Elizabeth? To have our own place."

"But we do."

"No, not a measly hundred acres partitioned off to us, like we were tenants."

"We're not tenants. Mother made it known on her death bed that we would have this land for as long as we live, and that it will go to our children. And, my brother promised it would be so."

"This will always be your farm—your family's farm. Your brother's farm. We have one hundred acres now, only out of your brother's kindness. And nothing on paper. And what

J. SCHLENKER

about our own children? Between your brother's children and our own, each parcel of inheritance becomes smaller. Do you want that for our children, Elizabeth? I don't. I want something I can call my own. Something to leave to my offspring.

"I've kept my ears open in the store. People are moving west. The government is offering land grants in Kentucky. Free land to anyone who served in the Revolutionary War. Not much, but we can buy more, a little at a time, as we can afford it. We could have a farm—as big as two thousand acres."

"I don't know, John," Elizabeth said, shaking her head. "We are getting older. What about the children? It would be hard to uproot them."

"We can do this. The children would love it. It would be a grand adventure for them. The land grants are available for the taking. We only have to prove we want to farm. We could raise tobacco like we do here. And our children would have something—a good future. They would own their own land. Having land is everything, Elizabeth. You know that."

"It's risky."

"Wasn't marrying me a risk?"

Elizabeth smiled and let out a heavy sigh. "You have me at a disadvantage there."

"Elizabeth, if you do this for me—for us, I promise I will make it work. It will be hard at first, but *I will* keep my promise."

"I can see you have your mind made up, John Leander. I know there is no arguing with you when you get this way. Tell me, how can we pay for this? The land might be free. But, there will be other costs. How will we build? We have no slaves to call our own. I know how you feel about slavery. The four slaves my mother said we were to receive on her death bed work for us in name only. We have never gotten it

32

in writing. You know my brother when it comes to such matters. I have brought it up to him on numerous occasions, and he always shrugs the issue off, saying we will attend to it later."

"The store has done okay. I've managed to save a little. We could hire hands."

"Are we to pack up the family and head to God knows what?" She walked away and looked out from their bedroom window. "This is all I've ever known, John. Am I to leave my fine dresses and become a pioneer woman?"

"I will see to it that you have the finest silks and a fine horse, one befitting your fine side saddle. You said you always wanted a white mare. I'll see that you get one."

"John. Oh, John. I do have the same desires as you. There is a part of me that wants to leave. Still, this is all I've known. I grew up on this farm. I don't like it that all the land was bequeathed to my brothers. I don't like answering to my sisters-in-law. But, living here is safe."

He walked over to her, placing his hands on her shoulders. "I know, Elizabeth. It will be hard at first, but eventually you can have your own grand house. You will be the mistress. Everyone will answer to you." Placing her hand over his, she turned her head. He paused and winked. "Even me."

Elizabeth's heart did a slight flutter. "After all these years of marriage, how do you still have this power over me, John Leander?"

"We can't wait any longer. Neither of us is getting any younger. You said it yourself. Although you don't look a day older than when I married you," he added with a smile. "Elizabeth, if you take this leap with me, I promise I will make us a good home—a good life. We'll have something we can leave to our children."

She turned back toward him, standing in a meditative

pose. She saw the desperation in his eyes—in his whole manner. She knew the situation had become more on his mind with each passing year. The loss of two children had taken its toll. They had four fine boys though, and she was pregnant again. She placed her hand over her bulging belly.

"John Leander, you've been a good husband to me, and a good father. I owe you this. Yes, all right. We will do it."

John grabbed his wife by her pregnant waist. He lifted her off the ground and kissed her with a passion she hadn't experienced in years.

"Oh, John, if I had known moving from my family's place would have evoked such a reaction in you, I would have suggested it myself."

"Of course, we can wait until the child is born before we depart."

"All right, John." She let out a sigh and straightened out the kinks in her dress. "We will start making plans to leave."

———

"IF YOU MUST DO THIS, Elizabeth, I will provide what you need." Her brother placed the documents that gave her full ownership of the slaves on the table before her.

She looked at the names on the paper and read aloud, "Nell, Ib, Henry, Jacob." She paused and looked back up at her brother. "Dear Brother, these are not the same slaves we have now. I know these slaves. They are not much more than children."

"Elizabeth, it will be planting time soon. I can't part with the others. You will have to take these or none at all. Mother only said you were to have four slaves. She didn't specify."

"But, Brother?"

"These slaves will do nicely. They are young and healthy and easily amenable to your wishes. Besides, that husband of yours, if he had his way, would venture into the wilderness with none at all."

"Yes, John Leander is a proud man." Elizabeth bit her tongue lest she should say anything to anger her brother into withdrawing the slaves listed. She hung her head, avoiding eye contact, and swallowed her pride.

"Now, now. Be of good cheer. These slaves will be fine. I won't let it be said that I sent my own sister and her family out in the wilderness with no protection."

"I thank you, Brother," she said in a muted tone. She took the papers from the table, careful not to smudge the drying ink, and gave him an embrace.

"So, when will you go?"

"John says early spring."

THE WAGONS SWELLED with ten years of the family's accumulations, what they could fit in. Elizabeth held Eliza, their newest addition, in her arms, and looked out in all directions over the land she had known all her life before handing the baby off to Ib. She climbed aboard and settled down on the wagon seat beside Henderson, their youngest son.

It was a cool spring morning when they said their good-byes. The two mules were hitched to the larger wagon, the horse to the smaller one. John Leander with a final wave of his hand and tip of his hat climbed aboard beside his son and took hold of the reins.

The four slaves with tearful eyes hugged their relatives with solemn faces. Henry climbed aboard the seat of the smaller wagon, taking the reins. Ib sat beside him, holding the baby. Thomas, the oldest, who was ten, along with his younger brothers, Robert, seven, and John Brandon, six, followed on foot behind the wagon. Jacob and Nell walked behind. All the slaves had new shoes specially made for the journey. Elizabeth craned her head around and shouted from the front wagon, "Now, Nell, you take good care of those shoes. You know I had to have them made special because of your extra toes."

"Yes'm. Thank you, ma'am."

John stopped the lead wagon at the edge of the plantation property. He leaned over and kissed his wife. "For good luck," he said.

It was slow going on the first day. After nine hours of travel, only taking breaks for lunch and water when they came to streams, and with the boys taking turns on the wagon beside their father, they made it to a grove of birch trees where they made camp. By John's estimation, they were still inside of Russell County. On the second day, they picked up some speed and crossed the Virginia border and made it to Piketon before nightfall.

By the third day, the boys had grown tired of walking, and John handed over the reins to Thomas for long periods of time, giving the younger boys room to squeeze in beside their mother. With an early start, they made it to Prestonsburg. While there they came upon the home of Samuel May, a Kentucky State Senator.

"John, we should stop."

"Stop? Why?"

"Why to pay our respects, of course," Elizabeth said with a soft voice and a nudge to his side before turning her head once again to admire the fine house beyond the trees.

John stared at her backside, noticing that her posture had become more erect, her comportment more in line with the girl who had stolen his heart that first time he laid eyes on her in his store. She reached back a hand, straightening a strand of hair that had fallen from her bonnet.

"Elizabeth, you're sure about this?"

"Why yes, John. It's the only decent thing to do, pay our respects and all. And besides, I'm so tired of all the dust and wilderness. Bring the wagon to a stop over there by that grove of trees," she commanded. "I'm sure they'll be gracious enough to offer us a place to freshen up. Boys, come here. You see that house in the distance?"

"Yes, ma'am," Thomas said.

"I want you to be on your best behavior. Thomas, use some spit and slick back your hair and help your brothers look presentable. Oh, and take your kerchief and wipe the dust from your shoes. Henry, Jacob, you help them. Nell, Ib, you help me. Get my best dress, the black silk one, from the trunk in the wagon and hold up some blankets while I change."

"Elizabeth, you're going to a lot of trouble," John said, leaning back in the wagon.

"John, after I change, you should put on your best outfit," she said, placing her hand on his leg in a flirtatious manner.

"Well, you always were the boss of the family," he said with a wink.

Within a half hour, they pulled the wagons up within fifty feet of the house. A servant ran out to greet them.

"Does you have an appointment with the massa?" the black man asked.

"No, we don't. We're traveling through," John Leander said.

"This is John Leander Erwin, my husband. And, I'm Elizabeth Dickenson Erwin, his wife. You might have heard of us —the Virginia Dickensons?" Elizabeth said with an authority in her voice while waving her fan.

"No, ma'am, can't say as I has," the black man said, taking off his hat and scratching his head.

"Well, of course, you haven't," Elizabeth retorted. "But,

I'm sure your master has. We have traveled from Russell County, Virginia."

"Well, yes'm that is where the massa is from," the black man said.

"What's your name?" Elizabeth inquired.

"Henry, ma'am," the man said.

"We have a Henry, too." Elizabeth pointed to Henry and he gave a nod. "Is your master home?"

"Yes'm. He be home."

"Might you announce us then? Being from the same county in Virginia, we must stop and pay our respects."

"Yes'm. Follow me, if'n you please." Henry took off on foot, and John drove the wagon slowly behind him and stopped in the front of the house.

Elizabeth leaned in close to her husband and whispered, "See, dear. Family breeding matters."

"Elizabeth, I do believe you could talk your way into any situation," he smiled. "But then, what was the man to say, being a slave, talking to white folks?" Elizabeth sighed and even though the day was cool, continued to wave her best fan, trimmed in lace. "But, I commend your efforts. It will be good to take a rest from this hard wagon seat."

Henry disappeared around the back of the house. In a matter of minutes, a man appeared in the front doorway. He made his way to the wagon. "Samuel May," the man said, extending his hand toward John.

"John Leander Erwin, sir. And this is my wife, Elizabeth, and these are our sons, Thomas Jefferson, Robert, John Brandon, and Henderson. And these are our slaves...." He felt Elizabeth's sharp nudge to his side and glanced up to see Senator May's bewildered expression. "Our servant, Ib, is holding our youngest, a daughter, Eliza."

"A mighty fine family, sir. I hear you have traveled from my own county."

"Yes, sir."

"Will you be settling in this area?"

"No, sir, headed for a place called Greenup County, Kentucky. Plan on starting a tobacco farm there."

"Yes, I know it. Not as mountainous as this region, that is if you find the right spot. You should do well there. The land is pristine, and there is a lot of money to be made in tobacco."

"I'm hoping it will be so, Senator May," John said.

"Won't you come in? You must dine with us."

"Oh, we couldn't impose," John said with a shake of his head. He felt Elizabeth's sharp elbow.

"Why nonsense, sir. I can see you are weary from the road. And, I'm eager to hear of news of Russell County."

"Well, that we can give you, kind sir," Elizabeth chimed in, lest John should say any more to dissuade their stay.

"The Dickensons, you say?"

"Yes, might you have heard of our family?" Elizabeth asked.

Senator May rubbed his fingers through his beard and squinted his eyes, looking off into the distance. "Yes, yes, I believe I know of the Dickensons," he said, as he led them onto the porch. Elizabeth and John crossed the threshold of the mansion behind the senator.

"Henry," Master May called out. "Take their wagons to the back. Make sure their horses and slaves are tended to."

"Yes, massa."

"Ib, you take the children with you. I'll summon them later," Elizabeth said, not breaking her rigorous waving of the fan.

"Yes, ma'am."

"Henry gave us a bit of trouble when we first got him. The lashings proved to work." John winced. "Do your slaves give you any trouble?" the senator asked.

"No, sir. We've been most fortunate. We've never had to

whip our slaves."

"Well, then you are a lucky man, Mr. Erwin. I see that your slaves are young."

"That they are, Senator May," Elizabeth said. "We hope to acquire more when we arrive in Kentucky."

"Only to get started," John Leander added.

"You will need them, starting out fresh. And, I dare say you will need them if you are to be successful. If it weren't for slave labor my family and I wouldn't have this fine house."

"It is fine, indeed," Elizabeth said, casting her eyes in all directions. "I hope we can build as fine a house."

"I would be happy to give you a tour after dinner. There are only six rooms, but I take great satisfaction in them."

"You designed them, yourself?" John Leander asked.

"Yes, indeed, sir."

"Your parlor is quite large," Elizabeth said, looking around.

"Yes, ma'am. Eighteen by twenty feet. We often use it as a community hall. I'm afraid we've had frequent Indian attacks. It serves as protection for the rest of the community."

"Oh, dear," Elizabeth said with an alarmed look.

"Now, don't you fret, ma'am. We haven't had any trouble for a while."

"Oh, well, that is indeed good to know, sir."

"My wife will be down for dinner, shortly. She is taking a rest at the moment."

"The dinner invitation is most gracious of you, Senator May, and we look forward to meeting Mrs. May," Elizabeth said.

"Nancy," Senator May called.

A girl, no more than ten appeared in the doorway.

"Nancy, won't you show our guests where they can

freshen up."

"Yes, massa."

——————

"WHERE YOU BE FROM?" one of the black boys asked John Brandon.

"We come from Virginia, Russell County," John Brandon said.

"That where the massa is from. Has you seen any Indians on your travels?"

"No," John Brandon said. "Do you reckon we might come upon some?"

"Oh, they's plenty 'round."

"Are they friendly?" Thomas asked. John Brandon's eyes, along with his brothers, got big.

"Some are. Some ain't. Mostly, they's just hunt in Kentucky."

"Sampson, get the boys some water from the well," Henry said.

"Yes, Henry."

"And when you's done, take my shirt in to Nancy, and ax her to mend it. I's done tore the sleeve on a fence this mornin'. Won't do for the massa to see it, as he gave it to me only last week." He removed his shirt. John Brandon let out a gasp.

"What's wrong?" Sampson asked. "Your daddy don't whip your slaves?"

John Brandon looked at him and staggered back. "No, never has."

Henry reached for an old muslin shirt hanging on the barn post.

Nancy appeared at the door. "Your mama say it time to come up to the big house for dinner."

"Sampson, give that there shirt to Nancy." She reached for it, eyeing the visitors.

"Follow me," she said.

"Nice to meet you, Sampson," John Brandon said as they left.

"Likewise," Sampson waved.

"OH, you will face hardships. Taming the wilderness, if one can actually tame something so contrary to being tamed, is beset with problems," Senator May said as he passed the boiled potatoes to Elizabeth.

"I'm determined to give it my best try," John Leander said.

"We are certainly inspired by all you've accomplished here, Senator May and Mrs. May," Elizabeth said, eyeing her surroundings with a satisfied smile.

The following morning, the smell of bacon and biscuits drifting up the stairwell into their room was enough to rouse the boys from the hard floors of the May house but not enough for Elizabeth and John, curled up beside each other on the feather mattress. But, with the first light of day, they were saying their farewells and thanking the Mays for all their gracious hospitality.

John Leander cracked the reins. "Are we ready for our next destination, Paint Lick Station?"

The fourth day wasn't to be as hospitable as midway they encountered a band of Indians. Arrows whipped by their heads at one point. At the very moment John Leander reached for the gun he kept behind the wagon seat, fate intervened. The Indians spied a herd of deer, which appealed more to them than the scalps of one small group of travelers headed northwest. Elizabeth, though, would make the story much more threatening in later years than it actually was.

The next day, John Leander snapped the reins with a determined fierceness to distance themselves from any Indians. They stopped before nightfall and camped between two creeks.

SALLY GREW SILENT. Alice watched as her eyes closed. She sat beside her, listening to a slight snore and watched the steady rhythm of her chest rising and falling. Without warning, her eyes opened, and she continued, leaving the last part of the journey a mystery.

"They's finally arrived. The missus say she know it was all worth it when she saw the look in her man's eyes as he surveyed the land. Say he stood there for the longest time, ponderin' all those hills and fields that was his own.

"Yes'm, I's know the feeling. Many a mornin' when I make's my way to the garden to hoe, and it just me and the land, I's feel God all 'round me and all through me. So, I's imagine what the massa and mistress feels when they's see all that land that lay 'fore 'em."

"THIS IS OURS?" Elizabeth asked.

"Are you pleased?"

"Yes, husband, I'm pleased." Elizabeth looked out from the hill where they stood. There were beautiful rolling hills for as far as the eyes could see.

"We will commence with two slave cabins first, and a small cabin for ourselves before starting on our house. I have sent word to Mr. Barnes as to my intent to enter into a contract with him for our labor needs."

Elizabeth squeezed her husband's hand. "I know how you

feel about this, John. But there is no other way. Winter will be upon us before we know it, and we have our work cut out for us. Slaves are our only hope. Henry and Jacob won't be enough to do such heavy labor. Nell will work out in the fields along with the men. She's a strong girl, big for her age. Ib, I need by my side. She's best with the children." She sighed. "I don't like Mr. Jesse Barnes any more than you do. When I saw you off in the distance talking to him, the mere sight of him, even afar, sent something crawling up my flesh. As far as slave overseers go, he is one of the worst. Not the worst, mind you. I've seen my share in Virginia. But he will see that the job gets done and that we have a garden in place and a proper roof over our heads before winter sets in."

John Leander grasped his wife's hand and squeezed as they gazed in reverential awe at the work that lay before them and the possibility of it all, but mostly their eyes took in the beauty of the untamed wilderness that now belonged to them.

AN ORDERLY WHEELED the dinner tray in. Alice looked at her watch, the word Timex written on the face, the new one her co-workers had presented her with at her retirement luncheon.

"Oh, my," she said. "I have to get home. John and I have a date, tonight." She got up from her seat and kissed Sally on the cheek. Both she and Sally jumped upon hearing a loud clang. The orderly almost dropped the cover he was lifting off the plate.

"I promise, Sally. I'll be back as soon as I can. Thank you for telling me your stories."

Sally's ashen lips broke into a wide smile.

5

"*C*arried this around all day for nothing," John said, as he came through the door and put the umbrella back in the stand. "So, tell me, how did it go today?" he asked, kissing his wife.

"There are a couple of pieces of cake in the refrigerator for later," she said with a wink.

"See, I told you so. Get any going away presents?"

Alice held up her arm. "A watch," John exclaimed. "Now, who would have thought of a watch as a retirement gift?" He laughed. "In another six months maybe I'll get a matching one."

"I doubt if your firm will get you a Timex. I think they can afford something much more expensive. A Rolex, perhaps."

"Yes, you're right. But, it's the thought that counts, and I know you will treasure that watch."

"Yes, I will. The people working there barely make anything. Giving me this watch was extremely generous of them. I also got this beautiful scarf." She pulled it off from the back of the living room chair.

"From Sheila?" John asked.

"Aren't you the funny one? So funny, that I will listen to your jokes over dinner."

"Not so funny. It's because you retired that Sheila got her job. She owes you."

"I don't think Sheila feels she owes anyone. It's from Ethel."

"That was nice of her. I hope she spent her husband's money on it."

"John?"

"Oh, nothing. Well, I'm starved. What's for dinner?"

"What do you mean? You said you were taking me out tonight to celebrate my retirement. You didn't forget, did you?"

"No, I didn't. I was kidding. I thought we might drive into Cincinnati and do it up right, have wine and everything. I made reservations at the Maisonette. You can wear your new scarf."

"The Maisonette. Wow. You are going all out. Will you be spoiling me in my retirement?"

"You deserve some spoiling."

"The perfect place to celebrate the other present I got today."

"Oh, yeah? What?"

"It's a surprise. I'll tell you over dinner."

"HAPPY RETIREMENT." John brought his glass of wine up next to his wife's. "So, what is this other present you have to tell me about? I hope it's not from that hunk, Mac. I don't have anything to worry about do I?"

"No, nothing like that. Sally was waiting for me this morning. Couldn't wait to tell me more. Can you believe it?"

"That's fantastic. Have you learned anything interesting?"

"It's all interesting. Tomorrow before I go see her I'm stopping by the store first to get a notebook. I have to start writing it down. I don't want to forget anything."

"Tomorrow? Tomorrow is Saturday. And, besides, you're retired now."

"Yes, yes, I know, but Sally's on a roll. And, at her age, she might not last that long. I don't know. This whole thing seems like some type of divine intervention, her showing up at the nursing home about the time I started working on my family history."

"Yes, I realize that sweetheart, but it's your retirement. You should be enjoying yourself."

"This *is* what I enjoy."

"Yes, of course. I see how happy you are."

"I didn't see Sheila all day."

"Oh, so doubly happy. She didn't come to your retirement lunch?"

"No. Probably didn't chip in on the watch, either."

John laughed. "Maybe she was off in the broom closet with Mac."

"Yeah, sure," Alice said, rolling her eyes. "What is this obsession you have with Mac?"

"I'm just teasing," he said with a grin. "Well, I'm starved," John said, picking up his menu. "Do you know what you want, sweetheart?"

"You know I love the chicken Kiev, here. And a salad."

"Yes, I guessed you might order that. Since this is your retirement dinner I won't protest, but in your retirement, you really need to shake it up a little."

"Yes, dear. I will keep that in mind." Alice smirked.

"So, what did Sally tell you? About Nell? About Docia? About Jesse Barnes?"

"Basically, she talked about the Erwins and Nell. Not

Docia. No mention of Docia at all, yet. She did bring up Jesse."

"Oh? What did she have to say about him? Maybe we had it all wrong about him."

"No, I don't think so. He consigned slaves to the Erwins when they first came to Kentucky. It's already apparent he was the unsavory character the family gossip made him out to be."

"But then, you suspected that. Maybe you can ease Docia into the conversation?"

"I've been letting her talk. I'm afraid if I interrupt with questions it might throw her off. It's as if she is actually back there—back in time. She talks as though it happened yesterday."

"Are you ready to order, sir?" the waiter asked.

"Yes. My wife will have the chicken Kiev with a salad. Oil and vinegar, dear?"

"Yes, you know me so well."

"And, I'll have the prime rib. Rare. Just have the cow jump over the fire once." The waiter wrote down the order with no expression. "And a baked potato."

"Very good, sir," the waiter said, before walking away.

"John, I don't think the waiter gets your sense of humor."

"I gathered as much. Do you think we need to change restaurants?"

"Change? We don't come here that much."

"We will. When I retire. Yes, when we are both not slaves to a schedule, pardon the pun, we will wine and dine and do a bit of traveling. But, back to Sally." He whispered in his wife's ear, "Do you think the waiter overheard me?"

"Do you mean about not getting your joke?"

"Yes."

No. And what if he did?"

"You are so flippant tonight. Is it retirement or Sally that has put you in this mood?"

"It's a little of both." Alice took a sip of wine. "So suddenly, she's saying she is seeing people in the room, like ghosts from her past."

"Oh, no."

"Yes, I know. I've told you about how a lot of patients do that before they die. But, somehow, I don't feel it is Sally's time yet."

"She's one-hundred-nine, and you don't feel it's her time?" John said, as he lowered his glasses, looking over the top of them with a penetrating glance across the table while reaching into his jacket pocket for a cigarette.

Alice grabbed his arm. "John, could you please wait until after dinner?"

"All right. It's your night." He took his hand away from his jacket.

"Call it a woman's intuition or a nurse's intuition."

"Well, if you say so. You are around this sort of thing every day and should know."

"Yes, well, she told me about the Erwins coming from Virginia to Kentucky. And get this. Nell was with them. Even mentioned having to have special shoes made for her for the trip because of her extra toes."

"Wow. So, the story is true?"

"I guess it is." Alice smiled and took another sip of wine.

"I haven't seen you this ecstatic in a while. You were becoming so depressed over retiring."

Alice tore off a piece of bread. "I think I'll have plenty to keep me busy in retirement."

"Going to the library?"

"Some, but mostly I want to talk to Sally, while there's still time."

"Will they mind you being there so much?"

"Why should they? I'll be camped out with Sally. It will certainly make Sheila happy that she won't have to fool with her."

"Sir, I hope the steak is to your approval. The chef said he stopped the cow before he tried to make the second jump. And, ma'am, your chicken Kiev. Will there be anything else?"

"Perhaps some more butter and sour cream. Thank you."

Alice laughed as he walked away. "I guess he did get your humor. But, honey, I really don't think you need to have all that butter and sour cream. When you *do* retire, I might have to put you on a diet. I worry about your eating habits."

"So, when I retire, no cigarettes and no pancakes? I'm beginning to think I want to keep working."

6

"*A*re you awake?" Alice asked.

"My law, child. What are you doin' here?"

"What do you mean, sweetheart?"

"I thought yesterday was your last day."

"Well, it was. But, I came in especially to see you."

"Aw, ain't that nice."

"Let me prop up your pillows and getting you sitting up a little. Tell me if you need to go to the bathroom, okay?"

"Yes'm. It seem strange to have a real toilet. Had to wait o'er a hund'erd years to have one."

"You never had a bathroom until now?"

"No, had a outhouse. That's what most folks in the country had. And we's all used the same one. I did, at least. Marthie see'd to that. Not like in town. I 'member plenty of times I had to hold it till I got home if I weren't near a colored toilet."

"I can only imagine, Miss Sally. That is so sad," Alice said.

"The missus used a chamber pot. I 'member plenty of times emptyin' it. But back early on, we's went out in the woods. The bushes didn't know no difference 'tween a white butt or a black butt." Alice laughed.

"And, when I's little, I just innocent. We's all innocent, black and white child'n alike. I plays with the white child'n at Boone. Some of 'em just as poor as us slaves. None of us young'uns didn't know color at first, but didn't take us long to learn."

"I'm sure it didn't. What is Boone?"

"Boone was where I's born. My mama tell me 'bout my birth. Nell was there. Nell was always there, somewhere in the background. Just like me—always somewhere in the background. They called me *Nigger Sal*, and they's called my grand young'un, *Nigger Nell*. It hurt the both of us. That's why it was 'portant she learn to read, know her numbers and come educated. Nell always be one to look to the future. She ne'er wanted any part of the past. She say it too painful."

"Sally, I know you are talking about your granddaughter, but when you said Nell was there, always in the background, are you talking about the Nell who had to wear the special shoes?"

"Yes'm. Nell tell me 'bout my birth later. 'Bout how's they all up on the hill pickin' blackberries when it happened."

IT WAS HOT, a typical late July day. Susan was away from Boone, and could finally breathe again. The heat of the camp was intolerable when the furnace was in full force. A fresh breeze stirred, a welcome relief from the heavy, still air that encircled her back at the camp.

Today she was on the hill with the women who were picking blackberries. She sat in a spot that had been carved out by a passing deer. Clean air filled her lungs. The grass was green and fresh, not trampled down and blackened by soot. A big basket overflowing with the first of the season's blackberries set next to her. She picked off an attached briar to one of the biggest, juiciest looking ones and plopped it into her mouth.

She touched her bony hand to her swollen belly, the only part with an ounce of fat. The arms and legs that protruded out of her muslin dress were twigs. The climb up the hill had taken a toll on her. Most work these days, to Master Barnes's chagrin, took a heavy toll on her.

The master looked forward to a strong baby boy, a boy that more than likely he would rip from her arms and sell off as soon as he was old enough to do any kind of work, at all. Her intuition told her it was a girl. She always knew the sex, even with the two stillborn babies.

Enclosed in the tight space of her womb, this child was clinging on to the last remains of freedom. This baby held tight to the walls of its protective case, refusing to come out. It reminded her of the doll the Russian family had brought with them to Boone.

Boone didn't have many pleasures for her, but one of the few was the Russian family who stopped there. Susan looked on from a distance as everyone around marveled at the woman, jabbering away in her native tongue, as she sat atop a colorful wagon, peeling back the layers of the painted doll she brought from her old country.

Susan looked down over the valley. The smoke from the furnace obliterated the thriving town full of laborers, politicians, preachers, the snake oil salesmen, and every sort of scoundrel to be had. But most who lived there were decent folk, barely getting by, eking out a living.

Susan called Boone a camp. That's how it had started. It grew rapidly into a village with its own little neighborhoods. Her neighborhood was the one for the coloreds. She was brought to Boone with her husband, William, in 1856 to clear the land, then to build the furnace that would make the pig iron. It was almost a year ago, another hot day in July, when the first blast took place.

Susan rubbed her belly. A week had pased since her mama had placed her six-fingered hands over her belly and shook her head and said, "That baby shoulda been here by now." Nell had been traveling back and forth, mostly on foot, twice a week, lest the baby be born without its grandmama being there.

Susan lay sprawled on the grass. *Where was she? She was supposed to be here today. Maybe the mistress wouldn't let her leave. Or, maybe her mama had given up on the baby being born.* There hadn't been many kicks. It was as if the baby instinctively knew that any action might propel it outward into a world it wasn't quite ready for—the life of a slave.

It must have been the fresh air away from the furnace that enticed the baby to finally want to see the light of day. The pains hit with a vengeance. Susan groaned and called out, "Mama? Mama? Where is you at?"

One of the women set her basket of berries down and called out to the others, "It's time."

In a synchronized sweep, the other women set their baskets down. All except for one. She carried hers on her head, steady, not missing a beat, as she walked toward her, the sweat on her bare black arms glistening in the sunlight. Or was it a mirage of her mama? She wanted her with her so badly. "Steady, steady," her mama, Nell, would say as she placed a small batch of kindling atop Susan's mop of hair. "This is how my own mama taught me, the way her own mama taught her back in our mother country, Africa."

The contractions were a relief. This pregnancy had been different. It was harder. There was nausea from the start, nausea that lasted all day. The hot, thick, dirty air produced by the smelting process burned her throat and stomach. William encouraged her to eat, but she couldn't. When no one was looking, she slipped the larger portions that were doled out to her to Henry. Henry had no more been weaned when Susan discovered she was with child again. She was one of the lucky ones. At least she had her man with her. And, she had Henry.

Susan was born in Kentucky. She hadn't known the cotton fields, but those who had been there agreed that furnace work was even more grueling. The white folks there far outnumbered the colored folk, but the most punishing work always found its way to a slave. When history was recorded there would not even be a trace of her or any Negro having been there.

The darkies were the ones farthest from the camp, the ones placed downstream, lest their filth muddy the waters. Still, the dark soot that sunk into everyone's pores acted as a leveling agent. It hung in the air and pervaded every aspect of life in Boone. It was a creeping evil. There was blackness all around. The only birds were vultures and crows. What hope did this child have? But this morning, as she and the other women left the camp, she saw a cardinal. Her mama always told her a cardinal meant hope. Maybe this child might have some of that.

The contractions grew closer. There was no time to move her back to the camp. This child would be born under a blue sky, in pristine air. Another good sign.

At her first scream, the women drew in closer. "Here, let's help her up to a squatting position," one of the women said. The baby was crowning. The women lauded on the birth. "Push. Push. Just a little more," they all chimed in.

Susan heard one voice above all the rest. It was her mama. Nell stood above her, as proud as any mama and grandmama could be. "I's here, Susan. It gonna be all right."

"Mama," Susan uttered. She stared up at Nell, raising a hand, covering her eyes from the bright sunlight.

SUSAN'S PAPA was long gone, a runaway traveling through on his way to Ohio. Nell kept him hidden in a nearby cave for a week. The missus and master were none the wiser. She took him food and applied a poultice to his leg, a gnarled piece of flesh ripped open by a hound. Moses, the papa Susan never knew, had come all the way from Tennessee. He was a sweet talker of a man, had his head in the clouds, her mama told her. He was going to cross the Ohio and find work up north. It was sheer luck he had made it to the Erwin farm.

"Why don't you go with me, Nell?" Moses pleaded. "We's could jump o'er the broom." But Nell knew it was foolishness talking. She would only slow him down. She had never even fancied being free. Slavery was all she had ever known, and she had a good situation as far as slavery went.

A month later, Nell knew she was with child. Everyone suspected it was one of the Lansdowne slaves, and that it happened on the night of the outing to the caves. The masters planned the outings, hoping the slaves would mate, creating a bigger work force.

Only Susan and her mama knew about Moses. "Don't tell Ib," she told Susan. "Lest she let it slip to the missus I's hid a runaway. She mean well, but she almost never leave the missus's side. I don't wanna tempt fate, but I's thought you oughta know who your papa be."

THE MISTRESS HAD GIVEN Nell permission to leave but didn't supply her with a wagon or a horse. She had only her feet to carry her, as many slaves did in the summer months. The missus still held a grudge against Susan. "Nell, I've given you a horse several times. I can't spare it today. You'll have to go on foot. Why can't your child be more like you? You never give me any trouble," the missus said.

Susan was weak—weak from Henry's birth and other pregnancies that went awry. But mostly it was from the hard pregnancy she endured at Boone Furnace.

The furnace had only started the year before but was operating at full blast. The work was hot and dangerous. Three men, Colonel Sebastian Eifort, Thomas Price, and John Eifort built the furnace. That is the historical version, at least. The truth of the matter was that it was built by the ones who were left out of the history books, the ones who did the dirtiest, most strenuous and backbreaking work—slaves. There were others, those a step above the slaves, the ones William worked alongside, the ones that worked for the lowest of wages. But, then, they got wages. Company store wages. The furnace was a law unto itself, functioning out of the normal realm of society but drawing all forms of society to it, like the Russian family, and the counterfeiter who used the smelting furnace as a way to further his crime. The furnace was where every opportunity seeker there was to be had, abounded.

THE BABY LANDED SAFELY in Nell's hands.

The young girl the women had sent to the nearest cabin when the labor pains started, came running up the hill, out of breath, carrying a blanket and bucket of water, only in time to see the cord being cut.

Nell held the baby with both hands, grasping it with all six fingers on each hand. She pointed it to the sky and voiced a prayer, something her mama had taught her. Her feet with the extra toes were planted firmly in the ground as she held the baby toward the sky with the severed umbilical cord dangling toward the ground.

Nell cuddled the baby in her arms, a baby as black as the berries they had been picking, covered in blood that looked as purple as the liquid from the berries against the dark skin. "I be your grandmama, child," she said, looking down into the child's eyes that were wide and brown. "Ain't she a big young'un," Nell exclaimed to the other women. The women nodded their heads in agreement. Nell finished tiding up the severed cord, cleaned the child in the water, dressed it and placed the new baby girl on Susan's shrunken belly.

Susan reclined on the gray wool blanket with her baby now in a white dress, the one Nell had carried with her. The missus saw fit to give the dress, a hand-me-down from one of the Erwin babies, to Nell before she left. It was clean, the only clothing on the hill, other than Nell's, without the suffocating mixture of sulfuric smoke and sweat from the furnace.

"Law, it was a wonder this young'un came at all," Nell said to some of the other women as she shook her head. Susan was too involved looking down at her new infant to even register what the other women were saying. "But it's a strong young'un," Nell added, looking down at her weary daughter who displayed a labored smile.

Nell studied her daughter as she lay there holding her baby. Susan had never been all that strong, and this pregnancy had severely weakened her. All winter Susan had coughed. The cough hadn't fully subside until late spring.

NELL WORKED out in the fields along with the men, for the most part. Mistress said Nell was stout and could handle the work of any man, which she well could. But Ib hardly ever left the mistress's side. Mistress was lost without Ib. She raised all the Erwin children, even though Ib was only a girl when she came with the missus to Kentucky. When Mistress Erwin was in a good mood, she would bandy compliments around about how she couldn't do without Ib, how she was indispensable. At other times she could be as harsh as any mother might be when scolding a stepchild—a stepchild who was *colored*.

Ib and Nell were the only ones still together out of the thirteen siblings. A couple had died as babies. The males were sold off to other farms back in Virginia. And a couple of the females, being too white to look upon by the mistress of the house, were sold off as well. But, that was all before they came to Kentucky.

Nell had hoped that the mistress would let Ib come with her, but it would be an unnecessary burden on her, as the mistress put it. "After all, she would see the baby in due time," Mistress Erwin said.

Susan was with them at the Erwin farm until she got her bleed. It was then that Susan started her wandering ways. She had the strap marks on her back to prove it. They were never administered by the mistress or the master. The mistress wouldn't dirty her hands with such things. She preferred the cruelty of words. Mostly her words boiled down to sarcasm. "Why can't you be like your mama and your aunt?"

Master Erwin wasn't keen on having slaves, always trying to wash his hands of the matter, pretending they weren't slaves at all but hired hands. There *were* hired hands who came and went, as there were only six slaves at any given time, not enough to tend to nearly two thousand acres. There was always a hired hand that excelled in punishing slaves even for the mildest of errors. But mostly, the punishment was doled out by Master Barnes. He rode about the country-side, dressed all fine and fancy like a proper gentleman, over-seeing, and wheeling and dealing in slaves. Even the white folks cringed in his presence.

Susan wasn't deterred by the beatings. She had slipped off so much to be with William, that the mistress said to sell her off if she couldn't stay there. Nell and Ib tried to talk sense to Susan. "If you don't stop runnin' off, the Massa Erwin gonna sell you to that Massa Barnes. That Massa Barnes be a mean man. Is that what you want, girl?" Nell pleaded. It was useless. Susan's head was turned by love.

Master Barnes was eager to have a woman for William, one of his more promising slaves. Susan wasn't Master Barnes's first choice. "Too puny," he said. William was a strong lad, a good foot taller than most of the slaves. Master Barnes had tried to pair him off with a string of buxom, wide-hipped bitches, but William wasn't interested. Nor did lashings make him interested. So, in the interest of business, he added Susan to the roster of slaves. He only hoped she might produce a slew of babies he could sell in the future or hire out to other farms or to the furnaces. Business was the bottom line with Jesse Barnes. Cruelty was a by-product.

Mistress Erwin did have a conscience and even one of the kindest hearts at times. If it had been on Sunday, she would have taken Nell in the buggy. That was the day she visited the sick and poor after church. She wore her finest silks and paraded around, taking little goodies that Ib had prepared along with some cast off pieces of clothing to give to the poor. Boone Furnace was sometimes on her route. But, Nell had asked to leave during the middle of the week.

"No, no, that won't do," she said, at first. Then after weighing the matter over, she disappeared from the main room for a moment. She returned with a baby's dress and said, "You'll have to go on foot. I can't spare the horse, and you'll have to walk barefoot. Your new shoes aren't done yet. This is quite inconvenient, Nell. How do you even know the child will come today? How many false alarms have there been? Surely that baby can wait until Sunday."

"Babies don't wait, Missus. I feels it in my gut. That baby gonna come today."

"That's what you said last week." Mistress Erwin let out a heavy sigh. "If you must, you must. I am a mother, myself, after all. Here, take this," she said, handing her the infant dress.

"Much obliged, ma'am. Susan will be, too."

"Well, you had better be off, then."

"Yes'm."

Most of the white people thought Nell's extremities to be a curse or at the least an oddity. Her own thought her special, as six fingers were mentioned in the Bible, not that she could read it herself. It was something that Missus Erwin read to her, said it came from the book of Samuel. *There was a war at Gath again, where there was a man of great stature who had six fingers on each hand and six toes on each foot, twenty-four in number; and he also had been born to a giant.* The passage made Nell smile, as she was also tall for a woman. She liked the thought of coming from a race of giants. Perhaps her own tribe back in Africa was tall. She didn't know. She only knew that people were fascinated by her fingers and toes and that the missus would often call her from the field and have her hold up her hands for visitors to see. Children were in awe as they held up their own fingers to hers seeing the extra digit off to the side.

SUSAN CUDDLED her new baby girl in her arms. Only a month ago one of the slaves delivered a sickly child. The master threw it out to the pigs as if it were slop. It was a hard thing to see or even hear of for any woman, slave or not.

The baby let out a whelp of a cry, exhibiting healthy lungs. "What you want to call her?" Nell asked Susan, as the child found her mother's right breast and began to suckle.

Susan whispered in a voice as worn out as her body, "Sally. Sally Ann." A smile spread across her mouth. She knew her baby would be saved from the fate of the other slave's baby.

While Sally lay atop her mother, there was a final swoosh and downward motion of Susan's stomach upon releasing the afterbirth. Her belly stayed caved in, losing the pregnant bulge that had given her any illusion of good health.

Susan lingered long enough to nurse Sally and see that she appeared to be a healthy child, romping about, before succumbing to the conditions of life at the furnace that made her mostly bedridden off and on. Her condition would have normally angered the master, but all the talk of war kept him plenty busy.

Susan lay on her deathbed in 1861 when she heard the war between the North and South had begun. She died the following day. Sally, nearly three, was at her side.

Sally was left in the charge of the other slave women at Boone. She saw Nell from time to time, mostly on Sundays when Mistress Erwin rode up in her fine buggy. She saw her papa at night until one night he stopped coming. When she asked why she was only told it was the fate of being colored. At least that was the way her Uncle Peter, her papa's brother, in the kindest way possible, put it to her. So, orphaned along with Henry, she played with the other children at the camp, mostly oblivious, and learned to avoid the men in the gray uniforms. Both the Yankees and the Confederates came through Boone, but the Confederates were the ones to fear the most. That's the warning all the slave young'uns was given.

"I 'MEMBERS ONCE, one of the Yanks, a man with blue eyes axed me to fetch him some water. He looks down at me and smiles e'er so big and say, *thank you kindly little miss.* He takes his hat off and puts it right on top of my head and say, *don't you look purty.* I wanna keep it, but he say he have to wear it. He say, *you don't want me to get in trouble with my sergeant, do you?* I say, no. I think some of 'em soldiers weren't so bad," Sally said.

Alice handed Sally a drink of water. She patted her delicate hand, looking on this aged woman with great admiration and reverence.

"Yes'm, after my mama died, Nell, Ib and the missus rode into Boone to fetch me."

7

*N*ell and Ib made sure to catch the missus in a good mood. "That color do look good on you, ma'am," Ib said.

"With the war starting, it's probably the last new dress I'll have for a while. I don't know whatever we are going to do. John Brandon has already talked about joining the Union. And, I do so worry about Mr. Erwin. That nagging cough returns every year."

"The poultice helped some, didn't it, Missus?"

"Yes, Ib. I don't know what we'd do if we didn't have your remedies. Did you say it was your mother's mother who was a witch woman in her tribe?"

Ib cringed. "No, ma'am, a wise woman." She looked over at Nell with a frown.

"Well, whatever you concocted, it did the trick for Mr. Erwin this past winter. I do so worry about him. I worry about my boys as well. And now, with this war starting, well, we can only hope it might blow over soon."

"Yes, ma'am."

"Well, Nell, what are you waiting for? Get the wagon.

We will go and fetch the child. I'm sure Jesse Barnes can't protest me taking a three-year-old off his hands. And after what happened to her father—an awful tragedy that was. She's no good as a slave to him. Her care slows the women at the furnace down. But, mind you, she's your responsibility. The other child, her brother…"

"Henry, ma'am."

"Yes, Henry. He's old enough to do some work. His master won't give him up, and we're in no position to buy him. But, we'll go get the little girl."

"Yes'm," Nell said, all smiles. "Right away, ma'am." Nell caught the approving look of Ib.

"I dread dealing with that Jesse Barnes, though," the missus said with a scowl on her face before stepping up in the wagon.

"JESSE BARNES SOUNDS AWFUL."

"Yes'm, he was. One of the meanest men to e'er walk the face of the earth, but I forgive him."

"Miss Sally, that's big of you to forgive him."

"He a product of his time. We all just a product of our time. And, the times, they be gettin' better. I watch Dr. King on the television in the big room. I see what he be doin' fer our people. Can't help but have hope. Nell can't talk 'nough 'bout Dr. King."

"I can imagine."

"Yes'm. And now here I is, sittin' out front with the white folks, with white folks takin' care of me. And they be carryin' out my bedpan on the days I can't get out of bed, like all those times I carries the white folks' chamber pots."

"Miss Sally, you do have a way of putting a positive spin

on things," Alice said, smiling. "I wish more of my patients were like you. Well, the patients I had."

"Oh, we's all alike when you get down to it."

"Yes, I guess you're right about that."

"Sometimes I make up a game in my head."

"And what kind of game is that?"

"Well, I reckon 'fore we come to earth, we all up in heaven, all the same, no color. And, we's all havin' a merry time. And 'fore God sends us down to earth, God gives us roles, like those soap opera people on television."

"You do like your soap operas, don't you Miss Sally," Alice said, smiling.

"You know everybody here do. It takes the mind off the aches and pains."

"Yes, I imagine they do."

"Well, God gives us different parts, like the good guys and the villains on the soap operas. But none of us are good or bad. We's all a mix of both. But, it's all a test.

"We be listenin' to God, like little child'n at God's feet, all lovin' each other. And it all seem so easy. We all be free up in heaven. Then we come to earth, and none of us be free. It a test to see if we can find our way back to God, to be free again, like Dr. King say, *free at last.* And like in the Bible, 'bout the prodigal son.

"I imagine God say it all a game. He send us to earth with different roles like the actors to get us to play good together. But, He make it hard. He takes 'way our memories, and we forget we's all loved each other at the start."

A tear rolled down Alice's cheek. "Miss Sally, that's an extraordinary way to look at it. If everyone looked at it that way our world would be so much better. But, I don't see how you can be so forgiving after all you've been through?"

"Like'n I say, it's all just a test. Don't you see? Oh, I don't guess you do. Nell don't see it that way either. Well, not 'xactly that way. But I have to look at it that way. Or, it don't make no sense. And after bein' on this earth over a hund'erd years, and seein' all I's saw, it have to make some sense, or what's the use in it all?"

"When you say it that way, I see your point, Miss Sally."

"Yes'm, God tells us it a test. Like in school. I don't know much 'bout school, but I know 'bout tests. I's had plenty in my day. Not the slate or paper kind—the life kind.

"I hear'd a preacher up on a stump at Boone Furnace once. I reckon that's where I got this notion in my head. He goin' off 'bout how it all a game we's playin' and how's we all got to love one 'nother. He say that e'en though he be a colored man and get kicked 'round by the white man. Oh, he lower his head like the rest of us when the white man speak to him, but he say it all a part of the game we has to play. When's we get to heaven we see how childish we was."

"But don't you wonder why you were a slave and someone like Jesse Barnes was a master?" Alice asked.

"Oh, I reckon I axed for it. Maybe I got the best part like that Miss Laura on the soap opera. And no one want to take the villain part, but Jesse Barnes were brave 'nough to raise his hand and say *God, I do it.*"

Sally let out a chuckle. "And God teases us. He say, *let's see how well you can play together?* And then we get bodies, all different, and then the hard part come. Some of us black, some white, some rich, some poor. It the same all o'er, no matter where you go. And I's traveled all o'er these parts, deliverin' and taking care of babies, goin' where's I's needed. It all the same. People all the same."

"Miss Sally, you should be the one to write a book. You are a wise woman. If children could read this in school, we would grow up learning to get along with one another."

"God sent Dr. King to remind us all. He doin' a mighty fine job. Don't need an old woman like me tellin' him how to run the show. And look at Miss Rosa Parks. No, don't be needin' me. 'Sides, I be leavin' this phys'cal body soon. This body be like old worn out clothes I gotta shed. I be in heaven where it be nice and cool. Not that fiery place, not like Boone Furnace. I 'member the heat from that place like it was yesterday. I was ne'er so glad to leave a place as I was that one. But it took me twice to get 'way fer good."

8

"*I*'m here to see Mister Barnes. Is he about?"

The strapping, thickset black man took hold of the bridle of one of the horses, eyeing the fine lady and two black women atop the buggy.

"He be here, ma'am, but he be in a frightful mood."

"What's your name?" Missus Erwin asked.

"They calls me Jobie, ma'am."

"Well, Jobie, I reckon what I have to say will put him in a better mood," Mistress Erwin said with an upward tilt of her head.

The man smiled suspiciously. "That would surely be somethin' if you could do that, ma'am." The man held his head down, turned and began walking away. "Follow me, if'n you please."

Nell jerked the reins and commanded the horses to follow the man. They rode past a circuit preacher, standing on a stump, holding up his Bible, yelling out the end of time was at hand. A meager crowd of white folk was gathered around, some shouting amen, some on their knees. In another section, they rode through to find a couple of politicians debating the war and what it meant for both the North and the South. Kentucky was a hotbed. Families divided. The crowd at the second gathering was larger and more somber.

Looking over the spectacle at Boone Furnace agitated Mistress Erwin. She wasn't usually one to be rattled, having stood up to her parents to marry someone they thought beneath her, making the move to Kentucky, with her husband, four young slaves, and five children, one merely an infant, in nothing but two wagons, as well as facing a minor skirmish with Indians along the way. No, if anything, she was a strong-willed woman, the Rock of Gibraltar of the family, but she now had grown sons and a husband, and all she could see was losing them to war, possibly brother fighting brother, as they were a divided family as far as slavery was concerned.

After about quarter of a mile, the slave held up his hand, motioning for them to stop. Nell pulled on the reins, and the horses came to a halt. "He be in there, playin' cards," the man said, tipping his hat to the ladies.

"Hardly a place for a lady to enter. Fetch him, if you please, but not until he finishes his game. Hopefully, he is winning. We don't want him in a sourer mood than what you indicated. Hmm, what did you say your name was again?"

"Jobie, ma'am."

"Well, Jobie, we'll wait here."

"Yes, ma'am."

It wasn't long until the scrawny figure of a man, known as Jesse Barnes, appeared in the doorway. He made his way over to the wagon with an entourage of outlaw-looking types following in his wake. "Aw, Mrs. Erwin. To what do I owe this pleasure?" Mr. Barnes asked. He lit up a cigar, took a puff and threw the match to the ground, all the while squinting his eyes dubiously at Mrs. Erwin.

"I trust your card game went well, Mr. Barnes," Mrs. Erwin said, eyeing him up and down.

"Why, yes ma'am, it did. Mighty obliged to you for asking," he said, as smoke rings escaped his mouth.

"That is good to hear, Mr. Barnes. Sir, I'm here to make a proposition."

The man smiled, showing a full set of rusty looking teeth, except for one gold one, smack dab in the middle. It glared in the sun. "A proposition, you do say?" The men around him snickered.

"Shush," Mr. Barnes said to them. They obeyed loyally. He paused as if giving some thought to what he was about to say. "I'm used to dealing with your husband. I hope he is well."

"He's well enough, thank you. However, we won't linger on niceties. I'd rather get straight to business."

"Whatever you say, ma'am." Unlike when Jobie said it, Jesse Barnes' way of saying ma'am had a slimy feel to it.

"What we are here about is the slave girl, Sally."

"Sally, Sally, I don't recall a Sally. I deal with a lot of slaves, Mrs. Erwin. Sally seems to be a common name among them."

"I'm sure you do, Mr. Barnes. You might recall her mother, Susan. She died a few months back."

Mr. Barnes nodded his head, "Yes, ma'am, I remember now. Always sickly. Not much of an investment. That husband of hers, though, a fine worker. God rest his soul. An awful accident—him falling into the furnace like that."

"Accident, indeed, Mr. Barnes." Mistress Erwin raised her eyebrow. "I understood you were of the belief that Negroes didn't have souls?"

"A figure of speech, ma'am. Anyway, not for me to decide."

"Amen to that," Ib whispered.

"What was that your colored woman said?"

71

"Nothing of concern. Now, back to…"

"Yes, right. You came here on business. Not to philosophize whether a Negro has a soul or not."

"We thought we might take the girl off your hands."

"I'm sure we could come to a price."

"No, Mr. Barnes, I'm not aiming to buy her."

"Ma'am, surely you aren't suggesting I give her away. I *am* a businessman."

"Exactly. And I have a business offer. One that we both can profit by."

"Profit, one of my favorite words. You have my attention," the man said, taking another inhale of his cigar.

"Surely, the child, that young, is of no use to you. She's another mouth to feed, and her care by the other women slows them down. I'm offering to take her off your hands for the time being—until she gets old enough to work. In the interim, I will feed and clothe her."

"And just why would you want to do that?" Jesse asked, removing his hat and scratching his head.

"Because her mother is the daughter to one of my two slaves here."

"Oh, I see. You want to make a present of the girl to her grandmother. While I don't hold to coddling slaves in that manner, I do understand a happy slave is a good worker."

"Sir, my slaves have always served me well. They are more like family."

"Well, ma'am," Jesse said with a laugh, looking back at his card playing buddies, "maybe I might take some instruction from you on how to handle slaves."

Mrs. Erwin let out a heavy sigh. "Mr. Barnes, why must we play this cat and mouse game? You know this arrangement would benefit us both."

He let out a hearty laugh. "You are the direct one, aren't you? A woman after my own heart." After some pause, he said, "Well, seeing it means so much to you, I'll accept your offer. I hear your boys may be heading off to war. This war is hard on us all. You might be in need of some niggers to work in your tobacco. I trust Mr. Erwin will remember this favor and call on me when he is in need of field hands."

"I will let you know." Mrs. Erwin nodded good day to Mr. Barnes and turned to Nell. "Let's ride over to where Sally is staying." Nell snapped the reins.

"That man be a snake in the grass if there e'er was one," Nell said as they rode off.

"I won't argue with you, there," Missus Erwin agreed.

The women entered the colored section, which consisted of nothing more than tents, lean-tos, and the shabbiest of structures, located on the farthest reaches of what was now the town of Boone Furnace.

After the death of Susan, the slave women at Boone took turns watching Sally to be best of their ability while they cooked and washed clothes. Mostly she scampered about on her own like a wild fawn throughout the camp. Although they often called it a camp, it had grown so that now it had its own post office. The women quit what they were doing, seeing the approaching wagon.

A man held Sally on his lap. "That be Peter, ma'am," Ib said. "He be Sally's uncle, her daddy's brother. He do a lot of driving fer the white folks. He good with horses and young'uns. All the young'uns love Uncle Peter."

"He's a lively sort, I see," Mrs. Erwin said.

"Bein' a driver, he see a lot of the countryside. Also, hear a lot. He always have his eyes and ears open. Hears a lot 'bout the war. Everyone start calling him Uncle Peter, 'round here, as that what Sally call him."

Uncle Peter wore a bright purple shirt covered in patches, a black leather belt, and a bright orange knitted scarf around his neck, even in the heat of summer.

"He certainly has a flair for fashion," Mrs. Erwin said, trying not to break out in a laugh.

"Sally's mama say he wear all of his belongin's, lest they be stolen. Some say he got them from a hanged nigger that was bein' et' by the crows. No one know the 'xact story. Peter make up a lot of stuff. So, you have to be careful what you believe, ma'am. He so used to lyin' to the master and curryin' favor, that it all become second nature to him. Still, if you in need of news of the war or 'bout anythin' 'round these here parts, Peter be your man, Missus."

Sally looked up to see the wagon. She wiggled off Peter's lap. "Nell, Nell!"

Nell brought the wagon to a halt, and the women got down. Sally reached for Nell's hands, putting her own small hands up against them, stretching her smallest fingers to Nell's extra ones, smiling.

"We are here for Sally," Mrs. Erwin said. "Ib, might you give the women the baked goods you made?"

Ib handed a basket over to one of the women. "Much obliged," the woman said with a wide toothed grin.

"I's take your horses to the water trough," Peter said.

"I hear you have news of the war, Peter," Mrs. Erwin said.

"Yes'm, I do. What I hear is the war ain't goin' well fer the Confederates. They's a hurtin' bad."

"Now, are you sure about this, Peter? The war just started, and the Confederates are already faring badly? I'm thinking that may be wishful thinking on your part."

"Maybe tis so, ma'am, but that is what I hears."

9

"*D*id you sleep well last night?"

"All's I do is sleep, it seem. But last night, I dreamt I was runnin' from the Yankees."

"But, Miss Sally, why would you run from the Yankees? The Yankees were on your side."

"Not all the time. They was better than the men in gray, but they all come and took what they wanted. At least that what Missus Erwin say."

"I guess times were harder than we can even imagine during the Civil War. You were so young then. I'm surprised you remember back that far," Alice said.

"Oh, I's 'member well 'nough. And lately, I's 'member more when I's young than when I's old. There were always some sort of ruckus goin' on. The mistress stayed in a tither. She brought a wagon load of valuables from Virginia, and she weren't 'bout to lose 'em to the Yankees or the Confederates. She was e'er on the lookout for new hidin' places.

"There was caves all o'er the place, and us kids knew every one of 'em blindfolded. We played all o'er those woods, white and colored together. It was one of the times we's 'membered who we was up in heaven 'fore we got older and started forgettin'."

"You lived near Carter Caves when you were young, didn't you?"

"Yes'm, but it weren't called that back then. A lot of the woods we used to traipse 'bout in was called Smokey Valley. Still called that to this day. And, it was called Trough Camp. Still called that, too. That's the name the soldiers give it. They camped all o'er those woods. There was an old man who had troughs set up all o'er the valley, sapping the maple trees for their syrup. Us child'n would eat some when he weren't 'round. Once, he caught us and threatened to take a switch to *us* all. The soldiers would take plenty, too, but he didn't threaten them any. 'Fraid to, I reckon."

"That's all so fascinating, Miss Sally. I've visited Carter Caves with my family—a family reunion."

"Yes'm, we have plenty of reunions there, ourselves, and we's used the caves fer more than explorin'. They made dandy cellars for food storage. And, they made dandy hidin' places, too. There was one time Missus Erwin carted us all off, ridin' her white horse atop her grand side saddle right up into one of the bigger caves where we's all hid from the Yankees. We's all walkin' 'hind her, carryin' what we could carry to hide in the cave.

"We sat in that cave way into the night, 'long with the horse, talkin' low, lest the Yankees should ride up and hear us. The missus weren't 'bout to let that horse or saddle be stole. I 'member there was the whole Erwin clan along with us slaves. There was Ib and Nell and Henry and Jacob and Docia and me."

"Docia?"

"Yes'm. Docia be Ib's daughter. We all curled up together, white and black folks alike. We slept there till the daylight crept in, and when we's know the coast was clear, we all carted the stuff back to the house. No, there was ne'er a dull moment durin' the war. And there was the share of sad times. The missus lost both her man and one of her sons durin' the war. Both succumbed to awful sicknesses."

When the Erwins came to Kentucky in 1836, they settled in what was Greenup County. In 1838, the section they were in became Carter County. When the Civil War broke out, Olive Hill was still forming. The locations of Buffalo Creek, Boone Furnace and what was yet to become Carter Caves, all in the area where Sally grew up were lit up with action. The cave area butted right up next to the Erwin Plantation. One would think that the war might pass up a rural Appalachian area such as Carter County, but that was not the case.

Elizabeth was right. The war between the North and South did take a toll on her family. The Civil War hardly left anyone untouched, especially in Kentucky, as brother was divided against brother. Elizabeth's third son, John Brandon, joined the Union army.

"Mama, I am a man of conscience. You know that. It's how you raised me. You know I have this strong aversion to slavery."

"Yes, John Brandon. I know you do. Like your father. But, might you reconsider? Your father has been sickly you know.

He's getting old. And Susan, your wife? What about her and your child?"

"Mama, I have no choice. I'm an able man. How can I not fight for what is right? If I can do anything to rectify this horrible situation of slavery, I must do so."

Elizabeth hugged her son. "If you must, you must. Your own father fought in the War of 1812. I understand a man's duty."

"I have made a deal with Jesse Barnes. While I'm off fighting to hold this here union in one piece and for the abolishment of slavery, I feel like I have made a deal with the devil, himself. But, he said he would see that the farm would be taken care of and that Susan need not worry. And for that, I'm much obliged to him."

"Might we never rid ourselves of that man?"

"Not when we live in these troubled times, Mama," he said, taking hold of his mother's hand.

John gave his mama another tight hug and walked off to a place he knew the Union soldiers were camped. Upon entering the campsite, John Brandon announced, "Boys, I'm here to join the cause."

Although John Brandon joined with a passion to do the right thing, he soon found the war to be sorely distasteful, and not what he thought fighting to preserve the union and freeing the slaves would be at all.

He wrote to his wife, Susan, in 1863:

January the 9th, 1863

Dear Wife,

I can't say that my health is good at this time. I have a bad diarrhea. But I am able to knock around. But I sincerely hope when it is come to hand it will find you all well. I received two letters from you the 7th of this month bearing date Dec. the 10 and 24. You can't tell how glad I was to hear from you, that you was all well. Wife, I was almost faintless with trouble and disgust at this war. But your kind letters has revived me some. But I am sorry that you did not tell me in your last letter whether you had got your money or not. Why did you forget it? You know I am all the time stewing about your welfare at home.

We are now at the mouth of White River two hundred miles from Vicksburg. Their occupation is stealing Negroes, robbing and burning houses, killing old milk cows and eating them, and my Dear Wife how can I stand this? I never was wanting to do this and if I can get money enough to take me home I am coming. I think we will get back to Memphis, Tenn. And stay there till we are paid off, and if so I will say good bye to the army, for I had rather be called a disserter than a Negro thief. So, I will say no more on this subject.

You stated in your letter that Jesse was gone. I am glad he is gone, but I druther he had not told a lie. He promised to tend the place, the last words I had with him. Now Susan I have written to you about the renting of the place. If you get it do not depend on me to tend it for I may be disappointed in coming. But if I come, I can find plenty of work to do.

Now I will say something about the health of this army. The health is no good. There is a great deal of sickness beginning among the soldiers at this time, and a great many deaths. There is none of our company very well, but none bedfast. But James Parry, John Cawhun and I think they will recover.

Now you seem to make light of my short letters. This is not very long. But if it is a long going as you say the others were, maybe it will grow some. So no more.

I still remain your affectionate husband till death.

John B. Erwin to Susan Erwin and John James

JOHN'S WIFE, Susan, was from the Lansdowne family. Dr. Lansdowne owned a number of slaves, as did a neighbor, Dr. DeBard, who lived a mile down the road. John Brandon knew that the slaves of both men, as well as most of the slaves in the area, visited each other on weekends and would sing and dance throughout most of the night. It was encouraged as the slave owners in the area hoped offspring would come of it, giving them more slaves to tend their farms.

John Brandon and his father-in-law disagreed over slavery. Dr. Lansdowne was appalled that his daughter's husband, whose family owned a small pack of slaves themselves, were Union sympathizers and that his own son-in-law would enlist in the Union army. John Brandon laughed at the recollection that the slaves were doing far more than mating on those weekend rendezvous. They were setting their sites on escaping when they learned the state of Ohio, where free territory lay, was only twenty miles away.

One night, four slaves from a neighboring farm, along with three of Lansdowne's slaves, while visiting the Lansdowne farm on the weekend disappeared. Both John's father-in-law and his neighbor, after the discovery, set off on horseback after them. At Greenupsburg, Kentucky, located to the south of the Ohio River, they made inquiries where they learned a strange white man had taken the Negroes across the river. The slaves were never to be recovered. Lansdowne and his neighbor turned their horses around, cursing the abolitionists the whole way back.

Although some of the slaves tried to escape, some remained on both the Lansdowne's farm and the neighbor's farm after the war, a surprising fact, since neither man spared the whip. The ones who did leave migrated to Missouri and Kansas.

IF THE WAR wasn't bad enough, the heat at the Union camp in Morganza, Louisiana, was. And, that was where John Brandon was stationed. There were skirmishes and battles, the largest fought at Sterling Plantation in September of 1863. The Confederates won that one, but the Union retaliated by burning the whole town down, not such a wise move, as they were subjecting not only the people of the area to the heat, but themselves as well, and most being from the Northern states, had much less tolerance for it.

To add to his misery, he received news some months later that his father, John Leander, had died on Christmas Eve of 1863. Susan wrote that the grave was dug in haste on the same day and left unmarked as Elizabeth had seen fit to bury family valuables with him, fearing either the Yankees or Confederates, whoever got there first, would more than likely rob them blind. She wrote in her letter that Christmas Eve was warm enough, forty-five degrees, a proper temperature for grave digging, but it was also warm enough to rain. The rain turned nasty. The temperature dropped enough to turn it into a blinding snowstorm. Overnight, the temperature dropped to twenty degrees below zero, a record low. They awoke to find a deep snow covered the ground. The men trudged through it, carrying the wooden casket. Luckily, the grave was only a few hundred feet away from the house. The immediate family, adults only, stood around the grave as the body was lowered. His sons did their best to shovel the frozen ground beneath the snow over the wooden box, not wanting their father to lay exposed.

John Brandon was already near the point of breaking,

both mentally and physically, when he read his wife's letter about his father's passing. His father was seventy-two.

During the following summer, the Union soldiers, between battles and skirmishes, spent most of their time constructing arbors and tents to shield themselves from the blazing sun. Between mandatory drills and sports games, they stripped off as many articles of clothing as the Union army allowed them within regulations and spent idle hours in shaded areas near the river. Along with the heat, the excessive rainfall also cursed them. Before long, a good deal of the soldiers suffered from scurvy, chronic diarrhea, swamp fever, and small pox.

John Brandon, growing tired of the situation, and worrying about the state of affairs back home and about his wife and child, saw it as a chance to run, to implement his earlier plans of desertion. He was apprehended and court-martialed and thrown into the prison on August 1, 1864. While in prison, he contracted yellow fever.

He was discharged on February 17, 1865, before the war ended. On March 13, he boarded the L. C. Swan and headed up the Mississippi River toward Memphis. He optimistically planned on making it the rest of the way home on foot. He died a couple of hours into the journey before the boat even reached Vicksburg. They buried him on the riverbank. Later, his family would place a monument, bearing his name, in the family plot.

While John was being buried on the riverbank, his mother was dealing with the war as a widow. It was shortly after the Yankee scare when Mrs. Erwin gathered her family, the valuables, and the slaves to hide in the cave, that Jesse Barnes came calling.

"I'm here to reclaim my property." The alcohol on his breath and his general mean disposition were enough to send the dog that lay on the porch running.

Elizabeth looked at him with a piercing hatred. The man was a menace, almost always with a bottle in his hand since the war.

Sally had been with them for three years. They had all hoped with everything else to keep him busy, he might forget about the child.

"Now, what use is the girl to you?" Elizabeth scoffed. "She's still young, neither old enough or strong enough to work."

"She's still my property, and I've come to claim her."

Elizabeth stood stalwart in her doorway, not inviting him in. If it were anyone other than Jesse Barnes, she might have invited him in to have a friendly discussion over a hot cup of sassafras tea so he might see how unreasonable it was to take the child, but Mr. Barnes was not a reasonable man. He was drunk and belligerent, and there was no dealing with him in his state. It was rumored this had become his constant condition. The war was going badly for the Confederates, and Jesse Barnes' livelihood was slipping through his hands.

Peter sat on the wagon. He had loosened his orange scarf enough that one could see the throbbing veins in his neck. Elizabeth's own face was livid with anger. She reared her head back and placed her hands on her hips in defiance. Ib stood rigidly behind her, clenching her jaw.

"I have the papers, Mrs. Erwin. You don't have a legal leg to stand on as far as the girl goes. As long as slavery is still legal in Kentucky, I have my rights."

"Indeed you do, Mr. Barnes. Indeed, you do," Elizabeth said. "For now," she added with inhospitable eyes that could easily have killed the man where he stood if her eyes could have killed. "If you will wait, I will have Ib fetch the child."

"Don't make me wait too long."

Ib stood tense beside her mistress, not moving until Elizabeth turned and commanded her with resignation, "Ib, go find Nell and bring Sally."

"Yes'm," Ib said with a contorted face, scowling at the man before she turned her back to him and walked away.

Ib returned followed by Nell who held tightly to Sally, who at almost six didn't yet grasp the enormity of the situation. But, upon seeing Master Barnes, Sally let out a scream before breaking into sobs. "No, Nell, no," she cried.

"We promise to retrieve you again as soon as possible," Mistress Erwin said, holding Sally's hand and giving it a pat while she was in the arms of her grandmother. Nell hugged the child firmly and kissed her on the forehead before she handed her to Peter who put her in the back of the wagon. The women watched as Jesse Barnes stepped up to the wagon seat, almost falling to the ground on his first attempt.

"Now, now, Sally. It will be all right. The women back at Boone will be glad to see you," Peter said. He took a wilting flower from his front pocket, handing it to her, trying to appease her. Still, Sally bawled and stretched her arms out from the back of the wagon toward Nell and Ib who stood on the porch. Elizabeth stood watching from the doorway.

"Shut that nigger up," Jesse Barnes shouted to Peter, throwing his empty bottle to the ground.

"I's doin' my best, Massa," Peter said as he jerked hard on the reins. The women watched the wagon disappear in a cloud of dust.

"Not to worry. We will get her back," Elizabeth said to Ib and Nell. All three had tears in their eyes. "That man is out for revenge, pure and simple. He claims he is not getting paid for hiring out his slaves. No wonder. The war has left none of us prospering. The Union is winning, and Mr. Barnes knows that soon he will lose everything. Yes, mark my words, Mr. Barnes will be humbled soon enough."

"So, sadly you ended up back at Boone," Alice said.

"Yes'm."

"But you eventually left?"

"Yes'm. There was a big blast that blew out the furnace fer good. The blast killed a lot of the men. Missus Erwin was gettin' old 'bout this time, but still, she was a lookin' out fer me.

"That's how I come to know Martha. Martha was a Burchett 'fore she married. The Burchetts and the Erwins was related by marriage. Almost everyone up that holler related in some way. Everyone called her Marthie. Marthie was one of the kindest women there e'er was. After she get older everybody take to calling her Aunt Marthie.

"She came into Boone as bold as you please on top of a mule. After some dickering with Massa Barnes, she paid him some money fer me, and I got atop that mule right 'hind Marthie. And we rode off, but not 'fore a man stopped us and took our picture together."

"Sally, I'm confused," Alice said. "When did this furnace close down?"

"The big blast done happened in March of 1872. I 'member it well. It be big news."

"So, you were around fourteen at the time?"

"Yes'm. I reckon so. Marthie wasn't too much older than me. But she was married, and her man was sick, and she needed somebody to help her. She had three young'uns and a sick man. What was she to do?"

"But it was 1872 you say, and she bought you from Jesse Barnes?"

"Yes'm."

"Are you sure, Miss Sally? Slavery was over. Jesse Barnes would have had no right to sell you."

"Yes'm, and Marthie reminded Massa Barnes of that, but it was of no use. It was her agin him, and he was drinkin' mighty heavy in those days. The man was meaner than a snake and as crazy as one, too. You ne'er know what he might do. Best just to keep the peace with him."

"What happened after that?"

"Well, we's rode off, and Jesse Barnes rode off, too, in the opp'sit' direction. No one e'er hear'd from him agin. That made a lot of folks happy, I 'spect."

"I'm sure it did. Too bad it couldn't have happened sooner." Alice tried to smile. At the same time, if it had happened sooner, she wouldn't have been born.

"Yes'm."

"Where is she?" Jesse asked.

"I don't know, boss. But she'll be here. Don't worry."

"We have to be leaving soon," he said, removing his hat and running his fingers through his greasy hair. "That nigger is the only thing that's holding me up. I want to be out of here by noon. I want to make Lexington by nightfall."

"Not to worry, boss. She'll come after her."

"Would you quit telling me not to worry." Jesse placed his hat back on his head.

"Yes, boss."

It was April, and the first vestiges of spring were showing. It was high noon as Martha, straddled like a man across the mule she had borrowed from a neighbor, rode into Boone Furnace. Martha had been there with her parents before the war. What she rode into was a different place than what she remembered. The once bustling little town was a shell of its former self. It had all but turned into a ghost town, with only a few stragglers here and there. Most had cleared out after the blast that shut the furnace down. She was to meet a man named Jesse Barnes. Elizabeth Erwin warned her about him. On the long ride, Martha practiced out loud what she might say to the man, asking the mule for confirmation on the proper approach. The mule gave none.

"Where's the child called Sally?" she asked of the first man she saw as she got off her mule. One of the few remaining Negroes turned his head in the direction of a girl, who stood off to the side, peeking from behind some rubble that must have come from the blast. Martha looked over her way, smiling, trying to reassure her.

"I's Noah," the man said, before taking the reins from Martha and leading the mule over to the water trough a few feet away. Noah had scars on one whole side of his body, scars that were etched in with permanent black soot against his light brown skin. He walked with a pronounced limp. A mulatto, Martha observed, and a rather beaten down one. Martha mustered a sympathetic smile. He quickly turned his head in the other direction as a white man walked toward them.

The clean shaven man wore a brown hat. Black oiled hair oozed from beneath the rim. He wore a black frock coat with a black matching cravat tucked into his white shirt. Martha summed him up as a small man trying to command a big appearance and knew immediately he was the man she was there to see. Elizabeth Erwin had described him well. His eyes appeared sinister and as black as the coat he wore.

Martha didn't flinch. She eyed him up and down, resting her eyes on his fawn colored pants and dusty black boots, what any other man out in the field might wear. The man was mismatched, a small man trying to exude an air of a gentleman. The moment he opened his mouth, she knew he was no gentleman.

"I'm Jesse Barnes. I reckon you might be Mrs. Musick," he said, turning his head to the side and spitting out a wad of chewing tobacco. The gold tooth that Mrs. Erwin had given as an identifying feature, glared in the sunlight.

"You reckon right. I'm here for the child called Sally."

"Well, before I hand the girl over to you, we need to conduct some business," Jesse Barnes said with a stern face. "And, besides, she's no child. I reckon she's commenced her bleed and can do the work of a woman now."

"Mister Barnes, you know slavery is no longer legal. It became illegal seven years ago, and you don't have any call to sell that girl to me," Martha quipped.

"Maybe so. Maybe not. The way I see it, Kentucky hasn't passed that law, yet. And if'n it were illegal, you don't have any call to take her off and make her *your* nigger."

Martha winced. "What I intend is to give her a roof over her head and food in exchange for her help. And some decent clothes and shoes. Those rags she's wearing are an atrocity. I guess you've heard I have a sick husband and need help. And, both her uncle and grandmother gave me permission to take her. Her uncle would take her in, but he can hardly feed and clothe the family he has."

"Well, that may be rightly so, ma'am, but still, I have to

make a living, and she became the property of this here establishment as she was born to the slaves I oversaw. And, as for slavery ending, all I can say is the damn darkies were better off before the war ended."

"That may well be your opinion, Mister Barnes. I don't share it."

"Mrs. Musick, if you don't pay me for the girl, then someone else will." A silence ensued as both stood their ground. Martha looked over to see Sally frozen behind the rubble. Her hair shot in every direction like a bush in need of pruning. Her skin was only a couple of shades lighter than a piece of coal. Noah stood off to the side like a statue, holding onto the reins of the mule. Even the mule stood motionless.

Jesse Barnes made the first overture. "Ma'am, you look like an honest woman. We *did* have an agreement. Do you intend to honor it or not?"

The tenseness in the air disrupted what had started out as a beautiful spring morning.

Martha walked off in a huff in the direction of her mule. She reached into her saddle bag and returned, extending two bills toward Mr. Barnes. "I believe this was the price that was agreed upon."

Jesse Barnes gave a smile of satisfaction and took the money from her, placing it in the pocket of his black frock coat. "It's been a pleasure doing business with you ma'am." He walked away, awaiting no reply, his boots leaving a trail of dust behind him.

Martha noticed the stiffness leave Noah's body as Barnes walked away. Sally stood like a dark silhouette behind the rubble.

"Sally, it's all right," Martha called out. She walked over to Sally. "I'm here to take you home with me. Do you want to go home with me? I'll see that you're fed and clothed."

Sally stepped from behind the rocks, and said, "Yes'm."

The ragged dress barely covering her looked to be nothing more than an old seed sack. She looked more like a feral cat than a young girl. She stepped in front of Martha, barefoot, more assured than before. "Do you wan' me to walk 'side you?" she asked.

"No, Sally," Martha said as Noah helped her up onto the mule. "I want you to get up here *behind* me. Sally's your name, right? That's what I was told."

"Yes'm. Sally Ann Barnes," she said, awkwardly with her head down. "I ain't ne'er been on a horse 'fore. I might'n be scared. I could walk 'hind you."

"Nonsense, girl. You'll ride up here with me. It'll be fine. And, it's not a horse. It's a mule. Do you know the difference?"

"Yes'm. A mule does the hard work, like a slave."

Martha smiled down at Sally. "Sally, you're making me feel guilty about this mule now." She laughed. "But not too much, as on the way here I talked to this mule, and it declined to answer me back." A grin shot across Sally's face. "And, Sally, you are no longer a slave. Do you understand that?"

Sally looked to the ground. "Yes'm."

Martha reached out her hand to the girl. "Well, come on now. Sit up here behind me."

Noah helped her up. "You'll take care of her, won't you ma'am?"

"Yes, Noah, I will. You're not to worry about Sally any longer. She'll be taken care of."

"Wait, wait," a man yelled, running up to them.

Martha pulled on the reins to steady her mule. "What, sir?"

"My name is Jackson. I'm a reporter. Do you mind if I take your picture?"

"My picture? Oh, my." Martha straightened her bonnet.

"Yours and the girl's. You can stay on top of your mule. Just try to keep the animal still."

"We'd be honored," Martha said with a blush, pushing a strand of hair up under her bonnet.

Mr. Jackson pointed his camera in their direction.

"Sally, keep as still as you can," Martha said, as she turned back facing her.

THEY RODE a mile out of Boone Furnace in silence before Martha spoke. "Sally, what happened to Noah?"

"Do you mean how he walk funny?"

"That as well as how he got the scars on his face."

"The limp, that come 'fore the war. People say he liked to run away. His massa whipped his legs hard so he couldn't run no more. And, the scars, they be burns that come from the furnace."

"Do you mean when the furnace blew out?"

"No, 'fore. It was sometime durin' the war. I's didn't see it happen, but everybody be talkin' 'bout it when it did. I's was young, but know what they be talkin' 'bout. One of the white men pushed one of the slaves into the furnace. Noah was one of the men that tried to dig him out, but all they got was burns on their bodies and a chunk of hot rock they shoveled into the creek to cool. Us child'n was told to stay 'way from it, but we's sneaked off plenty of times. All the hot pieces cooled down and become one big chunk of rock that was too big for anybody to move. If"n you looked close 'nough, you could see black bones buried inside of the rock. Some say that be my daddy. I's ne'er know for sure. I's was young when it happened. No one told me fer sure it be true or not, but that 'bout the same time he go missin'."

"Oh, child." Martha looked straight ahead, tears rolling down her cheeks.

"This is my husband, Campbell," Martha said.

Sally scrutinized the man, who sat propped up in bed. His eyes were bloodshot, and he was as pale as the white bed cover.

"Hello," he said, followed by a round of coughing. Martha reached for the tin cup on his nightstand and placed it to his lips. After the coughing susided, he said, "I'm sick. Probably ain't getting no better."

Sally had seen enough sickness in her day to know he was telling the truth.

"Now Campbell, don't say that," Martha said, while removing her bonnet. A strand of hair fell across her cheek.

"Might as well face facts, Martha. Ain't that why you rode all that way to get the girl. A dying husband takes up a lot of time." Martha wiped her husband's forehead with a wet rag. "But you are a sight for these sore eyes. As pretty as the day I married you." He reached for the fallen strand of hair, twirling it in his fingers.

He turned to Sally. "Ain't she pretty?"

"Yes, sir," Sally said, shyly, holding her head down.

"I got sick during the war. Cholera. Had to leave the army because of it. They called me a deserter. Thought we could get a clean start in Oklahoma. What a waste. We decided it best to return home. On the way back, the sickness started to return," Campbell Musick said, looking at Sally. "A sheer disappointment. No wonder they were giving the land away. A complete and utter waste. Yes, a complete and utter waste." He had repeated the statement enough on the way back from Oklahoma. That was when he wasn't delirious with fever in the back of the wagon where Martha bathed him with damp cloths.

"It was Martha's brother who enticed us to take the leap. *What did they have in Kentucky*, he asked. I'll tell you what we had. We had plenty. The grass ain't always greener on the other side. Sometimes you're better off staying put." He sat silent for a bit. Martha sat on the edge of the bed beside him. Sally stood on the wooden floor boards, in her dirty smock, looking her new surroundings up and down.

"Why am I saying this to you?" he asked. "It wouldn't have been wise on your part to stay put. I hear the grass at Boone Furnace ain't green at all." He started another round of coughing, and Martha reached, once again, for the tin cup of water and held it to his lips. He took a sip and coughed some more. When the coughing eased off, he said, "Martha tells me you're an orphan."

"Yes, sir, Massa."

"Master? Don't go calling me master," he said, his eyes drifting shut as he said it.

"Yes, sir. What should I be callin' you?" Sally looked at Martha.

"Campbell. Campbell will be fine. We don't stand on airs, here," he said with eyes shut, his voice trailing off before falling asleep.

Martha looked at Sally. "We're both dirty after the trip. I guess we should get cleaned up and start on supper."

Sally looked down, embarrassed by her meager covering.

"After we get you cleaned up, we'll find you something to wear. I have a dress that ought to fit you just fine. It's pink. I think pink would look good on you. We'll both take a trip down to the creek and wash up. We'll get rid of that dirty old smock."

"Yes'm, Missus."

"Martha, Sally. Or Marthie. Lots of folks call me Marthie."

———

"WHAT HAPPENED after you were with the Musicks? Are you too tired, Sally?"

"No, it does me good to talk 'bout it."

"Miss Sally, you talk all you want. I'm retired now and have all the time in the world. I got up this morning and thought what do I want to do? And the first thing that I thought of was coming in to talk to you."

"Lawd, child. Why would you want to do that fer? You can do what you want now, and you come in ever' day to talk to me?"

"Because it's what I want. My child is grown, and my husband is at work. If I weren't here, I'd be puttering around the house. No, you are much more interesting."

"Bless you, child."

Alice placed her hand on Sally's scrawny forearm. "It's Friday, and on the weekend you'll probably have visitors. We'll be visiting our daughter, Kelly. She's throwing me a little retirement dinner."

"Aw, ain't that nice. Don't reckon I's ever been retired till I's come here. I's worked all my life. Worked right alongside the women and the men. Most of 'em have died off now.

Don't have much family left. I reckon Nell might come and see me this weekend. But, she have her own family now. And you's like family now, too. I've been tellin' you my life story. Ain't nobody e'er asked me 'bout it 'fore."

"Really, Miss Sally? I find that hard to believe."

"Once a newspaper take my picture on my hund'erth birthday. But they didn't ax much questions. I's think they thought I's too feeble to talk. I wore my finest dress fer the picture."

"I bet you looked really pretty."

"Aw," Sally said, acting embarrassed. "Ain't nobody e'er called me purty. My grand young'un one fine lookin' woman, though."

"Yes, I've seen her. Doesn't she want to know about your life? The family history?"

"No. Too painful."

"Too painful about colored history?"

"Yes'm, and other things. Some things even too painful for me to recall. But there was plenty of good times. Well, where was we?"

"You were telling me about Campbell and Martha Musick."

"Yes'm. Campbell died the following spring. I stood 'long-side Martha and her three child'n at the grave at Bethel Hill Cemetery as he was lowered in. I 'member Marthie cryin' somethin' awful. She truly loved that man. There weren't no finer woman than Marthie, and her first husband was a good man. I's sad I ne'er got to know him better. But, the short time I did know him, he treated me awful kind.

"Marthie had so much heartbreak. It was mighty hot as I 'member on the day Campbell was buried. It was July 1873. Funny, I can't count numbers. I've always had someone else count out money when I went to buy things, but dates stick in my head, somethin' I memorize inside my skull. The next

97

date I 'member was December 1875, the time Marthie took her second husband."

"She didn't stay widowed long, but I guess back then being married was a necessity," Alice said.

"Yes'm. Marthie loved the first man. It was written all o'er her, but the second, was how you said? For necessity."

Sally's eyes glazed over. "Things started changin' from that day."

Sally drifted off to sleep. Alice bent over and kissed her forehead, whispering, "I'll see you next week, Sally."

13

"*Y*ou're home," John said, as he came through the door. "And I smell something good."

"Yes, I stopped off at the grocery on my way home. And, I made your favorite, prime rib. I hope I didn't cook it too long. "

"Prime rib last Friday and now again? What's the occasion?"

"Just felt like it. Go wash up and sit down before your steak gets too cold. I'm tossing a salad to go with it."

John returned, took the plates from the cupboard, and placed them on the table. "I know there is more to this. Sally must have said something. You are lit up like a Christmas tree."

"She said a lot. She mentioned Docia, today." Alice's face glowed as she waltzed across the kitchen floor and retrieved the salad from the counter. "Sally told about how she hid in a cave from the Yankees along with Docia and Nell, the other slaves and the Erwins during the Civil War."

"They were Confederates? I thought you said Sally told

99

you, and you found during your research that one of the Erwin sons fought in the Civil War on the Yankee side?"

"I did. And, he did. Sally talked about that, too. But, the way I understand it, Mrs. Erwin was always afraid the troops were going to steal her valuables, no matter what side they were on. And, they did have slaves you know. I mean, what would Yankees think if they came upon them and saw the slaves?"

"Yes, that would make sense. Do you have any steak sauce to go with this?"

"Oh, sorry." Alice got up and opened the refrigerator door. "I made garlic butter. I forgot to put it on the table. It ends up they hid in the cave for nothing. It was a false alarm."

"Garlic butter? You know, I could get used to you being retired and going into work every day to talk to Sally. Sally puts you in an awfully good mood."

"I wish. But, I'm not sure how much longer she's got or if her memory will hold out. Sometimes, I'm afraid I'm tiring her out or maybe subconsciously pushing her to tell me things. But at the same time, when she's recounting her past, she becomes animated. I swear her face changes, and I can see her as a girl."

"From the way you've described Sally, I don't think she would tell you anything unless she wanted to."

"I'm going to put the garlic butter on the stove to simmer. It will be just a moment."

"Okay."

"You're probably right about that. She clearly wants to talk about her past. I think it's been bubbling up inside of her for a long time. She got up to her teenage years today." Alice paused and took a bite of her salad. "John, what if I hadn't been in Sally's room that day the Erwins came to visit? Don't you think it was fate? I would have never made the connection if they hadn't come. After all, it has next of kin as Ted Bonzo on her chart."

"Yes, but seeing the name Barnes made you stop and think."

"Yes, but lots of people have the last name of Barnes. That could have been a fluke. Still, I don't understand."

"Understand what?"

"Why on earth Docia used the name of Barnes for her son."

"Jesse was the father, wasn't he?"

"Yes, that's how the story goes. But she didn't marry him. Back then, even if they wanted to get married, they couldn't. And neither could we." Alice put her fork down. "What if you had known? What if I had known when we got married?"

"But you didn't know," John said.

"No, but say I did, and I didn't tell you?"

"Alice, I could never imagine you lying to me."

"I don't think I would, but I fell in love with you. Love makes you do some crazy things. Maybe I would have omitted the truth. Maybe I would have been afraid if you had known you wouldn't have wanted to marry me."

John got up from the table, went over to his wife, and took her hand. "Come with me." He led her to the couch in the living room.

"But, your steak. It will get cold."

"Not important. Anyway, you know I like it nearly cold."

They sat on the couch, facing each other. "Now, first of all, I fell in love with you. Even if the color of your skin was black I would have been in love with you. I'm sure we would have found a way. Don't you think people come together for a reason? It's written in the stars." He held up her chin. "Look at me, Alice. So what if you have ten per cent black blood running through your veins? It doesn't matter. And what about your father and his father and father before him? They all ended up looking as white as you do. And what about Kelly?"

"Kelly. Yes, we have to decide what to do. She needs to know that her great, great, great grandmother was a black woman. But then, at the same time, I'm afraid if we tell her it will change things for her."

"Do you mean she may decide not to marry or have children because of it?"

"Possibly, or wait, like we did, and then only have one child. The whole time I carried our baby, I was afraid it would come out dark skinned. I've read of that happening."

"Yes, I know you did. But, it didn't happen. And, I don't think it will happen with Kelly's offspring. After all Docia was a mulatto. Any black blood has been so watered down by now, and even if something like that were to happen, things are changing for the better." John put his hand on the back of his wife's neck and took her hand with his other hand. "I don't know why we are discussing this. We've discussed it before, and none of it matters."

"But the law says it matters. Technically, we broke the law by marrying."

"Okay, for starters, we didn't know at the time. And lastly, these are stupid laws. Your birth certificate says Caucasian. Kelly's birth certificate says Caucasian. That's the way it is. Case closed."

"John, you're only a lawyer, not a judge. You cannot close the case." She kissed him.

He smiled. "I take it the kiss said I won the case, though, and all this about watered down black blood and stupid miscegenation laws is ridiculous."

"I haven't even thought about any of this in years. But meeting and talking with Sally has brought it all back to life. Don't get me wrong. I love that I have met Sally. It's a double edged sword, though. I so want to know about my family history, but at the same time I'm scared that this secret I've kept for so long, that we've both kept, will reveal itself. I'm afraid for you. I'm afraid for Kelly.

"That day my mom told me has come back to me so vividly. It was such a bombshell, and not to tell me until after I married you. And, why did she wait until after my father was dead?"

"Sweetheart, your mother did what she thought was best for you."

"It was always talked about in our family, in whispers, behind closed doors. I had heard the name, Docia and Nell, and about Nell having six fingers on each hand and six toes. I never suspected they were black. They never said anything about them being black. I heard the Erwin name in connection with the Barnes name. And, I knew I had an ancestor named Jesse Barnes who was a slave trader, but I had no idea Docia was his slave and that they weren't married.

"Last year when I was pouring over all the records I could find, and somehow miraculously found Docia listed as a slave of the Erwins, I was both elated and shocked. Why I felt shocked, I don't know. I guess it was seeing something in black and white, an actual public record. I'll never forget that moment, sitting in the library. I immediately put my hand over the document, lest anyone else should see. It was instinctual. I've never considered myself prejudiced, but a part of me was afraid of what it could mean for me, for you, for our daughter. Why would I even think such things?"

"Exactly. The only problematic issues to come out of this is that because of silly, archaic laws, you can't share what you've learned with other people. Sheila, in particular, comes to mind. And, the other issue is having such a tyrant as Jesse Barnes as an ancestor."

"Sally talked quite a bit about Jesse Barnes today."

"Really?"

"Yes, he was worse than I ever imagined. It's one thing to find out your ancestor was a slave trader, another to hear first hand of his dastardly deeds. No telling how many of his progeny are out there, how many cousins I might have."

"If you want to go the Christian route, then all of us are related as we spring from Adam and Eve," he said.

"You're right, I suppose."

"After thirty years of marriage, a very good marriage I might add, what does any of it matter?"

"Our history matters. The more I think about it, the more I think Kelly should know. All these talks I'm having with Sally will be for naught if we don't tell her. It's nothing we should be ashamed of. Kelly has a right to know."

"Yes, she does. We will both tell her tomorrow night when we go over to her apartment for the retirement dinner she's fixing for you. And, besides, maybe Martin Luther King, Jr. and all the marches we are having will cause everything to change," he said.

"Yes, we can hope so. I'm sorry."

"Sweetheart, nothing to be sorry for." He put his arms around her and hugged her. "What's that smell?"

"Oh, no! The garlic butter."

14

"*M*iss Sally, I can't tell you how good it is to see you again," Alice said. "Let me give you a hug." She steadied herself on her cane with one hand and wrapped her other arm around Sally. "I hope you didn't think I'd forgotten you. I've called almost every day to check on you."

"I know'd you did, child. They told me." Alice noticed a definite change in Sally. It was age, of course. And then, there was Dr. King. Dare she bring up his name? Did Sally know? "I's see you has a cane."

"It helps. It's so good to get out finally. And, you were the first person I wanted to see. My leg's healing. It was stupid, really. I should have known there would be ice on the steps."

"Well, you's here now."

"Yes, and how have you been doing?" Alice asked as she pulled up a chair close to Sally's bed.

"Oh, 'bout as well as can be 'spected for a woman my age."

"Do you need anything?"

"Maybe prop me up so's I can see you proper."

Alice raised Sally up in the bed, positioning pillows

behind her. There was a noticeable difference in her body. Her bones protruded. Her face was sunken in. Her eyes were more glazed over. As a nurse, Alice had seen this over and over. Also, as a nurse, she knew when a patient was ready to give up. There was still a spark in Sally. It could fizzle out any day, but for now it was still strong.

"They brought my breakfast in earlier."

"Was it good?"

"I's need to teach 'em how to make gravy."

Alice laughed.

"I's thank the Lord I made it through another winter."

"I thank Him, too, Sally."

"I's hear'd about Dr. King," Sally said, as if she sensed what was on Alice's mind.

"Yes, it was so sad. I've cried for days." Sally's expression was hard to decipher. They both lingered in silence for what seemed like an eternity.

Sally sat upright in bed, staring off into space, before she finally blinked and asked, "Where did we leave off?"

"Leave off? You mean where did we leave off when you were telling me about your life?"

"Yes'm. More 'portent than e'er I's tell you 'bout it, now."

"Martha's husband, Campbell Musick had just died. And you said she married again."

"Yes'm. To a Bonzo. That's how I come to be with Ben and Ted."

MARTHA HAD KNOWN the Bonzos long before Campbell died. Just a generation before, they traveled from France, making their way to Pennsylvania. Some ventured further south to Ohio and Kentucky.

Neither could say it was love—not at first. The Bonzo

men were looking for women, good, sturdy women. Most in the area were already married; however, Martha, widowed, fit the bill for Charles Bonzo, thirty at the time, and seven years Martha's elder. Campbell was only a year older than Martha.

Besides a wife, Charles was also looking for land—land he could call his own. Marrying Martha could give him the in he was looking for, an alliance with the Burchetts and with the Erwins.

Upon marrying, they settled on a patch of ground on the edge of the Erwin farm. It sat at the bottom of a steep hill, nothing prime. It would be hard to farm, but it was all that Charles could afford and all the Erwins were willing to part with.

Charles, along with the aid of his brothers, began laying the rock for the foundation of the cabin alongside a stream he would move his new bride into along with the three young Musick children.

Sally hoed, planted, and tended to the children right alongside Martha. When she wasn't helping Martha, she trekked on the well-worn paths through the woods to whatever Erwin household or other household needed her most. She knew every path, every field, almost every nook and cranny throughout the area. At an early age, she was already becoming known for her skills as a midwife and the care of children. Despite the risks of childbirth, women had plenty of them. Boys were prized the most. As soon as a boy was big enough to hold a hoe he was put out in the garden. Sally worked no harder than any of the rest. Life was a struggle for everyone. They were all eking by, trying to make ends meet to feed their families.

The only thing that separated her from the others was the color of her skin and the stigma of being born into slavery. Most would always think of her as a slave. If being born into slavery wasn't bad enough, what was to follow for Sally was in many ways worse.

When Martha first noticed the bulge in Sally's stomach, a wave of nausea spread through her. "Sally, do you remember when you had your bleed last?"

Sally stopped peeling the potatoes and looked at Martha in embarrassment. "I's don't rightly 'member, Marthie, but I's thinkin' it was back durin' the last harvest or maybe right 'fore it."

"Sally, that was five months ago," Martha said.

Sally sat her knife down and held her head low.

"Now, Sally, don't be scared," Martha said, although a wave of fear spread throughout her own body, the body that was also carrying a child. Martha wiped her hands on her apron and walked over, putting her arms around Sally. "Sally, I know you haven't been around any men of your own kind. There haven't been any around these parts in a long while. Can you tell me who did this to you?" Martha lifted up Sally's lowered chin and looked into her eyes.

"No, ma'am," Sally said.

"Now, Sally, don't go talking like a slave. You aren't a slave any longer."

"No, Marthie," Sally said with tears welling up in her eyes. "I's scared. Scared of what might be done to me if'n I tell."

"Sally, haven't we always talked? It'll be all right. Haven't we been more like kin than anything?"

"No, Marthie, it won't be all right," Sally said as she let out a full blown wail and ran out of the house.

SEVERAL WEEKS PASSED. The only word that passed between Martha and Sally was about chores. Sally continued to keep her head lowered whenever she came into contact with Martha.

"Sally is with child," Martha announced one night to her husband. He had just climbed on top of her with a playful lust in his eyes. The proclamation triggered a new expression, one of alarm, as if the full moon fell into the bed between them creating a barrier between him and his wife—a barrier that couldn't be breached, at least not on this night. He fell like a boulder back over to his own side of the bed.

Martha rubbed her hand back and forth over her own swollen belly which was much farther along than Sally's. Charles remained silent as if in contemplation before saying, "We'll have to send her away."

Martha sprang up. "Send her away? Why?"

"People will talk. And, keep your voice down. She'll hear you. She's sleeping in the next room. The children will hear you."

Martha lowered her voice to a whisper. "Won't people talk if we send her away in this condition? How can we do that to her? And, where would we send her? This isn't her fault. Sally wouldn't do anything willingly. No telling how many times that girl was taken as pleasure by a man. How many times has as she been traipsing through these woods unattended? It could have happened more than once. I've seen men's eyes on her at different times. They all think of her still as a slave, as a piece of property. That poor child. It's all she has ever known."

"You don't know, Martha. She could have met up with someone of her own kind." Charles said.

There was something in his eyes. She could see the coldness of them in the light of the moon. "You know that ain't so. Do you know who did this, Charles?"

"No, Martha. It could be anyone. What has Sally said? Does anyone else know?"

Martha hesitated as she studied her husband's face. "I am the only one. But, she will be showing soon enough. She won't speak about it. Whoever did it put some awful fear in her. She's afraid, and I don't blame her. It could have been one of the Erwins. Or even one of my brothers. Or one of your brothers. Which one of your brothers, Charles? Or was it you?"

"Me? Woman, how could you say such a thing?"

Martha turned and rested her head back on the pillow, facing away from Charles. His hand inched over her expanding waist. She jumped and jerked away. Her whole body tensed. Charles withdrew his hand.

With tears dripping from her cheeks onto the pillow, she said, "I'll talk to Mrs. Erwin in the morning. I'm sure she'll take her in until the baby is born. Ib and Nell can tend to her."

"Yes, she'll be better off with her own kind," Charles said resolutely. He turned and within minutes, began snoring.

A silence gripped and choked what little breeze came through the open window. Martha lay there for what seemed like hours staring out the window at the full moon before drifting off to sleep. When she woke, she found Charles had already left the bed. She looked for Sally first thing but was told by her oldest that Sally had left for the field, not wanting any breakfast. Her husband, nowhere in sight, had also asked after Sally, her oldest said.

***

SALLY LAY in the narrow straw bed that once belonged to Ib. Across from it was Nell's bed. Sally was in their cabin, the old slave cabin. Ib, with the passing of Master Erwin so many years ago, and with her children all grown and with families of their own, at the mistress's invitation had moved into the big house. The mistress, as they still called her, wanted Ib by her side almost constantly these days. And, she said, she reckoned it would be okay if Nell joined her in the house, occasionally. Ib and Nell were the only ones who stayed on after the war ended.

When Martha told Sally it was best if she stayed with Nell and Ib, the only explanation she gave was that the family thought it best that she be with her own kind considering the circumstances. "Now Sally, if you were to tell me who the daddy is, I might could help."

"No, Marthie," Sally said, tensing up.

"I just hope it's not one of the Erwins. I don't want to send you from the frying pan into the fire."

"I's be okay with Nell."

Sally spent her time in the fields alongside Nell up until the moment her water broke, flooding the patch of corn she was hoeing. She and Nell made their way back to the small structure that Sally was now calling home. Seeing one of the Erwin children nearby, Nell said that Ib should be summoned right away to the cabin.

Ib came through the door, followed close behind by Mistress Erwin. Nearing eighty now, Mistress Erwin still saw fit to take charge. After all these years, she hadn't lost her strong-willed nature.

While most were looking the other way, putting Sally's condition out of their minds, the missus had acknowledged Sally's pregnancy straight away. When asked by Mistress Erwin who the father was, Sally feigned deafness and looked away. Still, the mistress was kind and as sympathetic to her plight as was Ib and Nell. Sally's having a child by a white man was a way of life ever since blacks were first brought over from Africa. The mistress said it wasn't likely to change in her lifetime, nor in her children's lifetime. "I don't condemn this poor child of what was wrought upon her race," she said.

Sally remembered a time when the mistress could be swayed by idle gossip and would take the side of the man in this situation, as many women were prone to do, but the mistress had softened in her old age. She had seen much in her lifetime. Her voice had become softer with each passing year, so much so, that sometimes when she spoke to Sally it felt like molasses running over a warm biscuit.

"Bring her up to the big house. There is no sense in that child being born in this dusty old cabin," the mistress said.

Ib and Nell took to the task of boiling water and preparing sheets while paying close attention to the contractions, as experienced midwives would. Both concurred it would be a short labor. This was often the case for black women, who were leaner and tougher than their white counterparts. Sally lay in Ib's bed, on the fine feather mattress, reflecting on her short life of eighteen years between each painful contraction.

Sally pondered her decision of having this baby, although there was no turning back now. She could have done away with the child she was carrying. She knew the herbs to take. No one would have ever known. And, maybe it would have saved a lot of heartache. But she wanted something of her own—*someone* of her own, a soft baby to hold.

Sally was thrust into a situation where she lived between worlds. She had lived with whites for so long she was an oddity to both the black world and the white world, not truly fitting into either. The color of her skin, which others saw so prominently, forced her into a limbo. The limbo between worlds was all she knew. It was a hard road to follow at times. She did her best to carve out her own niche between these worlds. Her new circumstance forced her out of the limbo. The way she saw it, humans were pushed to the brink at different times in their lives where they were forced to make a decision.

She had sobbed into her pillow on the night she heard Charles tell Marthie she had to leave, that she'd be better off with her own kind. Weren't they are own kind? Her family? Isn't that what Marthie had always said? She saw her own life and the lives of those around her fraught with difficulties and bad circumstances. Wasn't likely to change. All Sally could conclude was that the bad times polished the soul. Sally took each difficulty as it came, adjusting and surrendering, finding a depth inside herself she used as a harbor of safeness.

She knew her decision to keep this baby would regulate the course of her and her baby's existence. After he began laying his hands on her, and when she stopped bleeding and knew she was with child, she made a choice. She would get something in return. She recalled the first kick, and how a wave of joy spread over her.

Another pain. "Push, child." The voices of Ib, Nell, and Mistress Erwin echoed in unison. She clenched her body tightly, gritted her teeth and gave it all she had. Sweat trickled down her skin. It wasn't like the drip of sweat out in the field. The smell was sweeter. It had a womanly aura to it, a new experience for her.

She relaxed, once again. Her mind drifted. Sally began to observe her surroundings from an undercurrent of stillness in which everything happens. When she could go deeper, she discovered she was, in fact, that same stillness. Within the stillness, she beheld the same power of the stars she gazed upon at night, the mist hovering over the garden in the wee hours of the morning, and the soil teeming with life as she struck the sharp edge of her hoe into it. The more she listened, the louder the stillness became. There was a void, a gap, between her thoughts where the stillness lay. There was a whole new identity in this gap, one that couldn't be labeled. Her identity couldn't be the labels people put on her.

There was the pity, the shame, the judgment, and the torment. She was more than that. She looked out from the deep place that others couldn't see into. She removed the mental sufferings from her mind dissolving them with the steady beat of her heart, a heart that became more determined to see love instead of hate. This baby would have it hard, but times were changing for the better. She had to believe that.

A sharp scream coming from her own mouth brought her back to the physical world. "Here, bite on this," Ib said, handing her a piece of soft cloth. Sally assisted with births as soon as she was able to boil a pot of water. She was there with the midwives looking on and taking orders. Now, she squatted over a blanket on a real feather bed, stunned that this process was happening to her.

Ib stood at the foot of the bed ready to catch the baby, while Mistress Erwin stood to one side of her and Nell to the other. "The head 'tis a crownin'," Ib exclaimed. Sally clasped her right hand tightly to Nell's bony, calloused hand with the extra digit and her left hand to Mistress Erwin's plumper, more supple hand.

"One last push, and it'll all be over, child," the mistress reassured her.

Ib held the squawking child up with the cord still connected. The baby girl was several shades paler than Sally. She exhibited a strong cry that belied strength, a quality that she would need if this child's life was to be anything like that of her own. The cry tapered into a whimper.

Sally lay on the bed in a state of exhaustion, harder than any field labor she had ever remembered. Ib put the baby up to Sally's breast.

"We have us a little Sally, here. She looks to be healthy

enough," Mistress Erwin said, exhibiting a pleased expression.

Little Sally. Sally held the baby in her arms and smiled as any proud mother would. She held the baby close to her heart. The two heartbeats intermingled, one strong, one faint. This was the real life doll she never had. This bond with the baby was the unconditional love she felt in the stillness. She felt a connectedness to all the other mothers of the world, whether human or animal. The instinct was the same. Two—mother and babe—together equaled wholeness. While holding her baby, all the separation became an illusion. Born out of an unspeakable act, this baby was God's gift to her. Didn't matter who the daddy was.

The fragile child with the dark body looked up at her with the darkest of eyes. Sally knew at that moment that everyone was born to love someone in life. This would be whom she would love, who she would give her own life for if necessary. Little Sally made all the suffering Sally had endured worth it. Little Sally was her family, her own kind.

15

*I*t was getting late, almost time for supper. John would worry about her but she couldn't leave now. Sally had a child by a man she wouldn't name. She had to know the rest of the story. At Sally's age, who knew if she would even last until the morning?

The doctor would make his weekly rounds tomorrow. She felt Sally's pulse. "What?" Sally jerked. She had fallen asleep.

"Nothing, Sally. It's okay. I'll be right back. I'm going to go check at the desk and see if they'll bring supper into your room tonight. Would you like that?"

"I reckon it'd be fine. What 'bout your husband? Don't you need to get home?"

"No. Not tonight. He's working late and won't mind if I stay," Alice lied. "He'll get dinner in town, close to his office. I don't want to go home to an empty house. So, you don't mind if I stay here with you, do you?" She didn't want Sally to become alarmed or feel guilty about her staying.

"No, I's could use the company, myself."

"I'll just see about your dinner. I'll be back shortly."

"All right," Sally said, closing her eyes once again.

Alice stood at the front desk. Ethel looked up. "Alice, what are you still doing here at this hour? Why are you here at all? You're retired now. I'd have been out of here after that last bite of cake."

"I guess I'm just married to the place, Ethel."

Ethel gave a shrug of the shoulders. "Myself—I can't wait until retirement. And what about your leg? Heard about your slip on the ice. Is it healing okay? Saw you walking around with that cane."

"Oh, my leg's doing fine. I'll be off this cane in a week or so. I've been visiting with Sally."

"That old Negro woman?" Ethel paused. "You've grown mighty attached to her, haven't you, hon?"

"Yes, I have."

"I think she's the oldest person we've ever had here. And, she's perkier than the young ones, if you can call eighty young."

"She's something. She's been telling me about her life, and I don't want to miss a word."

"I didn't think she talked a whole lot."

"Ethel, do you think you could have her dinner brought up for her? I'll leave when she falls asleep. Could I use your phone and call John and tell him I'll be a little late?"

"Sure," Ethel said, placing the phone on the counter. "Is the old lady doing all right? It's hard when you get attached to the patients."

"She's one-hundred-and-nine years-old. Who knows? She was doing okay when I left her room, but who's to say when I go back? And, how can you not be attached to her? She's the sweetest lady. Never complains. And, she's had a lot to complain about. I want to visit with her for as long as I can."

"SALLY, look what we have to eat tonight. Chicken and dumplings, mashed potatoes and green beans. Won't be as good as yours. I know you're a fine cook."

"Yes'm, that's what they say. My daughter turned out to be a mighty fine cook, too. She cooked fer a hotel."

"Until now, you've never mentioned your daughter—that is coming to visit you. I've only heard you talk about Nell. Is she…"

"Dead? Yes'm. She had a short life. Short when you look at mine."

"I'm sorry, Miss Sally."

"No, child. It's all right. She's in a better place. I's be joinin' her soon. I's can't wait to see her again. She had a hard life. I partly blame myself. But what was I to do?"

"SALLY, it's Peter and Lizzie comin' up the road," Ib said, her face like stone. It was anything but a joyous occasion as Ib and Nell stood on the porch by Sally who was holding her little girl, barely weaned, awaiting the inevitable. The missus and the rest of the Erwin clan had all saw fit to be scarce.

They arranged the undertaking to take place on Sunday morning, during church service. "I reckon the congregation is openin' they's hymnals 'bout now, commencin' to sing the first song," Nell said.

"Sally, you's don't has to worry. Me and Lizzie will take good care of her," Peter said, as he reached for the child. But, Sally clung to her baby with a fierceness that was making white indentations on the child's legs. The horrific scene of her as a child being handed over to Peter and carted off into a wagon when she was young, herself, was playing over in her mind. The saving grace was that Jesse Barnes was no longer in the picture.

"It ain't right. It just ain't right," Sally shouted, tears streaming down her face, all the while squeezing Little Sally hard.

Nell looked into Sally's eyes. "Sally, it be for the best. She won't be that far away. We'll go see her from time to time. Ever' chance we get. The mistress done said we could use the wagon to go visit," Nell said as she attempted to pry Sally's fingers, one by one from the child.

"Yes'm, Sally. You know if that child stay here it gonna cause a whole mess of trouble. It already has. Why, we's could have another Civil War on our hands," Ib said.

"Maybe I should say who is the daddy of this child and be done with it." Sally looked down at her daughter whose complexion had grown paler since the birth.

"Hush, Sally. That'll just cause more trouble. It best if the child be out of sight. Out of sight of the white folks. They's don't like to be reminded of their shame," Nell said.

"Amen to that," Peter chimed in. "I don't have long. You needs to say your goodbyes. I got to get the wagon back 'fore my boss gets out of church or I be in a whole heap of trouble."

"Sally, you's has got to let go. Peter has to go," Nell said.

Sally eased up her grip handing the little girl over to Lizzie.

"You's not to worry. We take good care of her, just like she's our own," Lizzie said.

"We's know you will," Nell said, with one hand on Sally's shoulder. Sally's arms were extended out to Little Sally as if Peter and Lizzie were returning her instead of taking her away.

Sally, Ib and Nell watched as Peter and his wife rode off

with Little Sally. All three stood there until the wagon disappeared over the hill.

"She be all right, Nell?" Sally asked with an uncertainty in
her voice and with tears running down her cheeks.

"Yes, she be all right," Nell said, rubbing her granddaughter's shoulder and squeezing her six fingers tightly into
Sally's dress. "Now, Martha be needin' you to help with
her baby."

Sally wiped the tears from her eyes. "It ain't fair I has to
hand my own baby off and take care of white folk's babies."

"I's know, honey. I's know. One day it gonna be different.
Might not see it my lifetime, but Little Sally'll surely see it in
hers," Nell said, staring down the road into the trail of dust.

"My child gonna stand up to the white folks," Sally
vowed.

"She is a feisty one," Ib said. "Lawd, I remember that
wallop she let out the day she was born. If anybody stand up
to the white folk, it be her."

"But she didn't e'en let out a whimper today," Sally said.

They stood behind Sally as she gazed off into the
distance. "I reckon they be shoutin' their amens to the
preacher's sermon 'bout now," Nell said.

Sally sat silent for a good bit before saying, "I don't think
I's be goin' back to church for a good smart bit, if'n ever."
Nell squeezed her six fingers even tighter into Sally's
shoulder as they all continued to stare at the trail of dust left
by the wagon.

"Aw, don't cry, child."

"I can't help it, Miss Sally. I can only imagine what it
would be like having a child ripped from my arms," Alice said.

"It happened all the time back then, to colored folks. But, it hurt just the same. Yes'm, it hurt somethin' fierce. But at least I knows she be with family and that they's take good care of her. That give me some comfort."

"But you must have gone back to church. You have a Bible beside your bed, and you said you have remembered a lot of the verses by heart?"

"Yes'm. In time I's went back. Marthie would give me the wagon on Sundays, and I drove it all the way to Vanceburg so's I could go to church with Sally May and Peter's kin. They's always gettin' our names mixed up. So, I decided to name her May causin' that's the month she's born. We went to the colored church there. There be a whole community of colored people in Vanceburg. And sometimes, she go back with me fer visits. When she do, we always stay in Nell's cabin, and Mistress Erwin look the other way. I knows she feel the guilt of sendin' her 'way like she did. Course, she weren't the only one. And each time I see Sally May it take her a little while to get used to me agin."

SALLY MAY RAN through the house, tearing out the bow from her hair. "That child gonna be the death of me," Lizzie said. "When her mama comin'?"

"I sees her now," Sam said. "She be comin' up the road."

"Now, you behave, Sally. Your mama walkin' up the path now."

"You my mama."

"No, Sally. Miss Sally your mama, and I want you to call her that."

"I ain't gonna call her that. And, how come we's got the same name?"

"Caus'n she your mama. You be named after her."

"No, she ain't my mama."

Lizzie shook Little Sally. "Now, you call her that, you hear? You'll hurt her feelings if you don't. We talked 'bout this. You 'member?"

"Yes'm, I 'member."

"And, you gonna do what I say? If you's act good, there might be an extra sliver of apple pie after church service. I hears Ib baked one up just fer you. And, you gonna sit by Sally in church and hold her hand when you's walk back home. It's somethin' special her go'n to church. She ain't been in a while, at least not back where she usually go."

"You's goin' with us?"

"No, Sally May. Your mama takin' you back in the wagon to her own church. She be bringin' you back sometime tomorrow."

"Why's can't we go here? You say she don't go to her own church no more. Why don't she go? You told me everybody 'sposed to go to church."

"Child you does ax a lot of questions."

"It good to ax questions, Mama. How else I 'posed to learn?"

"I reckon you is right. All I's can say is that she has her reasons." Lizzie muttered under her breath, "Some mighty fine reasons."

"What you say, Mama?"

"I say nothin'. And, you call me Aunt Lizzie when Sally come. You hear?"

"I's hear."

"Now, let's fix that bow back in your hair. Nell sent it special from Missus Erwin. It matches the red dress she sent you."

"Mama, how come we have the same name?"

"Sally, you already axed me that. You don't have the same

name. Your mama be Sally Ann, and you be Sally May. Do you 'member why you be Sally May?"

"Yes'm, you say I's born in the month of May."

"That's right. But your mama would know that better than me. One day you can ax her, but not today. Sam, you get the door. I hear her walkin' up the porch steps. Now, let's see a big smile when she comes through that there door."

"Oh, Sally, don't you look mighty purty. Why, you's a sight for sore eyes," Sally said. "Aw, child. Come here to Mama."

"Go on, now. Don't be shy," Lizzie said.

"She don't see me 'nough," Sally said, shaking her head.

"Give her a hug, Sally May." Sally May eased over to her mama, after a push from Lizzie.

"Aw, that's just what I needed," Sally said, squeezing her daughter tight.

SALLY LOOKED UP AT ALICE. "And then, after some years, all the same folks who sent her away start to likin' Sally May. Oh, she was a precocious child. But, people couldn't help but like her. Said 'xactly what she thought. Sometimes, more than not, it got her in trouble, but deep down I's mighty proud of her. When we go to the white people's church, she sat right 'longside Martha. And, I sat on the other side of her. It was mostly 'cause of Sally May I's went. Mistress Erwin was getin' touched in the head by this time, but she saw fit to buy Sally a red frock. Oh, that child. She was so happy. She spun 'round. She's so proud. If'n it weren't for her frizzy hair, she could've passed fer white in that dress. And the shoes. Well, the shoes was hand-me-downs, but Sam polish them up so fine that they's could've passed fer new. Sam be Peter and Lizzie's boy.

"Sally begged and begged. She said we's had to go to church. I reckon that be Mistress Erwin that put it into her head. The mistress felt guilty that I's had quit goin'. Thought it be her fault. So, we all loaded into the wagon and went off to church. Ib made a pile of fried chicken to take 'long for the picnic afterward. In those days, there was always supper after the sermon, the first sermon. Church went on for nigh a whole day on some days.

"But, we's all crowded onto two of the front benches. Sally insisted we sit up front. She wanted the preacher to notice her in her new dress. We bein' the only colored people there, me, Sally May, Ib and Nell, nobody's ne'er said nothin' to us 'bout sittin' up front. No, Mistress Erwin would have come down on 'em mighty hard if they had of. And Marthie, too."

"And did the preacher notice her dress?"

"Yes'm. He complimented Dora on what she was wearin'. That be Sally May's little friend. Then he turned to Sally May and say *Sally May, that be a mighty fine dress you're wearin'*. I think Mistress Erwin took him 'side and made sure he say somethin' to her. Sally May couldn't have been prouder. I'll ne'er forget that day."

Sally's eyes closed, and she drifted off to sleep. Alice bent down and kissed her forehead before partially closing the door to her room. She stopped off at the nurse's station. "I'm leaving now but will be back first thing in the morning. If anything should happen in the interim…"

"Yes, I'm on duty tonight. I'll be sure to call you," Ethel said.

*a*lice entered Sally's room. "You're up?"

"Yes'm."

"Did you sleep well?"

"Yes'm." There was a knock on the door. It was Mac with a tray of food.

"Aw, I see it's time for breakfast. Do you feel up to eating in the cafeteria? Might be good to go for a spin down the hall."

"Yes'm. Might be nice."

"Mac, do you mind taking her food down to the cafeteria?"

"Not at all."

Sally sat at the table with the lone vase with the silk rose with her newest, dearest friend, Alice. Sally ate slowly, gumming her oatmeal, sometimes moving the food to the back of her mouth. "Do you want some juice, Sally?"

"Yes'm."

The nurse helped Sally raise the plastic cup with the paper straw up to her mouth.

"I ne'er had orange juice till I come here."

J. SCHLENKER

"What did you drink?"

"We pressed apples fer cider. And, we's had plenty of milk from the cows. And there was moonshine on occasion—not that I e'er had a sip." Sally grinned showing her gums and tried to raise her hand in a gesture with her fingers. "Well, maybe just a smidgeon. Everybody in the holler had a still. Ben made the best moonshine 'round, but that weren't till later.

"Yes'm, Ben was born in the summer of eighty-two as I recollect. Marthie just kept havin' child'n. Up till then, I went back and forth a lot, 'tween Smokey Valley and Vanceburg. Vanceburg be where Sally May lived, with Peter and Lizzie. They worked in the hotel there, and Sally May loved that hotel.

"I always takin' care of somebody's child'n, always bein' a midwife. I goes where'er I's needed. I's tried to stay close to Vanceburg durin' Sally May's growin' up years, but after Ben was born, Marthie got in an awful state."

"What happened?" As Alice asked, she noticed how quiet the cafeteria had gotten. Everyone was listening to Sally—even Sheila, who was helping a patient at the next table.

"Well, after Ben was born, Martha's oldest, her firstborn by Campbell Musick, want to go off to Oklahoma with his uncle. His uncle was ready to hitch a wagon and head back out there to join the part of the kin who stayed there on the first trip. Marthie got mighty torn up o'er it. I can't say as I blamed her. Was only twelve when he left. Course, he wrote her from time to time. She got so excited whene'er a letter from him arrived. Marthie read 'em to me. Later on, he became sheriff. Marthie was so proud of him.

"It weren't till much later on, he and a whole slew of kinfolks come back to visit. They all come by train. I 'member us all walkin' up to church together. By that time Marthie was

SALLY

gettin' old. She was in a wheel chair, like'n I am now. Course, I was older, too, but I's 'member it well. We had a big family reunion. Ever' year we's had one. Always took a big group picture. I's was always in it, lots of times right in the front. In later years, after Marthie passed, people stood in line to come up and give me a hug. I's was the oldest, then. Why, law, I can still feel the warmth of their bodies like'n it was yesterday if I think on it hard 'nough. Many a time, Sally May went with me. And then, Sally May passed. Sometimes Nell went with me. Why, they's just treated like one of the family.

"Those reunions got so big that we started havin' 'em at Carter Caves. We cooked fer days gettin' everythin' ready. And Ben and Ted started polishin' up their cars days 'fore. They's so proud of their cars. Town cars, they called 'em. A lot of folks come ridin' in on big ole hay wagons, but we loaded up baskets of food and rode into those reunions like somethin' grand.

"That time Marthie's son come back, she was so happy. That's all she could talk 'bout. And, when she seen him, you'd a thought she'd seen a ghost. Growed into a right handsome man. Looked just like Campbell, he did.

"Yes'm. He was a mighty fine lookin' man. Marthie ne'er really got o'er Campbell. They say you ne'er get o'er your first love." Sally paused before adding, "My first love's Sally May.

"Marthie was always trying to clear him of the desertion charges. And, she finally did. But, that weren't till years after he passed—1891 or thereabouts. Got her some compensation and a gravestone for his grave. I was there with her the day they placed it on his grave. Yes'm, that was in ninety-one. Sure of it. I 'member that day well."

"Miss Sally, you sure are good with dates."

"Well, I guess since I ne'er learned to read or write, I had lots of room rattling 'round in my head fer somethin'. Might as well be dates. Lots of em to 'member at my age."

"Oh, I think there is a lot more up there than just dates. And, also, a lot right here." Alice placed her hand over Sally's heart.

"Sally, why did you never marry?" Alice noticed everyone leaning in closer to Sally, even Sheila.

BEN LOOKED up and adjusted his eyes to the glare of the sun. "It appears we have a visitor."

A mirage of a man was yet off in the distance. Sally looked to Ben, gripping her hoe, and then to the man as he approached them. Her loose bonnet strings flapped in the faint breeze as she looked in the man's direction. As he drew nearer, they saw that his skin was dark like Sally's. As he came closer, Ben nodded his head to acknowledge him.

"Hot day out," the man said.

"Yes sir, mighty hot day," Ben replied

"I's been walkin' fer days, takin' work where'er I's can find it." He took his handkerchief and wiped the beads of sweat from the back of his neck. "Just the two of you tendin' to this here garden?" he asked.

"Today, just the two of us," Ben replied, as he swatted away a fly with one hand and leaned on his hoe with the other.

"Might you be needin' somebody else?" He spoke to Ben but looked at Sally.

"Don't reckon we do," Ben replied. "We wouldn't have any money to pay you. Not many around these parts can afford to hire anyone outside the family."

"Might I have some water? Mighty thirsty." The man removed his hat and shook off the dust. He stole another glance toward Sally, taking in the full picture of her before returning his eyes to Ben. Sally turned away and continued to hoe.

Ben dropped his hoe to the ground. "Follow me," he said.

Sally looked up from her work and saw them talking by the spring, but couldn't make out what they were saying. After a while, they both returned. The man held his hat, fumbling with it with both hands, his eyes darting back and forth between the two of them. He hesitated. "If'n I might come to the purpose of my trek?"

"You may," Ben replied with a mischievous smile.

The man looked at Sally and then to Ben. "You don't know of any woman 'round here I could take as a wife do you?"

Ben looked at Sally with a sheepish grin. "I don't know, but you might ask this fine lady here." Ben followed with a hearty laugh.

Sally loosened the grip on her hoe, dropping it to the dirt, and ran back to the house. She hid behind a partially open door, eyeing Ben and the man over while they continued to talk. She could see Ben shaking his head. Her heart skipped a beat when she saw them walking toward the house, but they passed on by the entrance and stopped again at the spring. She watched nervously through the cracked door as Ben handed the man a Mason jar. The black man knelt at the spring, filling it before continuing on with his journey. Sally stood behind the screen door and watched the man walk off, all the while hearing her heart pound within her chest.

"Sally, you can come out now," Ben yelled out. "Lord only knows what you might have done if I had invited the poor man to supper."

"Ben, I heard you gave Sally quite a scare today," Martha said.

"Oh, Sally told on me, did she?" Ben said, reaching for another biscuit. "These are mighty fine biscuits, Sally."

"Now, don't go tryin' to get on my good side, Ben. It be too late fer that," Sally said.

"Yeah, Sally, you make excellent biscuits. You'd make some man a mighty fine wife," Ben said. Sally gave him a pronounced glare.

"You be too big fer your britches, Ben."

"Aw, Sally, I was having fun. I didn't mean nothing hurtful by it."

"Stop it, Ben," Martha said. "If Sally wants a man, I reckon she can find one on her own. She doesn't need your help. And after being around you all the time, I don't know why she'd want one. And, Ben, one day, these practical jokes of yours are going get you in trouble."

"What's gonna get him in trouble is that still he has down in the woods, if the law e'er comes out here," Sally retorted.

"He'd have to throw me and every fellow up in this holler in the jailhouse, and I don't think it would hold us all," Ben said, breaking out in laughter. "Did you make apple pie, Sally?" Ben asked.

"Why, yes sir, I did." She paused. "But not fer ever'body."

"Oh, Sally, why do you want to go and hold a grudge?" Ben asked.

"Ben, leave Sally alone. You're eighteen, now—a man. Why do you want to act like a child?" Martha scolded.

"I'm just having some fun. And there ain't no Negro men anywhere near these parts that ain't already married. Then one comes along looking for a wife, and Sally runs away and hides. But you didn't hide too well. I saw you behind the door, clinging to it the way a tick clings to a dog. Why are you so scared of men, Sally?"

"Well, Sally don't need your kind of fun, and who says Sally is scared of men?" Martha said.

"Yes'm who says I's scared of men?" Sally gave a glare in Charles's direction, who was finishing up his plate, unconcerned about the day's excitement. Sally turned back to Ben. "Like your mama say, you be a man now. Time you be lookin' fer a wife. Don't need to be worryin' 'bout me."

"What on earth do you mean, Sally? I'm too young to get married. Look at my papa, here. He stayed a bachelor until he was thirty. I reckon I can do the same."

"Ben, you finished that pie long ago. You have time to do some more chores before the sun goes down," Marthie said, taking his plate.

"Listen to your mother, Ben. We all live under this roof. We have to get along," Charles said, rising from the table. "Come help me out in the field before it gets dark. Doesn't look like you'll be getting any seconds on that pie."

Sally and Marthie started clearing the dishes. "Sally, don't pay Ben no mind. You know what a practical joker he is. He's a boy, a boy that doesn't know the half of what you've been through. One day, when he settles down, maybe he'll understand. Although, I don't reckon a man can ever understand the plight of a woman in this world."

Sally poured hot water from the wood burner into the pan and washed a dish and handed it to Martha to dry. Martha took it, standing there with it in her hand, in thought, and was still holding it when Sally handed her the next dish. "Sally, why have you never wanted to get married?"

"Aw, now Marthie, don't you start, too."

"Everyone deserves a little happiness. I know how some people treat you. You go around to people's houses, delivering babies. I see how you love children. And what happened at the Meade house was shameful. I don't know who that woman thinks she is, so high and mighty?"

"I was mighty proud of Sally May that day."

"MISS SALLY, what happened that made you so proud?" Alice asked.

"Mr. John have a farm up the road. He and his wife mighty fine people, and he always ax'n me to come and clean. His wife was a frail little thing. She was a hard worker but wore out easy. But she was always so kind. I just loved her to death. And, Mr. John, he pay me well. He paid me by the job, a little somethin' for cleanin' and a little somethin' for laundry. He be a generous man. Too generous fer his own good. So's on weekends I take Sally May with me. She a grown woman by then. She work as a cook durin' the week at the St. Charles Hotel in Vanceburg. Oh, Sally May be a mighty fine cook."

"I've heard a lot about your cooking. Mr. Bonzo mentioned your fried chicken and cornbread one day when I talked to him. I guess your daughter came by it naturally."

Sally laughed. "Aw, well, I don't know 'bout that, but I did teach her how to make pies. She had the flakiest crusts of anybody 'round. Sometimes she made pies on the side and sold 'em. Mr. John loved her apple pies."

"I'll bet."

"Then one day, we's got the news that Mr. John's wife up and died. Doctor said she had a bad heart, the reason she tired so easily. Well, Mr. John went away fer a while. Was Cincinnati, I think. Come back with a new wife. A younger one. People's tongues wagged. They's liked their gossip. A young woman, and she painted her lips red. I see's the other men lookin' at her, too. I guess all men get their heads turned by a purty face, even a good one like Mr. John. The second was nothin' like his first wife. God rest her soul. She was a good woman. But the second one—I don't like to talk 'bout people, but she had a sharp tongue on her. And lazy. Oh, that woman was lazy.

"Mr. John all but begged me and Sally May to come help. I ne'er liked to believe in the gossip. It was somethin' in my gut that say stay away. But, I's thought of poor Mr. John. So's, I ignored that feelin' in the pit of my belly, and we went. That house had gotten into a terrible state.

"The new wife was actin' ugly to us right from the start. She liked to have company o'er while we worked. She rang her little bell, sayin' fetch this or fetch that. While we's in the next room, we hear her boast to the company, *I don't have to work now 'cause I got two niggers to do the work.*

"Sally May, when she hears this, she be seething. She say to me, *Mama, we don't have to take this.* She holds her head up high, walks right past them women through the main room. We always come and leave through the back door. Sally May stops for a moment and says, *This nigger is a leavin'.* Then she looks back at me and says, *Mama, you a comin'?* I hold my head up high, too, and walk out the front door right 'hind her. I hold my head up high 'cause of my daughter. Had nothin' to do with those women. I so proud of her. There was some days I wished I could be more like Sally May. After she passed, I starts to be more like her. There was the one day on the bus… well, that happen later and be a different story."

Sally paused and smiled at the recollection. "Oh, and those women. I's could tell it's all they's could do to hold in not laughin' right out loud at Missus Meade.

"Within a day's time, ever'body in the countryside knows what happened. Nobody liked Mr. John's new wife. When what happened got back to him, he showed his new wife the

133

door. Well, I's don't think it was all 'cause of that one thing. We hear'd she left through the back door. Oh, my lawd, we's all laughed till our bellies hurt o'er that one."

"Bravo, Sally. That would have been something to see." Sally mustered a pleased smile.

"Well, everything settled down after that, at least fer a while. Then everybody start talkin' 'bout the turn of the century. I ne'er thought much 'bout it, myself. It just be another day, another year to me. Little did I know. I was out in the woods that night the century changed, and what I found out in those woods would change ev'rythin'." Sally abruptly stopped talking and looked around at her captive audience in the cafeteria. "I think I's tired now. I believe I's take a nap."

"I'll wheel you back to your room," Alice said. A disappointed silence hovered over the dining room crowd as Alice wheeled Sally out of the cafeteria.

"Sally, do you know what you have here?" Martha asked, her eyes wide. She looked down into the bag, once again, before closing it and clutching it tightly against her breast. "Where did you get this?"

"I didn't steal it."

"No, I didn't mean to say you stole it."

"I found it."

"Found it? Found it where?"

"In a cave. A hole in the ground."

"Where is this cave?"

Sally started to speak, but Martha cut her off. "No, no. Don't tell me. I don't want to know." Martha put the bag on the table and placed her hand on Sally's and stared into her eyes. "Sally, you keep the whereabouts to yourself. You hear me?"

"I don't rightly know if I's could find it again, Marthie."

Martha raised an eyebrow. "That's good, and that's what you say, you hear?"

"Yes'm."

Martha picked up the weighty bag again and held it to her

chest with both hands. She began to pace. "We got to think, Sally."

Sally stood like a statue, her eyes darting back and forth in synchronization with Martha's pacing.

Martha came to an abrupt halt and placed the bag with its contents spilling out onto the table. "Were you alone?"

"Yes'm. By myself. I hear'd people comin'. But I hid till they walked on by."

"That's good—that you were alone." She paused, looking at the burlap bag and its round, gray, partially dirt-covered coins. "Do you know what you have here?"

"Silver."

———

"RUN, SALLY, RUN," the little boy said, running off ahead.

She wasn't young anymore, over forty now. Running didn't come easy, especially in the woods, in the dark. An old woman, that's what she was. Old woman or not—what would these men care? They were drunk. She was a woman, a Negro woman out by herself, and it was getting dark. It was the eve of a new century, the last day of 1899. Men had started boozing early in the day. The calendar was turning a brand new page, a new century, an excuse for all kinds of mischief. Martha had warned her. Get home early or stay at one of the Erwins for the night. She had said there would be all kinds of wickedness about.

She had walked this path a million times, the path between the Bonzo's and the Erwin's. She didn't recognize the voices. Their whooping and hollering were getting louder. They were out for a good time. Already good and drunk. They would certainly have their way with her. She must get off the path—hide until they passed. Just run, she told herself. Oscar had the lantern. She was supposed to look out for him, not the other way around. He was just a young'un.

She stumbled over a rock and hit the ground hard. All grew silent. The men had stopped talking. She wasn't hurt, that she could tell. Just scared. She tried to calm her breathing that sounded deafening in the silence.

After a short while, one of the men called out, "Who's there?" They had hear her fall.

She rose to her feet. They were looking in her direction. They saw her. She started to run once again. Pure adrenaline drove her. But she could no longer see the lantern. Oscar knew his way back. His mama might ask where she was, but if she knew Oscar, he would make something up rather than face getting a whipping for running off with the lantern.

"Come back. We don't mean you no harm." She knew that to be untrue. She ran until she heard one of the men cursing. He had fallen, too, but not from a rock. She looked back, to see that the other men, all drunk, had stopped and were trying to pull him up. She watched from behind some bushes. It was a sorry sight, seeing those grown men falling all over each other. She nearly laughed out loud but caught herself.

There was a shattering sound, the sound of glass hitting a rock. "Now look what you've gone and did. That bottle was half full," one of the men said.

"I have another." One of the other men pulled out a new bottle from inside his coat. That appeased them for a time.

They got quiet, passing the new bottle around, until the first man said, "Ain't right to waste a good bottle of moonshine like that. Might bring us bad luck for the new year." They all chimed in agreement.

The misfortune over the spill seemed to make them forget they were chasing after her. While they were cursing over the lost liquor, Sally spied a cubby hole off in the bushes and lowered herself down and waited for the men to leave. Instead, they decided to continue their drinking where the man had fallen. She listened into the night. Sometimes one of them would break into song, and the others would join in. She could see the moon from the hole. A good two hours must have passed before she could no longer hear their voices. No use in trying to make it back now. She would wake everyone. She carved herself out a bed like a deer might and settled in for the night.

At the first light of morning, Sally woke. For a moment, she forgot where she was and why she was there. Then, she remembered the men. There were no more voices. They must have moved on some time during the night. All she heard was a wrestling against a bush. She peeped out to see a rabbit. While climbing out, something caught her eye, something gleaming in the light of the sun coming through the entrance. Something shiny through a small passage. The sun's rays flickered on something momentarily. The passage was tight. She could just edge part of her body through it. A torn piece of burlap. She could feel it but couldn't see it. She tugged at it, pulling it through the opening and edged back out of the narrow crawlspace. She brushed off the dirt and untied the rope but could see the brightness seeping through the torn spot of the burlap, what must have been caught by the sunlight just right.

Silver. It looked like coins, only different. She thought back to the stories. The stories of the Jonathan Swift Silver Mine. There were rumors he hid his treasure all over the place. Even when she was small she remembered people at Boone Furnace talking about it. Some had made it their life's mission to find it. And here, if this was indeed the lost treasure, she stumbled upon it by accident.

Sally gathered up some of the coins, the amount she could put in the pockets of her dress. She couldn't carry it all. It would be too heavy. What if she came across someone on the trail? She would be robbed. Even if she wasn't robbed, no one would allow her to keep it. She was still considered property in the eyes of most around her, even if the law did say she was free. How many times had her daughter told her to stand up for herself? How many times had she told her daughter to act respectable, that she was asking for trouble? Sally worried about her daughter, but Sally May was ashamed of her. She knew it.

She tore off part of the burlap bag and made a makeshift smaller bag. She took some of the coins out of her pockets and put them in the bag. Sally shoved the remainder back in the dark hole, careful to cover it up so no one else would find it, and crawled back into the light of day. Snow was coming down. She wrapped her shawl around her, careful to cover her bulging pockets and the bag.

As she walked back, she could feel the weight of her dress. It drooped down in the front. Her pockets might rip right off, and she would have to sew them back on. Why was she worried about ruining her dress? Even though she couldn't count, she knew she had enough money in her pockets and what was in the bag to buy whole bolts of fabric, even silk. Or fancy dresses ready-made, the kind of dresses she remembered Mistress Erwin wearing.

As a child, she had tried to touch Mistress Erwin's fine petticoats as she lifted them up off the muddy ground at Boone Furnace. Nell grabbed her hand right as she reached out and gave her a stern look. What did it matter? She was there, doing the Lord's work, giving to the poor. She was poor. She only wanted to touch the fine petticoats. Ib had thought it funny and laughed.

Then there was the time they all went to the caves for a picnic. They had stayed way into the night, having to carry lanterns in order to see how to get back. The silver could belong to the Indian Princess. Sally reached down into her pocket. She could be touching the silver of a real Indian Princess. Imagine that.

They had sat at the campfire, all of their bellies about to burst from the picnic food. She had helped Ib and Nell make the cornbread. Mistress Erwin had come riding into the camp as grand as you please, atop her white mare early one summer morning. She was the only lady in these parts who rode side saddle. She had a black hat on with a shiny black feather to match. Nell was right behind her in a wagon. She insisted on taking Sally along with them on the picnic that was planned for the next day. Nell and Ib had promised, she told Master Barnes. The war was over, and technically, he was no longer the master, but old ways died hard. "We just have to do our best to get back to normal around here. Don't you agree, Mister Barnes?" Sally heard Mistress Erwin say.

Sally didn't know exactly what the relationship was between Master Barnes and Mistress Erwin, but she knew they had some kind of understanding between them. Mistress Erwin wasn't someone you wanted to offend. At the same time, Jesse Barnes wasn't someone you wanted to mess with.

Sally climbed up beside Nell and off they all went, as grand as you please. That day was magical for Sally. Sally had spent the night with Nell. The next morning, they started early making all the preparations for the picnic. Ib made a big batch of fried chicken. By the afternoon, they loaded up all the baskets of food on the wagon and headed for the caves.

After they had their fill of fried chicken and apple pie, they gathered around the campfire, both children and adults, to hear the tale of the Indian princess, the oldest story in circulation. This story had fascinated her from the time she had first heard it and continued to do so with each telling.

The little boys loved hearing about the Indian warriors and would fashion makeshift spears and bows and arrows. They found plenty of arrowheads under the cliffs. The whole area was covered with cliffs and caves. They lived not too far from where the actual events took place if they did indeed take place at all. Somehow, Sally knew that they really did happen. And the adults wanted to believe it because of the silver.

The girls liked hearing the love story part, and the boys loved the treasure part. Sally had heard the stories all her life. The grown-ups talked about the silver and dreamed of finding it. Almost everyone had a theory as to where it might be.

The story started with the Cherokees but eventually spread to the tongues of the white men. Some said the bones of a woman, an Indian princess, were found in the saltpeter cave, although it wasn't known as the saltpeter cave then. That wasn't until years later when it was used for making ammunition. Some said no bones were actually found. It was an open grave. The last version was the scariest because it meant her ghost was out walking around.

It was her eleventh summer that Sally sat on a log at the entrance of the saltpeter cave and listened intently to the story about the Indian princess. Her skin blended into the darkness around her, but the whiteness of her eyes gleamed in the direction of the man telling the story.

He started with how the tale had been handed down by the Cherokee. The Shawnee had been in this area as well. Sally knew the Cherokee as the mean Indians and the Shawnee as the friendly ones. She wondered why some people were labeled as mean and others not. The story was about the Cherokee, and they had families and fell in love the same as the good ones. She wondered if the man had really heard this from a Cherokee Indian himself.

As the storyteller began to speak, no one else dared to make a sound, not even the most ceaseless chatterers of the women folk. Even Nell and Ib, responsible for the last chores before the story telling, had sat down in a grassy area behind Sally and the other children. It was the Cherokee who attacked Master and Mistress Erwin when they were making their way from Virginia to Kentucky. She didn't know for sure whether they were mean. She had to take Mistress Erwin's word for it. The only Indians she ever saw were the Shawnee. They had come into Boone Furnace on a few occasions.

The man said it was a story of unfulfilled love, much like that of Romeo and Juliet. Who Romeo and Juliet were, Sally had no idea as the man didn't explain that part, but she loved the sound of their names. All kinds of romantic notions were in the air, stirring like the sparks above the fire. While the other girls were encouraged in this way of thinking, Sally was advised against it. One of the girls once said to Sally that she could never marry because she was the last of her kind around here. Sally held back the tears and then silently went off and hid behind a tree where they couldn't see or hear her and cried.

When the children played, they would often re-enact this story. Sally never got to be the princess. That was always reserved for one of the white girls. But, tonight was different. She sat on the log, alongside the other children and in the night only lit by the fire, conjured up dreams the same as them.

The name of the Indian princess was Manuita, and the brave Cherokee warrior was Huraken, and he hated the white settlers and was always putting on Indian paint and feathers and making war against them and other enemy Indian tribes. He had a mean heart. The only one able to penetrate his mean heart was the Indian princess. Huraken fell in love with her, and she with him.

The storyteller went on to say that the Cherokee warrior was two sides of a coin, showing his tender face to Manuita and his mean face to everyone else, even his fellow warriors. This caused the chief, Manuita's father, to not trust him. But Huraken wanted to gain his trust, his approval, and his daughter's hand. Sally wasn't sure that Indians actually asked for someone's hand. Colored folks didn't. They jumped over a broom. Indians surely had their way, too, different from both the white folks and the colored folks. But it was a white man telling the story, and he had his own way of telling it. Sally listened with her heart, not her head.

One day after a victorious Indian raid, Huraken didn't return with the other warriors. He had been on another outing and discovered a vein of shiny ore. It was silver, but Huraken didn't know that. He only knew he wanted to use it to make beautiful gifts for the Indian princess and her father. Something had told him to keep his find a secret.

The storyteller said he found the ore somewhere in Smokey Valley, although it wasn't called Smokey Valley then. He stayed out camping for weeks, losing all sense of time. He had become preoccupied in melting the ore, making ornaments for Manuita and a tomahawk and peace pipe for the chief.

Huraken had been gone for so long, there were rumors of him being dead. He could have had an accident or have been killed by an enemy warrior or a white man. Manuita was heartbroken. Her father tried to console her but it did no good. This made him dislike Huraken even more, blaming him for his daughter's sadness.

Manuita began taking long walks by herself. She sat in solitude on the cliffs. She could see no end to her grief. So, one day, she jumped. When the man telling the story said this, there was a sad sound coming from everyone who sat listening around the campfire.

At the very moment Manuita took her life, Huraken, with great joy in his heart, carrying the gifts he had made, had started his journey back. But on his trek, he saw a mangled body, face down, on the ground below the cliff. He made his way down the cliff and turned the body over to discover it was his lover, Manuita. He roared in anguish. Huraken carried her body to a cave where it would be safe. The tribe held nothing for him now. He chose to live in silence and forever guard Manuita's grave.

When the Indian princess didn't return, her father sent warriors to look for her. Instead, they found Huraken. They questioned him, but he had taken a vow of silence. The chief suspected Huraken of foul play and sentenced him to death. But the spirit of the princess protected him. She sent heavy rains to loosen the binding around his arms and legs. He escaped and wandered aimlessly for weeks. His soul would not rest. He returned to the tribe and asked that he be allowed to return to the cave where he buried Manuita, who he loved dearly.

The chief granted his wish but had warriors escort him to the cave. The warriors camped outside the cave and waited, but Huraken never came out. Fearing evil spirits the Indians fled.

The story ended. All sat in awe and silence, the only sound being the crackle of the fire, waiting for the two lovers to reappear. Sally wanted them to live happily ever after. Most who sat around the cave wanted the secret of the treasure.

It wasn't just a story. There had been proof. There had been talk at Boone Furnace about one of the first settlers in the area. One day he passed under a rock cliff and noticed something shiny. He dug the partially buried objects from the ground. He wiped them with his coat to find a beautifully crafted tomahawk and peace pipe. The hunt for the lost vein of silver ore was on.

Could this be part of the same treasure? Who could she tell, if anyone? Sally mulled it over as she walked back. Martha was the only one she could trust. She would know what to do.

"WHAT DO WE DO, MARTHIE?"

"Well, first of all, we don't tell anyone outside of the family." Marthie looked Sally in her eyes and grasped onto her hands. "Sally, you know people would kill for this, don't you?"

"Yes'm, I's reckon they would."

Martha paced about. "Oh, my, Sally. We got to put our heads together and think of something."

"Marthie, I would like a new dress and a good pair of shoes, ones that don't hurt my feet."

Martha smiled. "Oh, honey. I don't think that'll be a problem."

"I's was thinkin' pink. Pink's my favorit' color. I 'member the first dress you's e'er give me. It was pink. Do you 'member, Marthie?"

"Yes, I remember." Martha laughed. "I don't know why I'm making so much of this. We can take the wagon. Go to another town, buy some new things for the farm. And real store bought dresses, pink for you, blue for me. Somewhere where people don't know us and won't question how we suddenly have come into some money."

"And shoes, Marthie. Don't forget the shoes," Sally added.

"Yes, some really comfortable shoes for the both of us," Martha said.

"Marthie?"

"What, Sally?"

"There's more."

"What do you mean? Some ribbons for our hair or hats to match the dresses?" Martha paraded around, laughing, swirling her dress, pretending it was new.

"No, I mean there's lots more silver."

Martha stopped and placed her hand over her mouth.

"I's couldn't carry it all. So, I's stuck it back in the hole where no one could see it."

"But you don't know where it is? You said you couldn't find it again. I thought for a moment maybe it was because you were rattled over the men who were drunk. But Sally, deep down, I knew it wasn't true. You know every inch of dirt up and down this holler."

"I's said I's don't know if I's could find it agin. Not fer sure. But, I's probably can. It depends."

"Sally, what does it depend on?" Martha asked.

Sally pulled up a chair and sat down. "My feet ache. They ache so much these days. I's 'member all those years I's go barefoot. I just want a good pair of shoes." Sally looked down at her feet and back up at Martha. "Marthie, I's don't mean to be selfish, but when I's found that silver, I's thought how can me, a Negro woman, carry that bag out of that cave? White people take what they want. Not you, Marthie. You be nothin' but kind to me. Everyone talks about it being 1900. It's been years since they say slavery is o'er, but people still call me a slave. Right to my face they say, *Nigger Sal*. I's act like'n it don't hurt, but it do. And 'fore I find the silver, I's be runnin' in the woods cause I's hear voices, men's voices, and they be drinkin', and I's so afraid of what they might do to me 'cause I's a colored woman and nothing more than a piece of property."

"Oh, Sally, I know how bad you've had it. Sometimes I

look at you and see that little girl who hid behind the rock at Boone Furnace." Martha let out a heavy sigh. "This could change everything."

Martha pulled up a chair and sat beside Sally. "Sally, we could buy land—good land. We could have a big farm."

"A farm near Sally May. I's want to be close to my daughter."

"You found the silver. If you say we buy land near Sally May, then that's the way it has to be. We have to talk to Charles. He'll know what to do. But, we'll keep it a secret between the three of us. We can't tell anyone else."

"I know's you know what to do, Marthie."

"For right now, let's gather all this up and hide it."

No sooner than the silver was hidden out of sight, the door opened and in came Charles. He looked around. "Why isn't food on the table? Why are you two sitting there with sheepish grins on your faces? You both look like you've been up to no good."

"Sally, do you know what tomorrow is?" Alice asked.

"No," she said, closing her eyes.

"It's Wednesday, Miss Sally. The doctor will come check on you. I'll be in bright and early. Is that okay?"

"Yes'm," Sally said. "You's so good to come and see me ever' day."

"I wouldn't have it any other way. All right, honey. I'm leaving now. Letting you get some rest." Alice kissed her on the cheek.

"HOW'S SHE DOING, TODAY?" the doctor asked, holding his stethoscope to Sally's chest.

"She's perked up quite a bit in the last few days, Doctor," Alice said.

"Aren't you retired now?"

"Yes."

"Then why are you here? If it were me, I'd be out playing golf."

"I like being here with Sally," Alice said. "And, besides, I don't like golf."

"She's like family, now," Sally said.

"She's a good nurse. It's good to have a nurse in the family," the doctor said, smiling, putting his fingers on Sally's pulse. He looked over at Alice. "Her pulse is a little fast. Has she been getting excited?" He turned his head toward Sally and spoke louder. "Have you been getting excited? Running around the halls?"

"Why no, Doctor," she said. He laughed.

"Miss Sally has been telling me about her past."

The doctor smiled. "I bet a woman your age has a lot to tell. A lot of secrets, I suspect." He grinned at Alice.

"You don't know the half of it," Alice said.

He laughed, picked up her file, wrote something and clipped it back to the end of the bed. "Okay, I guess you're good to go for another hundred. You ladies be good," he said, as he left the room.

Alice pulled the chair next to the bed. "Sally, do you want to sit up? Look out the window?"

"Yes'm, that be fine." Alice helped her out of bed into the wheel chair.

"It's a nice day out today. I think May is my favorite month."

"Yes'm, mine, too. Cause'n that when I's first laid eyes on my purty baby girl, Sally May."

"John asked me what my plans were for today. I said, *what do you think? I'm visiting with Miss Sally.* I so look forward to our talks. I could hardly sleep last night after what you told me yesterday. It was a good thing you didn't talk about the silver when we were out in the cafeteria. You sure had everyone's interest. If they'd heard about the silver, they might all be quitting and going out to look for it."

"Oh, there ain't none left. At least in that cave where I found it," Sally said with a self-satisfied look.

"Do you have a good view? I would wheel you outside, but it might be a little too windy for you today. Look at all those dogwood flowers. When they blow off the trees like that, it looks like snow coming down."

"It was snowin' on that first day of the new century, too. Came down heavy as I recall. Charles and Ben came in from haulin' some rock 'round. He was aimin' to lay a new foundation fer a barn come spring. The Bonzos were a close lot. They all stuck together and worked together. That all changed after the silver. Sometimes, I's wished I's never found it. But that a different story.

"A whole pack of Bonzos come from France. They's gonna make themselves rich in America. Some didn't get any further than Pennsylvania. Some made it as far as Ohio and Kentucky. I was with them so much a lot of people thought my last name was Bonzo. And, I did feel like one of 'em. E'en after what happened."

"What do you mean what happened? Something to do with the silver?"

"No, not that. This ain't somethin' I e'er told anybody." Tears rolled down Sally's withered cheeks. Alice gripped Sally's bony hand.

Sally stared with glassy eyes out the window at the white flowers coming down. "It was caus'n who got me with child. That's all I'll say. I ne'er want to say who done it."

"Charles? Martha's husband?"

"No, ain't gonna say."

"That's all right, dear. You don't have to say who it was, but why didn't you ever say anything when it happened? Before you knew you were pregnant."

"Caus'n I's scared. An' caus'n it would have hurt too many people. Marthie was like a mama to me. The one who did it, he was drunk the first time it happened."

"The first time?"

"It happened more than I care's to 'member. He's always be drunk when it happened. That be one reason I's so scared of the men out in the woods."

"Sally, why didn't you stop it?"

"Oh, Missus Alice, you don't know the shame I felt. That a lot of the reason I's didn't say nothin'. But people don't understand what it was like to be a Negro woman back then. It was just their right."

"Sally, it isn't anyone's right."

More tears flowed down Sally's cheeks. Alice handed her a tissue. "Maybe not, but it was the way it was, and people either mean or they's look the other way when people bein' mean. I's afraid if I's say anythin' that Marthie might shun me fore'er. Marthie was my best friend in the world. And, I's know how it would hurt her. Sometimes I's think Marthie 'spected who might have done it, but she ne'er say. I's just knows she sent me away. After that, there's no way I could tell.

"I think Ib and Nell 'spected who the daddy was, but they didn't judge. How could they? It was the same fer 'em. Ib had a child, Docia. She come out more white than colored. Why there weren't a handful of white men who would turn down climbin' on top a colored woman if'n they had the chance. That's why I run so hard and end up stayin' in the cave on that one night."

"Yes, I knew that was the reason you were trying to get away. Even a white woman would be scared in a situation like that." Alice paused. *Could Sally hear her heart beating fast in her chest?* "Sally, you've mentioned Docia twice now. What-ever happened to her?"

"It weren't the first time I's with child. I's was no more into my womanhood when it first happened. Everybody knows what happened then. It was Massa Barnes. He be's with any Negro woman he owned, and some, he didn't. I knew as soon as I got my bleed that my time with him be comin'." Sally let out a heavy sigh. "Same with Docia. Only Docia thought it somethin' grand to be with Massa Barnes, and when he left, she ran off after him. Broke Ib's heart. We's ne'er heard from her or him agin. At least, if'n she e'er did come back to visit, Ib didn't say."

Alice tried not to look deflated at Sally's revelation. Maybe she couldn't find out firsthand about her ancestor, but she had Sally, a living piece of her history, right here. And her story was important. "But, Master Barnes, he didn't own you when you were old enough to get pregnant."

"Made no difference. Things didn't change much. Maybe up north, they be different, but not 'round where I was. I's too young to carry a baby proper. Didn't have the body fer it yet. The baby born early, but it stillborn and deformed somethin' awful. Some of the white men at Boone take it and throw it like corn out to the pigs."

Alice gasped. "Oh, my god, Sally. Something like that doesn't even seem real. How can people be so cruel?"

"I hear'd 'bout somethin' like that happenin' 'fore. We's just nothin' more than animals to some white folks. I didn't eat hardly anythin' fer weeks. I's always sad.

"Then Marthie come into Boone and rode me out of that place right 'hind her on that mule. I's thought I's died and gone to heaven. She talked to me like I's her equal. She like a mama and best friend all rolled into one. Oh sure, I worked hard. But Marthie worked hard right 'long 'side me. So, you see how I could ne'er tell?"

"Yes, Sally, I understand."

"But maybe I's should tell someone." Sally motioned for

Alice to lean in closer. She whispered in her ear. "It feels so good to get that off my chest after all this time. You won't tell, will you?"

"No, Sally, never."

"Well, he be long dead now, anyway. And, you's like kin." Alice wiped a tear from her cheek.

"Sally, I noticed the other day that for dinner you didn't eat the pork chops on your plate. Is that…?"

"Yes'm. After that day, I's won't eat anythin' that come from a pig. Oh, I fix plenty a plate of bacon in my day, but I always push it to the side and say I's not so hungry."

"I don't blame you."

"After the shock of me bein' with child, the second time— none of 'em knew 'bout the first—most of the men in the family looked the other way when they saw me. They's all 'spected each other. They all carried the shame, too. And, the one who did it—he looked away the hardest. We's ne'er speak of it, but somethin' in our souls touched, that good part of the both of us, and we had an understandin'. He ne'er come near me again. Course, I's with Ib and Nell for a while, but when I's come back to help Marthie again, he seem to be a changed man. At least fer a while.

"Sally May never know her real daddy. I think, one day I's gonna tell her. I's should've telled her. It maybe could've stopped what happened.

"Sally May lied about who did it. I's saw it in her eyes. She say someone visitin' the hotel where she worked, a white doctor from Cincinnati, got her with child. But, I's know better. I know who did it—the same one who did it to me. I's feels sometimes like I's a bad mama, but I's always did the best I could." Tears rolled down Sally's face.

Alice held her hand and wiped Sally's face with a tissue and then took it to her own face to wipe away her own tears.

"Sally May have lots of problems, but she have a purty

baby girl, and she name her Nell. I telled her so many stories 'bout her grandmama. I's so happy she named her that.

"When I's first find the silver, the first thing I's think of is a better life for Sally May. But things almost always ne'er happen the way you want 'em to.

"In the end, after all the bickerin' and fightin' o'er the silver, Charles say I's ne'er has to worry 'bout anythin'. That I's always be taken care of. I say, *and my young'un, too?* He say, *and your young'un, too.* I's know Marthie talk to him. She said it was only right caus'n I's the one who found the silver."

"Did he make good on that promise?"

"Yes'm. I reckon he did. Ben always special good to me. Oh, he liked to joke a lot, but he always lookin' out fer me.

"It take the family a good while 'fore they found land and moved. And there turns out to be a lot more silver in that cave than even I's thought. Too much to keep secret. "'Fore long, the whole family knows 'bout it. And you know how money can split a family. Well, not any different fer the Bonzos."

"The Bonzo brothers, e'en 'fore the silver, they's always talkin' amongst theirselves how they gonna work the land. All the brothers talked 'bout tryin' their hand at breedin' horses. All four brothers had two mules 'tween 'em, but mules weren't no good for breedin'. Most everybody 'round those parts were mighty poor, 'specially the Bonzos. They just be known as dirt farmers, but they's wanted to make more of theirselves. Weren't their fault. All they had was rocky patches of ground up that holler.

"They were good at farmin', though. They'd had to be to grow food on that land. Yes'm, farmin' was in their blood, what they did back in France. Their name, Bonzo, meant farmer in French, or they said it did at one time, 'fore it changed when they come'd to America. Sometimes when they got together they talked like they was back there. I's didn't understand a word they was sayin'. But you could tell by their bodies a lot what they was talkin' 'bout, like when they was telling jokes or when they was angry or cursin'. But they's was always tryin' to make farmin' into a good business and always complainin' they's needed money to do it and always complainin' they's didn't have none.

"Me finding the silver was 'sposed to be 'tween the three of us, me, Marthie and Charles, but the next thing I's know is that they's all in a big meetin', all the brothers, 'bout the silver. And there was a lot of shouting and hollering and French goin' back and forth from time to time. Marthie and I sat there fer the longest time holdin' our tongues. I seem to 'member Marthie left the room and come back bangin' a pot. Oh, she had a mean look on her face. It took a lot to rile Marthie up, but when she got riled, well…" Sally shook her head. "They's looked at her like she was out of her mind. She was the only one there that was with a right mind. Marthie told them how it was gonna be—that I's had as much say in what was to happen as anybody did. More, if the truth be known. Oh, if you could see the look on their faces when Marthie said that."

"And you said Charles said you would always be taken care of?"

"Yes'm. And, they did do right by me. But in the beginnin' they's constantly havin' family meetins', making all these plans. They talk way into the night sometimes, e'en when they know they have to get up a few hours later and commence the farmin' work."

"WHAT'S this talk of living in town? Why, I won't hear of it. Farming is in our blood. That's all I've ever known. It's all our family ever did. And a farmer, a tiller of the land, is what I want to be carved on my tombstone when I'm lowered into the ground."

"But Papa," William said, "we don't have to work anymore."

"Papa's right. I don't want to give up farming. Why I might as well shrivel up and die. No, we all have to be agreed. We'll buy a big tract of land, and all of us will work the land together," Charles, Jr. said.

"We could have milk cows," his papa said.

"I hear Lexington has some dandy farms. We ought to take a trip and check out land there," William said.

"We could do better a little outside of Lexington. The land would be cheaper. We would end up with more acreage," Charles said.

Martha and Sally sat there while the brothers argued back and forth. Martha saw the tears rolling down Sally's cheeks.

She yelled out, "Just hush, all of you." Everything came to a standstill. Martha cleared her throat. "You keep forgetting who found the silver, and she is the only person who knows where the rest of it is." A person could have heard a pin drop at that moment. A large crackle and a log falling in the fireplace broke the silence.

"Now, Martha, darling," Charles said, placing his hands on his wife's shoulders. All of their jaws dropped. Sally had never known Charles to call Marthie darling. "Ben, why don't you get Sally her shawl? She looks a little cold." Ben's eyes got wide and his mouth dropped even more.

"No, I'll get it," William said. Martha slammed her fist down on the table, and William jumped.

"You've been in this room for over an hour, rattling off all these plans you have for money that's not even yours. Not only has the thought of money turned you against each other. But more important, not once have you asked Sally her opinion."

They looked at each other, partly dumbfounded, partly ashamed.

"THINGS SETTLED down after that night, but talkin' and plannin' went on for nigh three years. At the same time, they always be tryin' to get on my good side.

"The more they talked, the more divided the family 'came. The temptation of the silver was too much fer 'em. Some of the silver was exchanged. Marthie made sure I got my share. Sally May and I went into a store in Vanceburg, as proud as you please, and bought us each a mighty fine dress apiece and some shoes, too. Marthie went with us, on account it was a store mainly fer white people. And, she counted out the money fer us. Sally May could count, but we just let Marthie do it. It just be easier. White folks might question why we has all that money.

"And we wear our new dresses and shoes to the next Sunday meetin'. Why I ne'er saw such stares.

"I ne'er tell Sally May 'bout the silver. No, that be too dangerous. I see how money can divide e'en a close family. So, I just let it be. She thinks Marthie bein' particularly kind, buyin' us all that stuff.

"It 1903 when they finally get all the wagons packed and moved, I stayed behind."

"After all that, you stayed behind? Whatever for, Sally?" Alice asked.

"They be buildin' houses at first. And I was needed all over. One of the women I knew was havin' a baby soon. She practically begged me to come. Not a month went by that someone wasn't havin' a baby. They's all wanted me, but still…" Sally's voice trailed off.

"Still what, Sally?"

"One time, I was holdin' a woman's baby. I walked back and forth with little Roy in my arms, singin' him a lullaby, just the way my own mama sung to me. I's 'member all they's names. Well, most of em. The woman lay there in the bed. Back then, white women would stay in bed for weeks after their babies was born. Not like now. She woke up and saw me and let out a shriek, *what's that colored woman doin' with my baby*, as in if she woke up from a bad dream. I look down at that precious baby and say, *aw, I love him as if'n he my own*. Then, she 'membered why I was there and settled back down.

"I's went back and forth. That be 'bout the time Ben bought a car. Buyin' a car, not farmin', was the first thing that popped into Ben's mind when he hear'd 'bout the silver. I's think it was somethin' seeing a young white boy drivin' an older black woman 'round. I's thought people's eyeballs would hit the ground. Ben always have a car. I's think he liked cars way better than he liked farmin'. Now, Ted, he liked drivin' a tractor, but later on, he liked his cars.

"But, Ted weren't born yet. No, he not born till a couple years later. It was 1905. And, his mama, one of Marthie's girls, weren't married. Was off runnin' 'round with a married man. She knows how I's loved child'n, though, and she plopped that baby in nothin' but a diaper on the doorstep and took off somewhere's up north. I's mostly raised Ted.

"Yes'm, as soon as there was any new farm 'quipment out, the Bonzos, they had it. They was now makin' money at their farmin', but sometimes I's think it come at a heavy price."

"What do you mean, Sally?"

"Well, first there was the talk. People in three counties talked 'bout how they suddenly 'come rich. How they went from bein' down and out dirt farmers to owners of a big fancy house and lots of land. Weren't nothin' fancy about Marthie's house. No, she wouldn't have any of that. But, Ben drivin' a car 'bout, all shined up, didn't help matters. It was nothin' but jealousy, I tell you. And, there was the talk 'bout little Ted being left on the doorstep, but the talk of the money preyed on most people's minds.

"People was always ax'n me what happened—how they's

could suddenly afford such things? I's kept my mouth shut. Wasn't none of their business. Marthie was right 'bout not sayin' anythin'.

"The brothers couldn't 'gree on nothin'. When their papa died, they fell out even further. They's all set up their different households. They's only a few miles from one 'nother, but they's ne'er spoke. They's raised their families and they grew e'en further apart. Young'uns growed up not e'en knowin' who their uncles and aunts was.

"Years passed. There was three different branches of kin not knowin' anythin' 'bout the other. We was always havin' big family reunions, but they's always on Marthie's side of the family."

"Oh, Sally, that's a shame."

"Yes'm. There was a time—I's think 'round the early fifties that a older man come a callin'. It was one of Jacob's grand-sons. Said he had hear'd things 'bout the fallin' out 'tween the families in hushes and whispers all his life and wanted to reconnect.

"Why him, Ben and Ted was havin' a good ole time—talkin' and laughin'. I's think I told you how Ben loved to joke. I's 'member Ben takin' him out in the barn and showin' him his newest car. Ben had a lot of pride when it come to his cars. Always kept 'em polished up fine.

"And then he got to ax'n about me. Says he hear'd the family talkin' 'bout me, too. I's be out in the stable with the horses most of the time, but they weren't standin' too far off. I's could hear 'em talkin'. And Ben was just braggin' on Nell. My Sally May had been dead fer some years by then. Nell loved to travel. And Ben was just braggin' that Nell was a schoolteacher and all and was on a trip to Iowa. And then, the man up and axes just like I weren't in earshot, *I thought Sally never married. So how does she come to have a grand young'un?* It was then that Ben's face turned red as fire and told the man he needed to leave.

"After he left, I's talked to Ben and say, *now Ben, why did you want to go and do that fer?* And he say, *they stayed away this long, and suddenly they come 'round bringin' up stuff that don't need to be brought up.'* Well, maybe the man was up to no good, or maybe not. I's always thought he was genuinely interested in reconnectin'. And, I was kind of saddened to see him go. I's did hear later that he bought a piece of land back in Carter County and was plannin' on trying to find the lost silver. So maybe Ben was right 'bout him.

"I think people, to this day, lookin' fer that silver mine. Oh, what a ruckus it would cause if people knew a Negro woman was the one to find that treasure." Sally laughed. "An' it ain't in that saltpeter cave like'n the storyteller led everybody to believe."

"Oh, lawdy. Lots of things happened after they make the move. I's with Ted, mostly, but I's go where's I needed. Sally May needed me an awful lot durin' that time. Nell was born in 1907. Nell had a birth much like Sally May. No one ne'er sure who her daddy was. I's told you Sally May said he be a doctor from Cincinnati, someone who stay in the hotel where Sally May worked, but like'n I told you, I have my 'spicions otherwise."

"And, you think it was the same one who got your pregnant?"

"Yes'm."

"Oh, Sally, that's horrible."

"I's don't like to look at it that way. I's look at it like I got me a mighty fine grand young'un. I hope when she comes to see me on some weekend that you can meet her." Sally paused. "Course, she don't come that much, livin' so fer 'way and all."

"I would love to meet her. In fact, would it be okay if I brought my husband, John? I want him to meet you both."

"Aw, that'd be really nice."

"Sally, you said Nell's mother died. When did that happen?"

"It was December of 1929. By that time, Nell be married and lived up north in West Virginia. And her mama be stayin' with her. Everyone thinks I's old then. Little did they know. Everyone say the trip would be too hard on me. I's always regretted I weren't there. Also, Marthie gettin' up in years. Charles died in 1917. We both two old women, together. About all's we look forward to is Sunday meetin' and reunions.

"Caus'n the way her mama worked, Nell be with me a lot. You think after the turn of the century things would change, but they not changed too much. One reason Nell not like talkin' 'bout the past. She tried to fit in with the white folks, but it hard on her when she's a young'un. We always be visitin' back and forth and one time we's at the Erwins. All the child'n be playin' in the barn. Nell be climbin' up the ladder. They's all barefoot. Her foot slipped and went into Earl's mouth. He was climbin' 'hind her. He had an awful fit and wanted his mama to wash out his mouth with soap. Nell come runnin' to me, cryin'."

"Aw," Alice said.

Sally closed her eyes and started a soft snore. Alice kissed her on the forehead. "Sweet dreams."

*H*e walked through the front door depositing his umbrella in the stand. "Honey, I'm home." No answer. He walked through the hallway, peeking into the living room. All the windows and baseboards were covered with masking tape. The bucket of paint, mellow yellow honeydew, the color Michelle insisted on, even though it cost more than basic white, which was what he maintained it was, although Michelle begged to differ, sat unopened. Okay, what did he know about colors? It was Michelle who had the art minor.

But, it was the name of the color—honeydew. Synchronicity, she said. Michelle just finished reading a collection of short stories entitled, *Honeydew*, with her literature class. She said it would inspire her.

"Honey," he called out again, going through each room on the first floor, one by one. No answer. Michael bounded up the stairs. "Michelle, you're not taking a nap, are you?" he asked, entering the bedroom. The bed was unmade from this morning but no Michelle.

He headed down the hall to the room Michelle was

turning into an office and study, where she planned to write that novel during the summer, although she had yet to come up with an idea for it. Maybe something came to her and she was all zoned out, deep into her plot. He peeked in. Her laptop sat closed on her grandma's antique desk.

She must have had to go out. He ran all the way back down the stairs and out the kitchen door to check if her car was in the garage. It looked as if it hadn't been moved all day. A wave of panic shot through him.

"Okay, Michelle, you are making me nervous," he mumbled, using the sound of his voice to relieve some of his tension while flying back up the stairs. He stopped in the hallway, seeing what he hadn't noticed before, something sticking out from the cubbyhole at the end of the hallway. The attic stairs were pulled down. He climbed the stairs, sticking his head up through the narrow passageway, "Michelle?"

"Michael, you're home." She looked up in surprise. "I didn't hear you come in."

"Obviously. I've been looking all over for you. You had me worried. I thought I'd come home, find the living room painted and your novel finished, all those things you were going to do on your first day of summer vacation."

"You're too funny."

He climbed through the cut out in the ceiling and made his way over to where Michelle was sitting, bending his head to avoid the angled ceiling. "What on earth are you doing up here?" She sat cross-legged on the floor, surrounded by old shoe boxes, looking over a pile of papers and old notebooks.

"I needed something old to spread over the furniture and the floor for painting. I thought there might be something up here. Instead, I found these."

"And just what are these?" he asked, clearing off a spot on the floor, sitting beside his wife.

"Journals. My grandma kept journals."

"Do you think you should be reading them?" he asked.

Michelle tilted her head, her auburn curls falling over part of her face, with a *duh* look. "Really, Michael? "Grandma's been dead for almost twenty years. And Grandma left me this house, and all the contents therein. These shoe boxes are part of the contents. Besides, if Grandma had lived long enough to see that I married you, I know that she would want me to read these. She would want *you* to read these."

Michael scratched his kinky black hair. "Why would your grandma want me to read them?"

Michelle flipped through some of the loose pages and pulled out a picture.

"Okay, it's your grandma posing with a black woman. A very old black woman."

"Yes," Michelle turned the picture around, watching Michael while he read, appraising his reaction.

Sally Ann Barnes, age 109, September 1968, my great, great, great grandmother's cousin.

Michael read the back intently, flipped the picture back around, studying it, before looking back at his wife. "Are you serious?"

"You ask if *I am* serious? You should be asking Grandma if she was serious."

"You were eleven, right—when your grandma died?"

"Yes."

"And she never told you this?"

"Nope," Michelle said, shaking her head, puckering her lips.

"What about your mom?"

"I'm sure Mom never knew about any of this. Oh, she knew Grandma was interested in genealogy. You know Mom. Those kinds of things don't interest her at all."

"So, what you're telling me is that I thought I was

marrying a white girl, but in reality, I wasn't," he said with a nervous laugh. "All those warnings both of our families gave us were in vain?" He eased into a more relaxed pose, nestling his blue scrubs on the dusty floor boards.

"Yes'm."

"Yes'm?"

"That's how Sally said yes. It's all here in my grandma's journals." She stacked the journals and papers up, placing them back in the shoeboxes. "How about you carry these down for me, and I'll order Chinese and we'll look at them while we eat. I'm starved. I came up here right before lunch and haven't been back downstairs since. I started reading these and couldn't put them down. The next thing I know, you're home."

"Michelle, honey, we're trying to get pregnant. You can't go skipping meals. You have to stay healthy."

"I know. I'm this skinny white woman you married. Oh, no, make that skinny *mulatto* woman." She laughed.

Michael paused before getting off the floor and wiping the dust off his nursing scrubs. "How do you feel about finding this out?"

"Actually, I'm excited. It's all kind of surreal. I mean, look at me. Who would have thought? What do you think about it? You don't act at all shocked or anything."

"If people started tracing their DNA or doing their genealogy, I think everyone would uncover all kinds of things they didn't know about themselves. Do you know how many slaves were in this country? And more than likely, most of the women were getting taken advantage of by white males. So, if you go digging back far enough, I think almost everyone would find out they are from mixed heritages. Like maybe I'm actually Irish."

"Yes, now that you mention it, I did wonder about your fascination with pubs."

"Ha, ha. But, I could go for a beer about right now. Must be this dusty attic making me thirsty."

"Yes'm. That would go real good with Chinese."

"Would you quit saying that?"

"Okay, but do you think my watered-down black blood had something to do with why I was attracted to you?"

Michael laughed. "Maybe so. Are you saying like your ancestors were calling out from their graves telling you to marry me?"

"I don't know. Possibly."

"I'll take these to your office. That's where you want them, right?"

"Yes, thanks, Michael."

"I'd pull you up off the floor, but my hands are full of boxes."

"*I* knew I'd find you up here. It looks like I'm going to have to paint the living room." He looked at Michelle with a frown.

"Ha, ha, smarty pants. You will be glad to learn I didn't forget dinner today. I have a quiche in the oven."

"Yes, I could smell it as soon as I walked through the door. It's not burning, is it?"

"No. I have the timer set on my phone. See." Michelle held up her phone.

"So, besides making the quiche, what have you been doing today?" he asked, bending over her chair, peering at the bulletin board above the desk. It was filled with stickum notes of various colors and family tree charts. Red yarn criss-crossed, from push-pin to push-pin, much like what he saw on detective shows. It was a collage of evidence needed to solve the case. But, what case?

"I have been making an outline, a plan of sorts."

"Yes, I can see that. I can't quite figure it out, but you're definitely up to something. Let me guess. Is it something you are going to do with your class when school starts back in the fall?" His eyes darted back and forth from the ordered stacks of papers and journals on the desk, now organized into different colored folders with dates written across the top, and back up to the hand written notes with the picture of Sally and Michelle's grandma, dead center, on the bulletin board.

"No. Way off."

"Okay, I give. What kind of plan?"

"A plan to find out more about Sally and possibly Docia."

"Isn't it all here in these journals?"

"Yes, but I want to know more."

"What more? Your great, great, how many greats was that, was a slave and the father of her son was a slave trader."

"I want to know whatever more I can find out. The journals just stopped. I trace back to Docia and Jesse Barnes, and Sally talked a little about Docia, more about Jesse Barnes, but it appears that Grandma never followed up with any of it. We don't even know what happened to Sally."

"What do you mean what happened to her? She was seriously old. She died. End of story."

"But why didn't my grandma write about it? And Sally's death record is nowhere in these journals. Grandma would surely have mentioned Sally's death in her journals. Sally meant so much to her. That's obvious by the way she wrote about her. Why would the journals stop before her death?"

"Why don't you call your mother? Maybe she knows something," Michael said.

"She won't know anything," Michelle said and snarled.

"How do you know?"

"I know. She's never been the least bit interested in family history. I remember asking her some stuff once. I was filling out the family history pages in the Bible, you know, the ones that fold out from the center. She said she didn't know anything to tell me, and I should let sleeping dogs lie. I was only twelve. I asked her what that meant? She gives me that look, you know that look of hers, and says, *Michelle*, like Michelle with a question mark," Michelle said, puckering her lips.

"Do you mean that same look you're giving me now?" Michael asked. "You pucker your lips the same way your mother does, you know."

Michelle stopped mid-pucker and made a slight frown. "Have you ever asked your parents about your family history?"

"I never asked my parents anything about it. Pretty much knew slaves were in the picture. If you're black, it goes without saying."

"I'm determined to find out. Look. I printed out these Google images of where the Erwin farm might have been and of what remains of Boone Furnace. Michael, this is what I'm going to write about—the book I talked about," Michelle said, her face glowing.

"I think that's great—really. But, come on, Michelle. You and your mother barely talk. How do you think that makes me feel? I know I'm the cause."

"Oh my god, Michael." Michelle's eyes widened. "What do you think she would do if she found out about this?"

"If you write a book about it, then don't you think she will find out?"

"I doubt if she would even read it."

"Michelle, you know she would read it. She reads what you put on Facebook. I think you should talk to her. Maybe she knows something."

"Seriously, Michael."

"Look. Maybe she's known this all along. Maybe that's why she didn't want you marrying me."

"No. She's prejudiced."

"I think you're wrong. I know prejudice. I see enough of it. Like when patients request a white nurse."

"Michael, that hasn't happened in a long time."

"It's happened. I'm just saying, Michelle, she's a mother. She just wants what's best for you. Same with my parents. You got to remember what they lived through. They weren't all that happy about us getting married, but they accept it. Besides, this bit of information, if she doesn't know it, might improve things with your mother."

"Or make it worse."

"You know what I want?"

"What?"

"I want you and your mother to clear the air. After all, we are trying to have a baby. She'll be a grandmother one day, hopefully soon."

Michelle sighed. "Yes, and I worry about that with my mom. I don't want my child, our child, to have an estranged grandparent."

"She won't be. There's something about a little baby that brings out the best in people. I don't care what color it is."

The timer sounded. "Better see to that quiche," Michelle said.

"*M*om?"

"Michelle?"

"You act surprised."

"Is something wrong?"

"No. I just want to ask you something." There was a pause. "Mom, are you there?"

"Yes. What do you want to ask me?"

"It's about Grandma."

"Grandmother Alice?"

"Yes."

"She died when you were ten."

"Eleven. I distinctly remember. You came and got me out of Mrs. Parson's class. I was in sixth grade. We were in the middle of math. I was so glad to get out of the math assignment. Mrs. Parsons had this glum look on her face and told me not to worry about any homework until next week."

"You have a good memory."

"About some things, I guess. Did Grandma ever talk to you about some genealogy work she was doing?"

"I think she might have mentioned it. It was something she was doing when your Grandfather John got sick."

"Grandpa John. Yes, I wished I had known him."

"I wished you could have, too, but he died years before you were born."

"Well, what I'm calling about is that I found some papers in the attic."

"What kind of papers?"

"They were mostly journals."

"I don't know about any journals. Your Grandmother Alice never mentioned them. Your father and I meant to go through that house and clean things out long before you moved in but never got around to it."

"Before the divorce? Before Michael and I moved in?"

"Yes, before the divorce and before you and Michael moved in." Michelle thought she heard a change in her mother's voice when she said Michael's name, but she wasn't sure. There was definitely an irritation in her voice in repeating the word divorce. No mistaking that. But, she could be mistaken about the way she thought she heard her mother say Michael. Maybe Michael was right. She imagined so much. She was a mother wanting what was best for her child. And soon, she would be the same if all went well.

"Michelle, are you there?"

"Yes, Mom. You see, the journals just stopped."

"I doubt if she had time for journals when your Grandfather John got sick. He required her constant attention."

"You never talked much about Grandpa. I only know he was sick for a good while before he died."

"We never told you about Grandfather John?"

"Just that he was sick and died."

"He had a heart attack. Had to take early retirement. Smoked like a chimney. Oh, he quit when he got sick. But by then, it was too late. After he got sick, he never wanted

173

Grandmother Alice to leave his side. She really didn't have any time to herself at all after he got sick." She paused. "So, what's so important about these journals?"

"There was a particular woman in the nursing home where she worked that she had gotten close to. So close, that after she retired, she continued to go see her. Mostly, the journals are about this woman's life story. But they end abruptly, with no conclusion."

"Why don't you just throw them out?"

"No, Mom. I don't want to throw them out."

"Why on earth would you want to keep them?"

"Because this woman was related to us."

"To us?"

"Yes, she was a Barnes."

"Your Grandmother Alice never mentioned her. I don't know. Maybe she did. I don't remember."

"Maybe that was because she was black."

"*I*t can't be much further," Michelle said, looking at the map on her phone.

"It's out in the middle of nowhere," Michael said.

"Oh, come on, Michael. This is an adventure."

"I guess if you can call being in the heart of Ku Klux Klan country an adventure."

"Michael, you don't know that," she replied.

"I'll err on the side of caution if you don't mind."

"Oh, look, there's a house. This must be the place."

"Sweetheart, this looks nothing like an antebellum plantation house," he said, slowing the car and stopping a couple of hundred feet away on the gravel road leading up to the house.

"This is it. It's got to be it. The man, a mile back, the one out washing his pickup truck, said it was the house we were looking for and that it was the only house up here."

"The man with the Confederate flag on the back window? The one who is probably the Klan's leader?"

"I'm sorry, Michael. I didn't see that until after I told you to pull over. And, he seemed friendly enough." Michelle said, defending herself.

"I don't understand why he needed to know where we were coming from when we asked for directions. I mean, how does where you came from enter into the equation of giving directions to some place from where you are at that moment?"

Michelle rolled her eyes. "I think it's just something they automatically ask around here."

"Do you think he told us the truth? He's probably going to be coming up the road any second, now. Just had to go back, get his banjo, and his buddies, the men in the white hoods."

Michelle rolled her eyes. "Really, Michael."

"Yes, really Michelle. Ever since you opened those shoe boxes, you think it's the coolest thing in the world to be black. Well, let me tell you, it isn't. Why do you think I always drive under the speed limit, even when you say like a little girl, *Michael, go faster, go faster?* It's because I *am* black. I do not want to be pulled over by a cop."

"Okay, Michael." She put her hand on his. "I understand. But, there are no cops here."

"No, worse, rednecks," he mumbled, banging his head against the steering wheel. "And why do you think your grandma hid those boxes away in the attic and never told the rest of the family about her discovery? I'll tell you why. She discovered all this stuff about the time Martin Luther King, Jr. was shot."

"We've come all this way. Are you suggesting we turn around and go back?"

"No, no. We're here. So, what do we do now?" he asked, with a perplexed expression.

"We get out of the car and knock on the door."

"Michelle, are you serious? Okay, I know, it's 2009 and we have a black president, but we are out in the country where rebel flags fly, me a black man, you a white woman. These people may have guns." He shook his head, squeezing his fingers tightly around the steering wheel. "What do I mean these people may have guns? These people *do* have guns," he said to the steering wheel. He ducked his head, and cast his eyes upward, gazing out the window, observing as if an alien spacecraft was hovering over them. "What are those?" he asked, turning to Michelle.

Michelle broke her eyes from him and looked in the direction he was looking. "Birds."

"Not just birds. Buzzards. They know something. They are just biding their time—waiting for us."

"I hope you don't make comments like this to your patients."

He finally let go of the steering wheel as if a brilliant idea had occurred to him and reached into his pocket for his phone. He held it up, taking a picture of the house. He started typing in a message.

"What are you doing?"

"I'm texting my brother, giving him our last known whereabouts."

"Okay, this is getting ridiculous. Do you want to just turn around and leave?"

"I think it's too late for that. A woman with a baby on her hip just came outside and is staring at us."

Michelle looked over. She slowly put up her hand and waved from inside the car. "She looks friendly enough. I don't see a gun, just a baby. I'm getting out of the car. We can't just sit in here forever. And, it would look stupid to turn around and leave now." She opened the door. "Are you coming?" Michael opened his door. They walked toward the house.

"Hi, I'm Michelle. This is my husband, Michael." Michelle looked back. "Come on, Michael."

"Just tying my shoe, sweetheart. I'm right behind you," he said, bent down going through some sort of motion concerning his sneakers. Michelle rolled her eyes and looked back at the woman who grinned.

"Beautiful baby. Little girl?"

"Yeah, she's teething right now. I'm sorry. She's cranky," she said while bouncing the baby on her hip.

"You might try soaking a wash cloth in cold chamomile tea," the voice behind her said. Michelle jumped.

"Oh, I thought you were back there," she said. "Tying your shoe." The woman with the baby smiled. "Michael's a nurse."

"Thanks for the advice," the woman said. "Oh, I'm Debbie."

"Glad to meet you, Debbie. I guess you're wondering why we're here," Michelle said.

"Sometimes I get Jehovah Witnesses out here, but you don't look like Jehovah Witnesses." She smiled again, bouncing her baby on her hip. "I'm just kidding. I know you're not Jehovah Witnesses. Joe said you were here because you're doing genealogy research."

"Joe?" Michelle asked.

"The guy down the road. You asked him for directions." The woman had a perpetual smile on her face like she was one up on them. "He called to say you were on your way up here. So, you're an Erwin descendant?"

"No, not exactly," Michelle said. "Actually, it has to do with the slaves the Erwins had."

"Oh," she said, looking at Michael. "So, you're a descendant of one of the slaves they had here?"

Michael blinked and swallowed. "No, they would be Michelle's ancestors."

"You're joking," she said, laughing.

"No, we're not," Michelle said.

"Oh," she said, her bottom lip almost dropping to the porch floor.

"So, is this the original house?" Michael asked.

"The log part is original. And the fireplace is original to the house. All the back part was built on about fifty years ago. I know there was a fire once. Every once in a while when the wind blows right you can smell it—the smoke. We don't use the fireplace. We have a wood burning stove insert in there now. My husband and I just rent the place."

"So, you're not an Erwin?"

"No. The last lady who lived here was. She died about ten years ago. Too bad you didn't come back then. I hear she was the family history keeper."

"Yeah, too bad," Michelle said.

"The well over there is original to the property. And, one of the cemeteries is just over there." She pointed. "A bunch of the original Erwins is buried there. The slave graves are marked with rocks. They're under the big tree. You're welcome to look around. I need to get this baby down for a nap."

"Do you mind if we take pictures of the property?"

"Like I said, we just rent. It's fine with me."

"Okay, well thanks a lot," Michelle said.

"Yes, thanks," Michael echoed.

"That went well," Michael said, in a more relaxed state of mind than previously, as they walked in the direction of the cemetery.

"Don't say that just yet. I still see those buzzards circling." Michelle laughed.

"They're above that other hill. Probably a dead deer or something over there," he said.

Michelle rolled her eyes. "You're not worried about them anymore?"

"No. Debbie seemed nice enough."

"I was so hoping she would invite us in," Michelle said.

"Maybe on the next visit," Michael said.

"Oh, so now you plan on coming back?"

"Maybe, assuming we get out of here without getting shot. Don't forget to wrap up some chamomile tea as a present if we do come back," he said.

"Good idea."

They walked through the wooden gate into the cemetery. Michelle walked straight toward the tree. "It's eerie, isn't it?" he said.

"Have you never seen slave graves?" Michelle asked, wrapping her arm around his waist.

"Sure, once on a school field trip, but I was only ten, and it didn't really mean anything to me. I was just thrilled to be out of the classroom and stopping for pizza afterward. I'm glad we are doing this," he said, bending down, giving her a kiss.

"We are probably kissing over Nell and Ib's graves. Maybe even my great, great, how many ever greats there are, grandmother's grave."

"Do you think she was buried here?" Michael asked.

"I have no idea. There was nothing in my grandma's journals about where her grave was. Probably not, though. Sally said they never saw her again. It's so sad, isn't it? These graves not being marked, when all the others are."

"It's ironic, too, that the ones who settled here, Elizabeth and John Leander's graves aren't marked. That's what I read in your grandma's journals," Michael said.

"I bet we walked right over their graves. Kind of puts them on an even playing field with the slaves, don't you think?" Michelle let out a sigh. "Are you ready for some hiking? There are a couple of other cemeteries around here."

"Sure," Michael said. "As long as we get back on the road before dark."

"You got it."

They walked back toward the car. "Look," Michael said. "Her curtain's open, and she's peeking out at us. She's on her cell phone. I bet she's talking to Joe, giving him the low down. Wave, Michelle," he said, giving a salute-like wave and friendly nod of his head, as they walked past.

"Okay, Michelle. Enough is enough. Am I going to have to paint this living room myself? This bucket of paint has set here for two weeks."

"Honestly, Michael, I had good intentions today, but I got to thinking that this couch isn't going to match at all."

"No, no, no. We cannot afford a new couch right now."

"I wasn't suggesting we get one. I went into the shed out back this morning. I knew there was furniture piled up out there. And, I was looking for old rags to cover the floor for the painting project. Like I said, I had good intentions. Anyway, Grandma's couch is perfect. And, it's in better shape than this one. I thought we could swap them out. Tomorrow's Saturday. What if we tackle it then?"

MICHAEL STOOD at the entrance of the shed, Michelle behind him. "Your grandparents sure did hoard."

"No, I don't think so. I think my mom and dad moved

pieces out here when they were going through Grandma's stuff. Remember they rented it for a while until we decided we wanted to live here."

"We are going to have to get this one out of here before we can squeeze in the one we have now."

"How about we leave our old one out on the curb. Someone will for sure pick it up. I can call Goodwill or ask around. I'm guessing college kids would want it or someone starting out."

"Sounds easier than hauling it all the way out here."

They eased the couch onto the curb. "One thing down. I hope it doesn't rain," Michael said.

"We'll cover it with a tarp if it looks like rain. Hopefully, someone will see it and want it. It's not in bad shape, even though it is a hand-me-down."

"I just hope my mother doesn't happen to pay us a visit and see it out here. If she does, then you can do the explaining," Michael said. "Are you ready to get the other one?"

"Might as well," Michelle said.

They walked out back and entered the shed. "Okay, have you got your end?" Michael asked.

"I think so. Ow," Michelle yelled.

"What's wrong? You okay? I'm going to let my end down. Is that okay?"

"Yeah, go ahead. I banged my leg."

Michael went over to her. "Let me see." He examined her leg. "You're going to have a bad bruise."

"Is that your expert opinion as a nurse?"

"No, my expert opinion is that we should take a break. Why don't you sit down, and I'll go inside and bring us out some beers?"

"Now, you're talking. Ow," Michelle yelled again.

"Now what?"

"Something sticking out of the cushion of this chair." Michelle jumped off the seat and pulled the cushion up. "A notebook. The wiring in the binding part was hitting my leg —my other leg—my good one."

"Are you going to be okay?" Michael examined her good leg. "You're not bleeding. It's only a scratch. Should I go inside and get those beers or not?"

"Oh my god, Michael."

"What now?"

"This is another of Grandma's journals." Michelle paused. "And, Michael, look at this chair," she said, sliding her hands back and forth on the threadbare arms.

"What about the chair?"

"Look. Closely. Aren't you seeing it?"

"Seeing what? That it's kind of ratty?"

"No. Look. *Really* look."

"What am I looking at, honey?"

"Overstuffed? Pink flowers?"

"Well, I guess if you look close enough and try to imagine the color under the stains, you can tell they might have once been pink once," Michael said while standing with a blank expression.

"Duh. This is Sally's chair. And this is probably the last journal that Grandma left. It will tell us what happened. At least I hope it will."

"I can see we are not going to get this couch moved into the house today, are we?"

"We'll get both the couch and the chair moved in tomorrow."

"The chair? Michelle, you've got to be joking. You were worried about our old couch not matching the walls. Look at this chair. It's hideous. Not to mention dirty."

"We don't have to use it in the living room. We can put it in my office."

"That's a flight of stairs," Michael groaned.

"It will inspire me." Michelle stood with the journal in one hand and massaged her husband's shoulder with her other hand.

"*A*lice, what are you doing here? Is John okay?"

"Yes, I'm only out for a little while. How's she doing?"

"You mean?"

"Sally."

"Of course. For someone one-hundred-and-ten, I'm surprised she's doing at all," Ethel said. "I won't lie to you. She's been going downhill fast."

"I missed her birthday."

"Well, we don't exactly know when her birthday is, do we?" Ethel said.

"Is her chart still blank?"

"Yes, but her granddaughter said she would be more around one-hundred-and-ten now, so we went with that."

"And I missed her granddaughter's visit. I so wanted to meet her." Alice sighed. "And no one has bothered to write in a date?"

"No."

"Ethel, do you think you might pencil one in? Sally deserves a birthdate, even if it is the wrong one."

"I really don't think it would matter at this point. Do you have a date in mind?"

"She was born when the blackberries were ripe. So, sometime in July. It was hot, she said. So, maybe toward the end of July? And on a Wednesday. She knew it was a Wednesday because her grandmother had to walk on the day her mother delivered her because her master wouldn't let her have the wagon."

"My, my, you do know a lot about her, don't you? I will somehow find out what day Wednesday was on the year she was born. 1858?"

"Yes, that would be great, Ethel. Has she been talking?"

"Not that I know of. Hardly says a word these days. Mostly sleeps." Ethel put the files she was working on aside and stepped out from behind her desk. She put her hands on Alice's shoulders. "Alice, you shouldn't be here worrying about Sally. A woman her age? What can you do? What happens, happens."

"I know. You are right. But, I feel so guilty. Like I abandoned her."

"Alice, what are you saying? You've done more than your duty when it comes to Sally." Ethel shook her head. "I mean, it's not like she's a relative." Ethel laughed.

Alice clenched the edge of the desk. "Yeah, of course, I guess you're right." She tried to smile.

"There's been several here to look in on her. Like I said, her granddaughter came, and the Bonzo man that brought her in comes on most weekends now."

"I would have liked to talk to them both. Doesn't look like I will. I can hardly leave John's side. Only to go to the grocery store or to the bank or to pick up a prescription. And, the doctor visits keep me busy. I was on my way to the grocery store this morning and couldn't stand it another minute. John expects me to go straight there and back. Oh, Ethel, I never thought retirement was going to be like this." Alice shook her head and tried to hold back tears. "I'm sorry. I didn't mean…"

"Now, hon, it's going to be okay."

"I wish. John and I had such plans. He was almost there— to his own retirement. Then, the heart attack. I told him to quit smoking. Begged him."

Ethel rubbed Alice's shoulder. "I know, hon. I feel so bad for you. John's such a good man. I always envied your marriage. My man's always ran around on me. In the best of health, too. And, he's older than John."

"Ethel…"

"No use trying to say something polite. It's a small town. Everyone knows it. Doesn't help we live on a rural road and are on a party line, either."

"You're right. John is a good man, a good husband. We still talk about all these things we're going to do when he gets well, but the truth is, both of us know he's not going to get well. The whole bottom part of his heart is dead. He gets winded going from the bed to the living room. We had to move our bedroom downstairs. I needed a diversion today. Some clarity. Somehow, Sally gives me that. And, I felt guilty. I just had to come check on her."

"Well, hon, if it puts your mind to ease, go look in on her. Whether she knows you're there or not, God only knows."

Alice sat by Sally's bedside. She watched Sally's chest move up and down. Frailer than she remembered, a mere skeleton of a woman. Alice took her hand. It felt cold. "What keeps you going, Sally? Is there something more you want to tell me? Do you even know I'm here?" Alice asked, talking to herself more than to Sally.

Alice looked over at the empty bed next to Sally. "I guess it's the one advantage of being the only colored person here right now. You get a private room." *None of the white people want to be in the same room. Could Sally hear her thoughts?* Alice got up and pulled the curtain back peering out the window before sitting back down by Sally's side and taking her hand again into her own. "It's snowing. Started this morning. March 15. I was hoping those few warm days we had would have lasted, but I guess we had to have one final snow. It's not sticking, though." Alice smiled. "I remember that's how it started. It was snowing on the day you began telling me about your life. We were looking out at the snow, and you said, *it was snowing that day, too.* The day you said you buried John Leander Erwin."

Alice reached over and kissed Sally. "I can't seem to leave your side, but I have to go. John gets so nervous when I'm away too long. His heart is so bad." Alice sighed. "I'm really scared, Sally." Tears fell from Alice's eyes. "We didn't plan this at all. I never thought I would retire from nursing only to be nursing my husband."

Alice rubbed Sally's bony hand. "Would you listen to me? I'm doing all the talking, now. I wish we could go back to where we were, you telling me about your life. I felt like I was back there with you.

"Sally, I never told you. I was scared to tell you, but you told me your secret. So, now I'll tell you mine. My maiden name is Barnes." There was no change in Sally's face. Sally's hand was limp in her own. Alice took a deep breath and let it out. "Wow, that felt good, just to say it." Alice let out a heavy breath. "I have to go. I need to go." Alice sat frozen. "There is so much I want to say to you. I wish I had said to you. I just let you tell me your story. Docia was my great, great, great grandmother. We're related, Sally. Really related." Alice felt Sally's fingernail squeeze into the palm of her hand ever so lightly. Was that a slight smile on Sally's face? More tears came down. Alice used her other hand to wipe them. "I hope that means you heard me." She leaned over and kissed Sally again. "And that you are pleased we are related. You said we were like kin, and we really are."

———

TEARS FELL from Michelle's eyes. Michael leaned over in bed and kissed away the wetness from his wife's cheeks. "Are you finished reading?" he asked.

Michelle nodded with downturned lips. She passed the journal over to Michael. He opened it up to the first page. A couple of hours later, he said, "Wow."

"Yes, wow is right."

"Do you plan on sharing this with your mom?"

"I don't know. Maybe. When the time is right."

"I mean, there is a lot in here about your grandpa, too."

"I know. I feel like I know him now. I've only ever seen pictures of him." Michelle rolled over in bed and hugged Michael. "I think I will work on Grandpa's side of the family, too, after I work on Sally. There were abolitionists on his side, you know."

"I know. You told me. I think your grandma would like that. She would like all this stuff you're doing."

"Mom said Grandma wanted me to have the house, but I was too young when she died. Then, it went through numerous renters and sat vacant for a while. It was like all this was here waiting for me."

"You may be right. Let me see your leg." Michelle removed her sore leg from underneath the sheet. "Yep, a bruise is forming." He bent down and kissed it. But, he didn't stop there.

"What are you doing?"

"We've lain in bed all morning, right through lunch. And, we never did get those beers. Might as well make it count."

"But Ethel didn't pencil it in, did she?"

"No," Michael said. "But she must have told the doctor at the last minute. It's clear someone at the hospital wrote it on her death certificate. But then, it's also weird that the date just happened to be the same date that Ted Bonzo signed off on it."

"Yes, one of those coincidences or synchronicities. Maybe Sally had a hand in it somehow."

"Maybe so," Michael said.

"The widowed part looks scribbled in at the last minute, too. It's written in the same pen as July 21 is written," Michelle said.

"It was nice of Mr. Combs to send you her death certificate."

"Yes, I'm lucky to have found him. Who knew someone else was so interested in Sally? So much is wrong, though. Or at least I think it is. Under married, it has her as widowed."

"I'm sure Mr. Bonzo must have told the hospital that. He's the one that signed off on her death certificate."

"Yeah, I'm sure he would have wanted to protect her reputation. Things were different back then."

"Or maybe she actually was at some time during her life. Did Mr. Combs know anything about it?"

"No," she said, shaking her head. "I finished reading his book last night, *The Isle of Regret.* Sally's mentioned briefly. She made such an impact on him when he was young that he wanted to pay tribute to her in some way."

"I would say she's made an impact on a lot of lives and still does so from her grave. Look at the impact she's making on you," Michael said. "So, you've been emailing Mr. Combs?"

"Yes, and we've talked by phone. He didn't tell me a great deal. Didn't remember all that much. When he was young, he went to the same church as Sally. Mostly, he talked about how nice she was and how she always wore the same pink flowered dress to church and house shoes. Her feet must have really hurt."

"Probably grew up without proper fitting shoes as a child, that is when she wasn't barefoot," Michael said.

"It's strange, isn't it?"

"What's strange?" Michael asked.

"That Grandma's last visit with Sally, or last visit that we know of, was right before she was taken to Haywood Hospital?" Michelle held the copy of the death certificate. "Grandma saw her on March 15, and Sally was admitted to Haywood on March 16. I can't believe she lasted until March 31."

"Sally was one strong woman."

"Yeah."

"As for your Grandma seeing her on that particular day, I don't think it was strange at all. I hear a lot of stuff like this, being a nurse. If I could write like you, I could write a book on all the anecdotes people have related to me."

"Yeah." Michelle sighed and smiled at her husband. "If I ever get Sally written, maybe one day I'll write it for you."

"I think your Grandma was meant to go see her that day. It was to clear the air. Just like you were meant to clear the air with your mom."

"I was so surprised to know that Grandma did actually tell her about Docia. But, I'm still kind of pissed."

"That she kept it from you?"

"Yes."

"And your dad. Do you plan on telling him?"

"No. What's the point? He and Mom have been divorced for years. He has his new family now."

"At least we know your mom being descended from a black woman had no bearing on why they got divorced."

"No, breakup story of the ages—he found a younger woman."

"And, that's a lot of the reason why your mom is the way she is. You now know the reasons she never told you."

"Yes, I know. I've always known, deep down. Well, the dad part. He was cheating, but she didn't want to bring him down in front of me. So, she kept it all to herself. Said she thought plenty of times about telling me about our family history or what she knew of it, but the time wasn't right, and with everything going on with dad, she was barely coping. I understand. I really do. In fact, I admire her for not wanting to burden me. She was keeping two secrets in a way."

"And you marrying a black man made her feel guilty about not telling you.'

"I guess."

"Maybe if we tried to get your mom fixed up?"

"Michael? Please?"

"Okay. Just saying."

*M*ichelle sat in the chair—Sally's chair—peering out her office window into the back yard. Her grandma recorded in her journal there was snow on that first day Sally opened up about her past. There was no snow, today. It was mid-summer. Nor were there dogwood flowers blowing in the wind, mimicking snow, one of the other things she remembered reading in her grandma's journal. There was only the large oak which needed pruning.

She found herself sitting in the chair more and more, instead of at her desk, trying to get a feel for Sally. She closed her eyes in meditation and tried to evoke scenes of Sally and her grandma together in the nursing home.

With her eyes shut, the odor was more prominent. It wasn't just one odor but a mixture of smells that permeated the room. Shortly after moving the chair into her office, she rented a carpet cleaning machine with upholstery attachments. She scrubbed until flecks of pink roses appeared—that is the ones she didn't completely scrub away.

A lingering mustiness competed with the lemon scented cleaner she had used. Sometimes, she imagined a third smell, something she couldn't define. It was a smell with a life of its own. Sometimes it was faintly sweet like fresh water flowing in a creek bed. She pictured Sally as a young girl doing laundry in a stream, beating the clothes with rocks. Was that how it was done? She would have to look that up. On other times, she reached her finger to her nose to block a putrid odor. She recognized it as the smell of oldness, the smell of death. It was the smell in the halls of Haywood Hospital where she had gone to visit her grandma right before her death.

She was in sixth grade. Her mom checked her out of school. They were gathering the family. Grandma's time was near. It was her first experience with death. Grandma had a stroke. Grandma's face looked all strange to her. Her mom told her that sometimes that's what happens when you have a stroke. Her mom held her hand as they walked up the steps of the hospital. As they climbed, her mom explained how Grandma looked different. "Don't be scared," she said. "She's still your Grandmother Alice."

Her mom always referred to her as Grandmother Alice. She referred to her dad's mother as Grandmother Hazel. "Grandmother Alice asked for you in particular," her mom said. Of course she wanted to see her. She was the only grandchild, but maybe there was more to it. She looked around at the stacks of papers in her office, once Grandma's office, all organized better than she ever kept her desk at school. This had to be it—the reason her grandma asked for her, in particular, as her mom had put it. There was a special glint in Grandma's eyes that day as she took her hand.

Her mom had said Grandma wanted her to have the house. She wanted her to one day find her journals. She was sure of that, now. Grandma probably knew her own daughter wouldn't do anything about them.

Her grandpa and grandma both died at Haywood Hospital. Sally died there, too. Haywood sat abandoned now, atop a hill, overlooking the town. It was a creepy, foreboding structure. Although it was boarded up, it was a rite of passage for almost every teenager growing up in Maysville to explore it. She had grown up on its ghost stories. Was Sally's ghost lingering there? What about her grandpa? Maybe Grandma was there with the both of them right now. All of them looking down on her, waiting for her to finish this project, whatever it was to be before they could leave. It had been nearly forty years since Sally and her grandpa died and eighteen since Grandma died. Ghosts were a patient lot.

Her grandma never wrote about Sally's smell. Sally was old. It came with the territory, and Michelle had been in nursing homes before. The smell could almost knock you down when you entered. She had always been extra sensitive to smells. Michael, being a nurse, was immune to them. He could go from vomit and bed pans to freshly brewed coffee with all the ease of a dolphin in the ocean. Michelle reasoned her grandma would be the same.

The chair was definitely more presentable, not that it mattered. She and Michael were the only ones who were ever in her office.

The room had become a Sally shrine. Black and white pictures of the Erwin place adorned the walls, along with pictures of slave cabins and slave life in general. Some were pictures she had taken and others she had printed off from the internet. She removed the pictures of the rocks marking the slave graves of the Erwin cemetery as they gave Michael the creeps. There was the picture of Boone Furnace or the remains of Boone Furnace. She had stood on the hood of her car and taken the picture from across the AA highway. What she longed for the most was a picture of Sally, other than the one of her with her grandma, one of her in her younger days. There had to be some, somewhere. Besides writing something that would make both her grandma and Sally proud, finding pictures of Sally was number one on her to-do list.

Michelle found herself sitting in the chair on a daily basis. It was a ritual, an attempt to travel back in time, before banging away at her keyboard. The writing had been progressing nicely although it was nowhere near what she wanted it to be before showing it to Michael.

Today was different. She sat in the chair because she was perplexed. She held a piece of paper in her hand that didn't make sense. Today, she understood writer's block. Today, the writing that had been flowing so fluidly, had come to a dead halt.

She wanted more to write from than her grandma's journals. She wanted documentation. She opened an account with a genealogy site. There was nothing to be found on Sally. There was plenty on the Bonzos and the Erwins. Sally was a non-entity. Sadly, those born into slavery were, even after slavery was over.

There was the day Michael came home and found her crying. She was more upset over the plight of black people than he was. Maybe it was something he chose to ignore or kept buried. Why stir up the past? He never asked his family questions, but he heard them talking once when he was young. He related the story to Michelle that he was descended from a man who had killed a white man in Atlanta in the late 1880s. Michael didn't know the exact reason, only that it had something to do with the Klan. He merely said, "Michelle, it wouldn't matter even if it was in self-defense. Killing a white man back then was an automatic death penalty." His ancestor escaped a lynching by running away and changing his name. He left a family behind and took on a new one. Michael didn't know the previous name. Maybe if she searched old newspapers, she might find an article, but that was a project for another day. Michael had a whole other family branch he would never know. Did Michael even want to know?

"WHAT'S WRONG?" Michael asked.

Michelle held the photocopy in the air, an exasperated look on her face. "This doesn't make sense," she said.

"What is it?"

"I went to the Kentucky Gateway Museum today. At first, I was so thrilled. I found Sally's obituary. Right on the front page of the Lewis County Herald. Front page, Michael. I laughed out loud. The lady at the center must have thought me callous or mad. She knew I was looking for an obituary. Grandma would have been so happy about Sally getting front page. I wondered if Grandma might have seen it? But, then I thought, no. For starters, there was no copy of it in her stuff. She said in that last journal we found that Sally died a couple of days after Grandad died. That Ethel had called her to let her know. So, there would have been no way she would have even got to go to the funeral. She only mentioned getting Ted Bonzo's and Nell's address and sending them condolence cards.

"Then, I started reading it. The whole thing was a compilation of both Sally and her daughter. How could they write something like that? Wouldn't Ted or Nell see that her obituary got written correctly? Here's the copy." She handed it to Michael.

Sallie Barns

   Dead At 110

   Miss Sally Ann Barnes, believed to be the oldest resident in Lewis County, died Monday, March 31st, in the Maysville hospital. She was 110.

A native of Lewis County she resided with the Ben Bonzo family in St. Paul and was a member of the Mars Hill Church of Christ.

The aged Negro woman was a daughter of the late "Uncle Peter" Barnes, and a sister of the late Perry and Sam Barnes, all of whom will be remembered by our elder citizens. The deceased sixty years ago was a cook at the St. Charles Hotel, and the last thing local people knew of her, she was cooking in the home of the late Charles and Jesse Hammond. The last time we knew of her whereabouts, she was living at Weirton, W. VA.

Funeral services were conducted at 1 PM Thursday at South Shore, with Rev. Clyde Callihan officiating. Burial was in Green Cemetery at St. Paul.

Michael looked up from the paper.

"You see how wrong it is, don't you?" Michelle asked.

"Yes. Or do you suppose Sally was confused when she talked to your grandma? Maybe she mixed things up. She was one-hundred-nine, after all."

"No. I don't think that at all. Look." Michelle pointed to the sentence, *The last time we knew of her whereabouts, she was living at Weirton, W. VA.* "We have a copy of her death certificate, courtesy of Karl. She died at Haywood Hospital. The death certificate can't be wrong."

"No, I suppose you're right," Michael said.

"Since I've been home, I've been calling people."

"Calling who?"

"The people listed in the obituary. That is, the ones I could find. Most are dead. I started with the man who preached the funeral."

"And?" Michael asked.

"Dead. But, his wife is still living. She told me about how nice Sally was and what an honor it was for her husband to preach the funeral. Wasn't even the same church she went to."

"Why do you think that was?" Michael asked.

"I asked Mrs. Callihan that same question. She didn't know."

"I suppose, too, people don't remember. It was a long time ago," he said.

"Yeah. I also called the funeral home."

"Oh, yeah?"

"Yeah. They kind of shrugged me off. They basically said, *no, they didn't make mistakes in their obituaries.*" Michelle rolled her eyes.

"What's this?" Michael picked up a piece of paper. On it was a long list of names and phone numbers and notes with arrows pointing to different names. Michael read, *loved to cook, churned butter, dog named Pup, one child scared of her at family reunion—looked up her dress—Sally said she was the same color all the way up, Mr. Veach's son worked at store, as a boy he remembered Sally brought in eggs... somewhere around the 1950s...* He flipped to the back to find similar scribblings, all with names and phone numbers beside them.

"Oh, those are the calls I made. Most were suspicious at first. Thought I was a telemarketer, but then after a while, they loosened up and if they didn't know anything, they gave me the name of someone who might. I think some of them were lonely. Most were old and had lost their spouses. I would go from elation to despair. Almost everyone told me of a person that could answer all my questions. When I asked how to contact *said person*, I was told they died just a short while ago. What is that saying? A day late and a dollar short?"

"How many people did you call? Looks to be around ten?"

"Yeah, probably. I've started keeping a daily log." Michelle held up a notebook. "See. I record all my findings about Sally.

I started with the trip we made to the original Erwin house in Carter County."

"I even tracked down the doctor who signed off on her death certificate."

"He's still living."

"Yes. He was really nice, but he didn't remember Sally. That added insult to injury. I thought how could someone not remember Sally?"

"Do you know how many patients I see in a day?"

"Yes, I suppose that's the reason."

"And, it was a long time ago."

"Yeah." Michelle sighed.

"You are so involved in this."

"I know, but I can't help it. It's like an obsession. I make notes. I search the internet."

"Maybe you should ease up a bit."

"Why?"

"I think it's making you sick, all this work. Your voice is hoarse."

"My voice is hoarse from shouting into the phone. Most of the people I talk to are hard of hearing. Don't worry. I'm not always shouting into the phone. Sometimes I write a little. And then, before I know it, you're walking through the door."

"You've started writing on Sally?"

"A little."

"Let me see."

"No," she said, closing her laptop. "I'll let you see soon enough." She smiled.

"Well, it's the weekend. You can give it a little rest."

"No, I can't. Are you up for a little trip tomorrow?"

"Where?"

"I'll tell you during dinner."

"THIS IS IT. It's the next right," Michelle said.

"Nice gravestone as far as gravestones go," Michael said.

"Yes, and buried here alongside the rest of the Bonzo family. A lot different from the rocks with no names marking the slave graves back in Carter County."

"Yes. Your grandma did say in her journals that Sally would be taken care of."

"I want to find the house."

"You mean the house where Sally last lived?" Michael asked. "I thought someone told you it was no longer standing."

"Someone did, but then someone else said that person was wrong and that it *is* still standing."

"So, we're kind of on a wild goose chase?" Michael said.

"Everything about Sally, so far, has been a wild goose chase. But, it's around here somewhere. I know it is. I don't have an actual address but have some directions in my notes."

"*M*ichael, stop. This is it. I know it is."

Michael pulled up alongside the house.

"No, in the driveway," Michelle said.

He gave his wife a look of disbelief.

"I don't know why you're looking at me that way. You know I'm going to get out of the car and knock on the door."

"Yes, of course you are, Miss Daisy," he said, shaking his head. He backed up the car and pulled into the driveway.

"What is the point in coming if we don't get out?"

"I don't know. I thought we might do a drive by. Go up and down the road a few times. Pretend we were lost. Enough to get a good look at the house. Take a quick picture if no one is home."

Michelle rolled her eyes. "Look. We don't even have to knock on the door. A man is coming out."

"Yes, of course, he is, like the woman at the Erwin plantation, and I'm using the term *plantation* loosely here," Michael said, gripping tightly to the steering wheel.

"The way you've been hugging that steering wheel lately,

you're going to have to buy it a ring," Michelle said as she got out of the car.

"Michelle, wait." But it was too late. "Please don't have a gun," Michael whispered to the steering wheel.

"Hi," she said, standing a few feet from the car.

"Hello," the man on the porch said.

Michelle walked up closer, her hand over her eyes, blocking the sun. "I was wondering. Do you know if a black woman by the name of Sally used to live here?"

"Long time ago. At least that's what I heard," the man said.

"I've been doing research on her," Michelle said.

"Research?" the man asked.

"Yes."

"Something like genealogy? My sister does that."

"Yes, something like that," Michelle answered.

"I guess the man in the car is related to her?" the man asked, staring at Michael.

"My husband? No, not actually," Michelle said.

The man raised his eyebrows and ducked his head, getting a closer look at Michael. Michael rolled his window down and waved.

"It's a long story. The short version is, I'm an English professor in Maysville, where Sally died. My grandma knew her, took care of her at the nursing home, and I've decided to write a story about her—about her life. I'm trying to find out as much as I can. I thought seeing where she lived before going into the nursing home would give me a better feel for her."

"Oh," the man said. "Well, I don't know anything about her, except that she was old when she lived here. We bought the house from a lady she used to work for—a woman named Hammond. She's dead now, too. I heard the woman, Sally, was buried up the road, at the Greene Cemetery with the Bonzos, the people she worked for." Michelle flinched, hearing the words that she only worked for them.

"Yes, we just came from the gravesite. And since we were so close to the house where I heard she once lived, I had to stop and check it out. Like I said, I'm trying to get a feel for how she lived, where she lived. You know, what the neighborhood was like. Do you mind if I take some notes and take a photo of the house?" Michelle held up her notebook and camera.

"I guess it's okay. As long as you're not from the government, or anything like that." He laughed. "Don't know what I can tell you about her, but ask away." The man stepped off the porch, walked down the steps and stood in the yard. Michelle turned and motioned for Michael to get out of the car. He got out, leaving the door open.

"This is my husband, Michael. I'm Michelle." The man gave a nod but didn't offer his own name.

A calico cat came up to Michael, rubbing its fur around his legs.

"He likes you, Michael." Michelle reached down to pet him.

"Ain't that something," the man said. "The cats around here aren't usually a friendly lot."

"Someone told me Sally had a dog that she called Pup."

"That's what you're writing about?"

"No, not necessarily. I thought it was interesting she didn't give the dog a name."

"Probably a stray. Most animals around here are. I doubt if she named any of the animals. Too *many* to name. And don't want to name a critter you're gonna eat."

"Eat? A dog or a cat?" Michelle exclaimed.

"No," the man said with a straight face. "A cow or a chicken or a pig. They had those here, too."

"Oh, yes, of course. Someone else told me she had an old

wringer washer that she had on the back porch where she washed clothes." Michelle craned her neck, looking to the side of the house that might lead to a back porch. The man made no offer to walk her back there.

"Don't reckon it was old back then," the man said with a chuckle.

Michael laughed.

"Your man here don't talk much," the man said, looking Michael up and down.

"Michelle does the talking for the both of us, usually."

"Yeah? I'm married, too," the man said. Michael laughed.

"Play basketball?"

"In high school," Michael said.

Michelle looked up at her husband, who was a good foot taller than her, and back at the man. "Michael is kind of my sidekick in this research. He humors me. Have you seen the movie, *Driving Miss Daisy?*"

"No," the man said, bluntly. He looked at Michael, "What do you do for a living, young man?"

"I'm a nurse."

"A nurse? Not a doctor?"

"No, a nurse."

"Do say? Don't reckon I've ever met a male nurse," he said, scratching his head. "My wife's had a real bad sinus infection. Went to the doctor. On antibiotics. Doesn't seem to be helping. She has an awful time with her sinuses. Probably comes from living near the river. Or could be allergic to the damn cats."

"Have you tried a Neti pot?"

"No, what's a Neti pot?"

"It's a little pot that you put a saline solution in. You pour it into one nostril and let it drip out the other. It irrigates your sinuses. It will come with directions. It's a good thing to do it every day. I guarantee they work wonders for sinus problems. Next best thing to spending time at the beach and taking in the salt air. I don't go to the beach much myself. Built in tan."

The man laughed.

"Where do you get them? Are they expensive?"

"Health food store is your best bet. But your drug store might have them or you could order one online. Shouldn't run you more than twenty dollars."

"Don't say. Sure beats the price of those pills she's taking. Neti, you say?"

"Yes, Neti."

"Well, don't know how much I can tell you. Used to be a big farm when the Bonzos lived here. Oh, I raise some chickens, myself." He pointed out back. Michelle glimpsed a woman with a straw hat wearing a work smock hitting the top of her rubber boots. She disappeared behind the coop. Michelle only saw her backside, causing a sudden chill to run through her, as for a brief moment she envisioned her as being Sally.

The man saw her looking and turned his head. "That's my wife, Gladys." He turned back. "As you can see, we mostly raise cats. They come and go. I would get rid of the whole lot of them, but need them for the mice. The house is old and has more holes than that road out there the state never seems to fix."

"Yes, there were quite a few potholes, we noticed," Michael said.

"I heard that Sally always used an outhouse," Michelle said.

"Never even had running water. A lot of people around here didn't, at least not until the fifties or sixties."

"No running water? How did they get water?" Michelle asked.

"Had a pump. And, the river's right back there. The

people who lived here before me hooked up to the water line and put in a bathroom. The pump's out back. Still works. My wife and I put the aluminum siding on the house. The house could use more work, but we're both getting old. Don't know how much more we'll do."

Michael looked at Michelle. She knew the cue. "Thanks for your time," Michelle said.

"Not a problem," the man said.

"Oh, a picture," Michelle said. "I almost forgot."

"Do you want me in it?" The man asked.

"Sure, why not?" The man gave a big grin as Michelle snapped.

"Will be trying that Neti pot," the man said, shaking Michael's hand.

Michelle opened her door and got in. Michael stood at the driver's door. "One of his cats is in the car," Michelle said to Michael.

Michael looked at the man still standing in front of the house. "One of your cats is in the car. He went under the seat. I'm trying to get him out."

"Just keep him," the man said, laughing. "We got plenty."

"Can we, Michael?" Michelle pleaded.

"The man's kidding, Michelle."

"No, I'm not," the man said.

"We don't need a cat, Michelle."

"You don't have to bother with him. I'll take care of him."

"He'll have to be fixed. Actually, we don't even know if it's a he," Michael said while feeling around under the seat. "Got you," he said, pulling him out and holding him up for inspection. "*He's* a she," he said.

"She's so cute. And a tabby like Garfield. I love tabbies." Michelle got back out of the car, standing on her side of the door, looking over the hood. "Does the cat have a name?"

"Kitten," the man said, and Michael laughed.

"See, like Sally's name for the dog," Michelle said. "It's a sign. I think we should take him."

"Do you have something old we can make a bed for the cat on the way home?" Michael asked.

"Just a moment," the man said. He returned from the garage with an old rag. "Will this do?"

"Yes, that's fine," Michael said.

They backed out of the driveway, waving and smiling.

They were a mile down the road. "That rag has oil all over it. It will get on the upholstery. We passed a McDonald's. We'll stop, get a Coke. I'll throw out the rag and wash my hands."

"I'm surprised you didn't say anything when he handed it to you." Michelle smiled. "I'm glad you didn't. He warmed up to us after you gave his wife advice on what to do about her sinuses. Same with the woman with the colicky baby. You're my ace in the hole." She leaned over and kissed him.

"Neither one of them invited us in."

Michelle let out a heavy sigh while petting the cat on her lap.

"What?" Michael asked.

"I'm imagining what this area was like when Sally lived here. It's so dead and dull now. We passed those buildings with boards over their windows. This had to be a thriving place once."

"I don't know about thriving," Michael said.

"I mean, thriving as in for a place out in the country. There used to be kids running around. And, they all liked Sally, from what I was told. It was probably like a scene out of *Andy Griffith.* Sally walking down the road to church or to the country store, taking her eggs, kids going there, getting a Nehi," Michelle said with a nostalgic smile.

"You mean more like *Huckleberry Finn,* don't you? There were no black people on *Andy Griffith.*"

"What shall we name the cat?" she asked.

"Oh, we're not going with Kitten?" Michael laughed. "And, you do know he said that because he knew you would be a sucker and take the cat after that, don't you?"

"What can I say? It worked. Your wife is an easy mark."

"No, I'm an easy mark. I said yes to us keeping the cat. I suppose you want to name her Sally?"

"No, too obvious. I'll think about it. I'll come up with a name."

They drove another mile. Michelle stroked the cat on her lap, looking out the window. "You're quiet," Michael said.

"I keep imagining what this place looked like back in the day. One lady I talked to, told me how Sally did her canning outside over a big fire. And, I'm picturing her doing laundry on the back porch with that old wringer washer."

"New."

"What?"

"Remember, the man said the washer would have been new back then."

"Oh, yeah." Michelle smiled. "There were probably sheets, overalls, and dresses hanging on the clothes line, flapping in the breeze. One woman said she was a little girl, and all the children loved her. Like I said, I bet kids were all over the place back then. We haven't seen one child around here."

"They grew up. More than likely had to move away to find jobs so they could buy washers and dryers. And, if there are kids around here, now, they're inside playing video games."

"Yeah, sad."

"The video game part, yes, maybe sad. But, do you want to go out in the dead of winter to an outhouse or run clothes through a wringer washer that you had to haul water to from a pump?"

"No, but we did lose something along the way."

"What?"

"Simplicity."

"Maybe, but living back then wasn't all that simple. At least it wouldn't have been for me. I would have been using a toilet for coloreds, drinking out of a water fountain for coloreds and sitting at the back of the bus. And, we wouldn't be married. You probably wouldn't have even looked my way. I would have been beneath you."

"No, that's not true, Michael."

"Don't be naïve, Michelle. It is true," he said with a frown on his face.

She grew quiet.

"There's that McDonalds up ahead." Michael put on his turn signal.

ichelle entered her office, teacup in hand. She picked up the cat from the chair with her other hand and sat down with it on her lap. "Do you think this is your chair, now, Marthie?" Marthie purred. "It's okay. I'm sure Sally would have shared it with you."

The phone startled her. "Now, who calls this early? Someone, no doubt, who has been up since five. Someone who eats dinner promptly at four o'clock, goes to bed at sunset and gets up with the roosters," she said to Marthie, setting her teacup on the desk and reaching over for her cell phone. "Hello."

"Hello," came the sandpaper voice on the other end—a voice honed from decades of cigarettes. "This is Inez. We talked a few days ago."

"Yes, Inez. I remember. How are you?"

"Oh, arthritis is acting up."

"Oh, I'm sorry."

"I'm used to it. Hard to get out of bed in the morning, but once I get moving around…" She paused. "Well, you don't want to hear about an old woman's problems."

"No, Inez, not at all. I'm sorry you ache so much."

"What I called you about was the Erwins. Of course, I'm not an Erwin by blood but was married to one for nearly fifty years."

"Yes, you told me that when we talked last."

"I got to thinking. I remember my husband talking about a woman who did a family history. Her name was Knisley."

"Knisley? Do you have her address or phone number? Can I contact her?"

"Well, only if you can reach the heavenly realms," Mrs. Erwin said, laughing, following with a croupy cough. "She died, but I made a few phone calls, started checking around, and I was told that everything she did is in Frankfort."

"Frankfort?"

"Yes, at the Kentucky Historical Society. I was told there was a picture of Sally there." Michelle dug into Martha's fur, causing the cat to let out a screech and jump from her lap.

"Sorry, Marthie."

"What?" the woman on the other end of the phone asked.

"Oh, sorry, I was talking to my cat who was on my lap. She took off down the stairs. Sorry, it startled me. Anyway, I'm so excited there is a picture of Sally. I have one of her in the nursing home with my grandma beside her. I would love to have one of her when she was younger."

"I don't know how young she is in the picture. I haven't seen it myself. I could make some more calls and see if anyone else might have seen it."

"Oh, no. You shouldn't go to any more trouble. I so appreciate you calling me with this information."

"Not any trouble. Nothing better to do these days. I didn't even know if I could pick up the phone this morning. Arthritis is acting up something awful. Had to put the heating pad on my arm last night."

"I'm sorry to hear that."

"Oh, well, as I was saying…"

Michelle sat her cold tea aside and opened up her laptop after the forty-five-minute conversation. She looked down at the cat who had returned. "A two-hour drive, Marthie. I better shower and get dressed if I want to make it back home in time to have dinner for Michael."

Michelle walked up the steps to the second floor where the records were kept. She went to the desk. "Hi, I'm here looking for a report I was told might be here on a family called Erwin. In particular, I'm looking for information on a woman named Sally. I was told there was a picture of her with the report."

The woman at the desk laughed. "My name is Sally."

"Oh, wow," said Michelle. "A good sign."

"I hope so. Follow me. I'll point you in the right direction." They stopped at a row of filing cabinets. "Anything on the Erwins should be here. You can take it over to the tables and look at it. Nothing can be checked out or leave the premises. If you want copies, we do that here and charge for the copies."

"Okay, sounds simple enough. Thanks."

Michelle pulled the file from the cabinet and took it over to a table. She flipped each paper over as she perused through them. There were two sets, all photocopies, that were held together by black binder clips. There were pages of family history that looked to have been typed on a bad typewriter. And there were copies of ledgers and reports in old-fashioned handwriting—a rhythmic flow of penmanship, a lost art, indecipherable to her. She imagined a store clerk with blackened fingertips dipping his quill pen into an inkwell.

Michelle spread the two reports out on the long table and looked around observing this new circle of people she had joined—avid genealogical and historical researchers. Their briefcases, papers, and laptops were spread out in front of them, all soaking up the hard work of the pioneer researchers, like Mrs. Knisley, who did the grunt and time-consuming work before laptops and the internet. Serious scholars. She was a novice. More than likely, they were studying their own family histories. She was looking at a family that had no connection to her family other than they enslaved one of her ancestors.

She looked back down at the papers before her. She came to a bad photocopy of two women, standing side by side. Sally was a strong, stout looking woman, nothing like the whittled down lady who sat in the pink-flowered chair with her grandma standing beside her. She wore what appeared to be a long bib apron over a dress and a sweater over both. Too bad it was in black and white. Too bad it was so grainy. The white woman carried a purse, holding it with both her hands in front of her. Sally had none. The woman had clearly come to see Sally. They were standing to the side of a house with automobiles in the background. The automobiles were maybe forties or fifties models. She knew nothing about cars. Michael might know although he was more into football or basketball than cars. Michelle looked at Sally's feet. The photocopy was faded, but she appeared to be wearing house shoes, and her feet were turned in. Was she pigeon-toed? She remembered what Michael had said about Sally's feet hurting. There was typing above the picture:

On the left, Allie Erwin Caudill, a descendant of John L. Erwin through William Jefferson Erwin, son of Thomas Jackson Erwin, oldest son of John L. Erwin.

   On the right, the slave Sallie, who was born the same year as

William Jefferson, Erwin - 1859. She died 1968. She was a descendant of the slaves John L. Erwin and Elizabeth brought from Virginia.

Mrs. Knisley was more than likely the one who typed the information above the picture. From the stack of papers before her, Mrs. Knisley had given her typewriter a run for its money. But how much of the information was wrong?

Sally's name on the photocopy was spelled, Sallie with an *ie*. But her gravestone read Sally with a *y*. Mrs. Knisley also stated Sally's birth was in 1859. Her gravestone and death certificate gave the year as 1858. Her grandma wrote in her journal that Sally was born in 1858. Surely, Sally would have known her own birth date, but then, those were different times. She also discovered that census reports weren't always accurate. Dates were all over the place as was the way names were spelled. One old-timer joked with her that back in the day census takers were given so much moonshine as they went from house to house, it was a wonder anything got recorded. And the date of her death was given as 1968. She was sure Mrs. Knisley got a lot of second-hand information. Wasn't that for the most part what she was getting? But, Michelle had both her grandma's journal and Sally's death certificate, definitely first-hand information. There was no doubt in her mind about the year of Sally's death, the same year as her grandpa's.

Michelle flipped through Mary Jane Knisely's report. It was massive. There were copies of letters she had written. It looked as if each family member had a page.

There was the account of hiding in a cave from the Union soldiers. It was a little different from the way Grandma had recorded it in her journal, Sally's relating of it. Sally was a child after all. Still, she was there, and Mrs. Knisley wasn't. It read:

When the union soldiers came to Carter County, Elizabeth was a widow. It was expected that the army might come. County officials had taken the records to a cave for preservation. Land owners were on the alert, and no doubt had scouts out, with relays to warn the inhabitants.

When the warning came, Elizabeth called her slaves together and drove all the hogs up the woods to a deep ravine. She also took her prized white mare, and tied her in the deep woods.

When the danger was passed and the troops had gone on to other areas, Elizabeth and the slaves brought the stock back to the plantation.

It read more like a news report. Sally's version was more colorful. Sally had also said the horse was in the cave with them. Had to be a big cave. They did live in the Carter Caves area. Michelle had been there a few times. Some of the caves were definitely big enough for a horse.

One of the first pages had the heading of *Stephan Erwin.* Mrs. Knisley typed the name of the woman he married, who her parents were, and proceeded to say after having six children, he came home one day carrying a seventh, told his wife who the mother was, handed it to his wife, and said, "Here, raise it." She did. *Would a woman stand for that today?*

The next page was headed with another Erwin—Eula. All the pertinent information about her was listed, when she was born, who she married, and their children. Her husband was found dead in the barn. There was much speculation over whether it was murder or suicide. The insurance company ruled suicide and left her with three small children to raise.

But Eula got a job teaching school and built herself a fine home, according to Mrs. Knisley. Mrs. Knisley was struck by Eula's kindness. She took in an old man who had no place to go because he got kicked out by his own family. She gave him odd jobs to do. Then one day a car hit him. Eula took care of him until he died. Michelle looked at the dates. This would have happened around the last decade of Sally's life. The woman, Eula, had the tenacity of her ancestor, Elizabeth Dickenson Erwin, Michelle thought.

There was one couple with the last name of Erwin who had a troubled marriage, yet they had twelve children. The report said the woman was a pouter. When things didn't go her way, she pouted. Her husband built her a pout house in the back yard, where she stayed for days at a time. The children took her food or whatever she asked for.

One of the children, Dora, the last to be born, died as a child. Could this have been Sally May's best friend—the one her grandma wrote about in her journal? The timing would have been right.

The Erwin man ended up leaving his wife and keeping house with another woman. But, the oldest of the children became an attorney and brought suit against his own father on behalf of his mother. He ended up coming home.

The next page started with an illegitimate birth. According to Mrs. Knisley, the woman who married the illegitimate Erwin son, took an avid interest in Erwin history, so much so, she could have written a book, Mrs. Knisley had commented.

The next page was about how one of the Erwin women, at the turn of the century, married a bootlegger. He wore expensive clothes, kept his wife in expensive clothes, and bragged how he would never be caught by the feds. What happened on the day he died at age thirty was in dispute. The Erwins claimed the feds shot him. But a witness said he shot himself rather than be caught by the feds. His widow, on her deathbed, said the thing she regretted most was leaving all those pretty clothes behind.

She had come looking for the picture of Sally but became

engrossed in the skeleton's closet of the Erwin family that lay before her. The report read like a soap opera. Was everyone's family like this if you dug deep enough? Why didn't Mrs. Knisley write a book?

Michelle glanced at her cell phone on the table. She was so absorbed in what she had found that two hours had slipped by. There was so much more to read, but she had to head back. And, she had yet to get copies. She gathered the file and went back up to the desk.

"Find what you wanted?"

"More than I anticipated. Thank you, Sally. If I could have copies of all of it, please?"

30

*M*ichelle settled into the familiar spot, cross-legged atop the faded fabric, Marthie in her lap, a cup of tea in one hand and the copy of the report with The Kentucky Historical Society stamped on each page, in her other hand.

"I saved this until this morning, Marthie. I wanted to be undisturbed. See, I've even turned off my phone. I don't want you to be startled like you were yesterday morning when my cell rang. Okay, this is the part I wanted to read." She rubbed the cat's back. "Are you understanding a word I'm saying? I think I'm getting as bad as these old people I'm talking to. I'm talking to my cat. I've become the cat lady."

She situated the report on her lap and read "Prologue. Can you believe it starts out with a prologue?"

Michelle read aloud.

Although it is essential to furnish documentary proof of lineage, the discipline should not be more strict than science. Science does not rigidly define the interpretation of the word proof. Ceram in his book, *Gods, Graves and Scholars* has this to say:

Hypothesis belongs to the working method of any science, it is a legitimate form of speculation proceeding from established results.

Michelle flipped through the report. "There are several pages like this. Footnotes and everything. I had no idea genealogy was this involved. She talks about the field of literature and Plato. Maybe she traced the Erwins back to Plato. I haven't read that far into the report, yet, Marthie. I'll read some of the rest silently. I'm afraid these parts might bore you. When I get to something good, I'll read it aloud, how's that?"

The cat closed its eyes.

"OH, OH, HERE WE GO, MARTHIE."

An Account of the Slaves Presented to Elizabeth Dickenson as a Wedding Present

One of Elizabeth's wedding presents when she married John L. Erwin was a "parcel of four slaves." They were named Ib, Nellie, Henry and Jacob. They served the Erwin family from this time (circa 1818-1819) in Russell County, Virginia, and accompanied them when they moved to Carter County, Kentucky, about 1836, to become pioneer settlers in the Smokey Valley.

Nellie could have been put in a circus—she was born with six fingers on each hand and six toes on each foot.

"I hardly think that could be grounds for being in a

circus. Do you, Marthie?" Marthie purred. "Was that a yes or a no? Also, I don't think this was the same set of slaves. Grandma's journals said Elizabeth's brother replaced the slaves Elizabeth had with young kids when they came to Kentucky. Also, in Grandma's journals, she always referred to her as Nell, not Nellie. I suppose she was called both." She read on.

> The Erwins had to have special shoes made for her. The slaves and their offspring continued with the family and were well treated.

"Okay, Marthie, I have to interject here—again. I'm afraid there might be a lot of commentaries on my part regarding this report. So bear with me. Don't all slave owners say their slaves were well treated?" The cat stretched out a paw. "I will take that as a yes."

> Nobody ever tried to run away. After the Civil War, one of the men went to Lexington, but most stayed either with the family or in the area. One, Sally, survived until 1968, ending her life as a ward of the Erwin family.

"We know that's not true, don't we, Marthie? She was clearly staying with the Bonzos. And, they were the ones who put her in the nursing home."

> Sally was born in Carter County—some said in 1859. However, the 1870 census sets us straight on when she was born. It shows the following blacks living with Elizabeth: Ibba 45, Nellie 40, Docia 16….

"Docia, my ancestor, Marthie. And if the census report is right, Docia would have been four years older than Sally."

Jacob, 10. The blacks on the 1880 census shows: Evaline 50, Nellie 46,…

"Funny, how Ib, that is if Evaline was Ib, and I believe that to be the case, only aged five years, and Nellie only aged six years from 1870 to 1880. Nellie must have had it a little harder than Ib. After all, Ib was the house slave, and Nellie worked out in the field. But, whatever those women were taking, I want it. Or, their ages could have been the result of the moonshine the census taker may have been drinking." She rubbed Marthie's back.

Sarah 4. Obviously, these ages are not true. So, we cannot rely entirely on them, but if Sally was born in 1859, she would obviously have been older than four in 1880. Since her name does not appear on the 1870 census, she must have been born after the census taker made his records. All that can be said is that she lived to an advanced age.

"Obviously—Mrs. Knisley liked to use that word a lot— she didn't have all the facts. Sarah had to be the second Sally —Sally May. Plus, the name listed is Sarah. For some reason, I don't know why, Sarah and Sally were interchangeable names—I guess a lot like John and Jack, something else I never understood. Mrs. Knisley *obviously* didn't know Sally had a child, an illegitimate child. And, *obviously*, these ages can't be right. According to Grandma's journal, Ib and Nell were young girls walking alongside the wagon when the Erwins came to Kentucky. And, that was more than likely 1836. They were probably ten years older than what this census says. Black people do age well, especially the women."

Elizabeth had two waiting maids until the day she died in

1895. We do not know their names, but probably one was Sally.

"I don't think she was right, there, either. I would bet those two maids she refers to are Ib and Nell."

She then went to live with Thomas Jackson Erwin, the oldest son of the family. In 1914, she went to live with the Bonzo family, and when Mrs. Bonzo died, she was veritably the children's "mother."

As Sally became too old to work, the Erwins put her in a nursing home in Maysville, Kentucky as a ward of the family. Sally never married and said she felt the Erwin family were "her own." She was the last of the slaves and died in the Carrigan Rest Home in Maysville, March 1968. She is buried in St. Paul, Kentucky.

Sally is said to have had two brothers, Sam and Henry, but she lost track of them over the years. Lenora Stamper, kin to the Erwins, of St. Paul, Kentucky, says she well remembers Sam as a grown man when she was a little girl.

Michelle flipped over to the next page.

Sally

Sally was a slave, a descendant of the slaves given to John L. and Elizabeth when they were married. She was born in 1859 into slavery, and the date was kept by the fact she was born the same year as Thomas Erwin.

Slavery was in effect when she was born. She stayed with Elizabeth until Elizabeth died, and then went to work for Thomas Erwin, Elizabeth's son. She remained with the Erwin family as a slave until she became too old to work, and the Erwins put her in a nursing home. She lived to be 109.

This is pretty good evidence that the slaves in the Erwin family were never mistreated—despite all the talk of cruelty to slaves.

Another evidence was that as the slaves died they were buried in the Erwin cemetery—the same as the Erwins. They were considered family.

"Okay, a lot of this is repetitive. The same as the Erwins? Hmm, the Erwins, except for Elizabeth and John Leander, had headstones. The slaves had unmarked rocks over their graves. And do you notice Mrs. Knisley refers to Sally as a slave until she became too old to work? Slavery was supposed to be over a hundred years by that time."

She looked down at her lap. "Asleep again? Marthie, I really need your input here."

31

Michelle drove up to the small narrow building that was once a residence, now a center for historical research for Lewis County. The front room was a museum of sorts, for Lewis County. Since she only had two hours before they closed, Michelle didn't bother to look at the exhibits. She would need those two hours to look through old newspapers.

"Hi, I'm Michelle. We talked by phone."

"Yes, I'm Karen." Michelle followed her down an aisle lined with tables and chairs on one side and large document cabinets on the other side. "Would you like some coffee?"

"Oh, no thanks. Not a coffee drinker."

"Well, there is a kitchen in the back. We also have tea if you prefer. Make yourself at home."

"Thank-you, I will. If you could point me to the newspapers for Lewis County I guess starting in the 1920s?"

The first thing Michelle found was the obituary for Ted Bonzo. Three short paragraphs, one of which was the date and time of the funeral service and another stating Morton Funeral Home was in charge—the same one that was responsible for Sally's funeral. One of the people she talked with told her both Ben and Ted hunted with Old Man Morton. The obituary read: *Age seventy-five. A farmer and veteran of World War II. A resident of Carter County and St. Paul. No survivors.* Michelle thought, if only there would have been survivors, this could have been easier.

She went back further and found Ben's obituary. Age eighty-one. Died in 1964. Sally did say she outlived them all. Ben died in the office of a physician. How often does that happen? One of those men who doesn't go to the doctor until it's too late?

"I think I found something for you," came the voice from across the room. These women were so nice. Not only did they hand her newspapers, they also helped her look.

"Oh, wow," Michelle said. "Sallie Barnes. This, I think was her daughter. Except Sally was spelled, Sallie with the *ie* at the end. The newspaper was dated February 7, 1929.

Sallie Barnes, colored, aged 47, died Tuesday at the home of her daughter, in Weirton, W. Va., after an illness of four weeks duration. She was well and favorably known by all, and was born and raised here. Surviving her is one daughter, Mrs. Nellie Williams and two brothers, Sam Barnes, of this place, and Perry Barnes, of Cincinnati. Final funeral arrangements have not been made, but the remains are expected here Thursday afternoon.

"Strange, how they felt the need to put colored on the obituary back in 1929," Michelle said.

"I think you'll find that a lot for that time period," Karen replied.

"If they were bringing the body back on the following Thursday, there should be something about the final funeral arrangements in a later newspaper," Michelle said.

Both Michelle and Karen searched. Nothing.

"Maybe they didn't bring her body back after all," said Karen.

"Or maybe it was because she was *colored*," Michelle said with a sigh. "There was a mention of Sam in my grandma's journals. Perhaps I can find something on him."

SEPTEMBER 15, 1949

Old Resident Dies Suddenly

Sam Barnes, well known colored citizen, passed away Tuesday morning about 8 AM having apparently suffered a stroke sometime during the night at his home on East Second Street.

He was discovered by Wilford McClain and Mrs. Virginia Esham who had gone to Barnes' home to get the key to her beauty parlor of which Barnes was the caretaker.

Dr. Bertram was summoned and found life almost extinct.

Just how old he was is unknown. Last year he told us that at the time of the hanging on the hang tree (which was in July 1876) that he was a small boy anywhere from nine to twelve and distinctly remembered his father, Uncle Peter Barnes, taking him to see the man. He said at the time they lived in a small cabin just this side of the present county infirmary. So that would place him at least in the late 80's.

When Mr. Samuel Pollitt came to town in 1898 and started the livery stable, Sam Barnes started working for him and did so as long as he was in business. Hundreds of trips he made taking guests to Glenn Springs and Esculapia Springs during the hey-day of those famous watering places. After Mr. Pollitt went out of business, Sam became a general factotum and all around handy man for many persons in town. He had complained of not feeling well Monday.

In the old days of horse drawn carriages, and with the cemetery road being bad everyone wanted to get into Sam's carriage, as his reputation of a careful driver was well known. He is survived by a niece, daughter of his late sister Sally, and another niece, daughter of the late Perry Barnes.

Funeral services will not be completed until the arrival of his niece Nellie, from Steubenville, Ohio. The body is at the Plummer Funeral Home.

"Here's a later one," Karen said. "It's dated September 20th."

Vanceburg's "Sam" Dies, Almost Legendary Figure

Sam Barnes, aged and highly respected colored citizen of Vanceburg who was one of Lewis County's oldest residents and one of its few remaining links between a by-gone era and the modern age, died Tuesday morning at 9 o'clock at his home on Second Street in the east end of Vanceburg. Although his exact age was not known, since he himself did not know the date of his birth, he was at least 90.

Sam, as he was familiarly known to every man, woman and child in Vanceburg, died within half an hour after being found unconscious in bed at his home where he lived alone. Mrs. Virginia Esham, who operates Virginia's Beauty Shop, discovered the aged man's plight. She had gone to his home to get his key to her place of business, where he cleaned and did odd chores, after finding she did not have her own key. Although unable to gain entrance to Sam's modest abode, Mrs. Esham peered through the window, saw him in bed and knew that he was ill. She notified County Attorney Charles Reldinger, who looked after the affairs of the nonagenarian. Mr. Reldinger summoned Dr. H. M. Bertram, Sr., and the two men had to cut the screen in the front door to gain entrance to the house. They found the man unconscious and dying as the result of a stroke suffered during the night. He died within half an hour without regaining consciousness. The aged man had been out on the streets Monday.

Sam, who was a native and lifelong resident of Lewis County was born before the Civil War and during his long span of years built for himself an enviable reputation as an honest, upstanding and industrious citizen. For a number of years, he had served as janitor and had done odd jobs for the people of Vanceburg. It being estimated that at the time of his death he was working for some thirty business establishments and homeowners.

During his more active years he was employed at various livery stables in Vanceburg and became a familiar figure as he drove carriages and hacks about the town and into the country. Back in the days when Glenn Springs near the headwaters of Salt Lick Creek, was a famous resort known throughout the Middle West, Sam drove carriages to and from the resort while carrying guests who traveled by train to Vanceburg. At various times he was employed by the Parker and Samuel Pollitt livery stables. In those days he also drove horse-drawn hearses for the Plummer Funeral Home. He started working around livery stables when he was a lad of fifteen or sixteen years.

The deceased is survived by only two nieces. Mrs. Sam Bradley of Vanceburg and Mrs. Nellie Williams of Steubenville, Ohio.

"One more, if it's possible?" Michelle asked. "I know approximately when Peter Barnes died. Do you have papers back as far as 1910?"

"A few," Karen said. She brought a small stack from the back.

"At least there won't be many to look through," Michelle said.

Death of Peter Barnes

Uncle Peter Barnes, colored, answered the final summons Monday night and was buried in Woodlawn Cemetery, Wednesday at the foot of the hill. He leaves a wife, two sons and two daughters to mourn his loss. "Uncle" Peter, as he was known by both young and old, was born in Bath County. He never knew just when, but from conversing with him and the years people have known him, all are agreed that he was not far from 100 years of age. "Uncle Peter" was well liked by all who knew him for thirty-four years, and many's the time he would come to our place of business and relate incidents of his past life which occurred before the war when he was a slave.

He had varied experience in life; in earlier manhood he served about hotels in Maysville, and later did odd jobs and looked after several offices. He used to remark, some morning you will be asked if you have hear'ed the news and will be informed that "Uncle" Peter died last night and so it was, and so we are passing away one by one. We shall miss him. The bereaved family desire to thank all who so kindly assisted them in various ways during the sickness, death and laying away of their loved one.

Michelle thanked Karen and left with copies of her findings and a membership to the Lewis County Historical Society. All the information was spinning around in her head like a time loop. Grandma's journals made it simple. Sally told her story. All this digging only brought up questions. And

Docia, if she were to go down that road, she wouldn't even know where to begin.

She spent her days talking to people she didn't know on the phone, like a reporter trying to uncover the past. And, she made numerous road trips, knocking on doors of people she didn't know—people who surprisingly opened up to her after their initial suspicion of her wore off.

There was the old couple who said Ted used to cut their hay for them. They remembered seeing Sally at a school Halloween function. She had made candy.

There was the lady who had married a Bonzo. Michelle had stood on her front porch forever trying to get her to provide some relevant information on Sally. She knew of no child. Finally, she snickered and said, "Well, I could tell you some stuff, but it's not anything you'll want to write about." Michelle wanted to say, *really, try me,* but thought better of it. Ted was having an affair. The transgressions happened while the husband was away at work. Ted boldly walked in through the door after her husband left and crawled out the back window when the man returned. Sally had said, "Ted, don't think I's don't know what you're a doin'."

There were numerous stories. Everyone had their own versions, and memories were faulty. She was only twenty-nine, would be thirty next week, and couldn't remember sometimes what she did the previous week. How could she expect people in their eighties and sometimes nineties to remember what happened when they were young, or what their parents had told them? If their parents told them anything? Her parents never told her about her own history. Nor did Grandma.

The summer was fading away. Classes were scheduled to start in two weeks. She was no further on writing about Sally. It had grown too complicated. Michael sensed her frustration. "You'll never know the whole truth. Write it as fiction. It's the only way," he said.

He was right. How did she expect to do research and write a book, any type of book, non-fiction or fiction, in a time period of three months? How long had it taken Harper Lee?

Wednesday was her birthday, and Michael was taking the day off. The big 3-0. Michael had his big 3-0 last year. They were planning an outing to the National Underground Railway Freedom Center and a Mediterranean dinner. Mediterranean wasn't necessarily Michael's favorite, but it was hers, and he said he would suffer through it for the Turkish coffee and baklava at the end.

She needed to get her mind on something else. She turned on the radio. "An oldie but goodie, *You're Having My Baby* by Paul Anka," the DJ on the radio announced.

32

"Hello," Michelle said, answering the phone.

"Hi, you don't know me. I'm Rebecca, and I live in Olive Hill. I heard about the black woman you were researching, and I think I might be able to help."

"Oh?" Michelle said.

"Yes. I have a picture of Sally. I'm related to the Burchetts, and it was taken at a family reunion."

"Oh, my god. I've been looking for a picture."

"Yes, Inez called. Said you wanted one. It was taken in September of 1959. All the reunions were in September and the picture is dated 1959."

"Let me see. That would make Sally one-hundred-and-one."

"It's in one of our family albums. You're welcome to it."

"Really? That would be fantastic. When could I get it? Do you have it scanned? Can you email it?"

"I don't have a computer, but I could mail it to you."

"Rebecca, would you mind if I drove to your house today, to pick it up personally? You're only an hour away."

"Okay? Yes, I guess it would be all right."

"Hold on just a minute. Let me get a pen and paper and get directions to your house." Michelle grabbed a pen from her desk and a blank sheet of paper. "Okay, I'm ready."

After getting the directions, Michelle folded the piece of paper and put it in her purse, along with her cell phone.

"Thank you so much. I'm leaving in about thirty minutes."

Michelle looked down at Marthie. "Do you know who that was? The branch of the family you were named after. Looks like another road trip. One that calls for a celebration if everything pans out. A bowl of milk for you and possibly a bottle of wine tonight for Michael and me."

"I CAN'T BELIEVE I'm holding this. I can only hope I look this good if I reach that age, although I can't imagine reaching that age," Michelle said to Rebecca.

The picture had a thin strip of paper stuck to the back where Rebecca had cut it from the family album.

"Did you ever meet Sally?"

"No, my mom knew her. I was only five when this picture was taken."

"Is your mom...?"

"She passed some years ago," Rebecca said. "Why are you so interested in her? Inez said you were working on a book?"

"I can't thank Inez enough for contacting you. I don't know about the book. Maybe. We'll see. I've been working on her history all summer. It all started with some journals my grandma left in the attic. My husband and I live in her house now. I stumbled upon them by accident and found her talks with Sally so fascinating. My grandma was her nurse while she was in the nursing home. I teach English and Literature at the community college where I live. I've always dreamed of writing a book. We'll see.

"Since working on this Sally project, though, I've come to know what writer's block is. There is the story Sally tells in Grandma's journal, but, when I try to find actual records to back it up, all I find are conflicting reports. Sally had a daughter according to Grandma's journal, but there is no actual record on any census report that I can find that says this.

"Her death certificate says she was widowed, but no husband is listed. Her newspaper obituary is a fusion of two different women."

"Oh, she wasn't married. And, she *had* a daughter," Rebecca said.

"How do you know this?"

"I have a photographic memory. Sometimes it's a blessing. Sometimes, it's a curse. I remember my mom and other adults talking about it. There were two Sallys."

"Do you know who the father of the first Sally's baby was?" Michelle asked.

"No. There was talk. Some said one of the Burchetts. Some said one of the Erwins. Others said the Bonzos."

"So, Grandma's journal was right. She wrote Sally wouldn't reveal the name."

33

"*W*hat's wrong?"

"I don't know, Michael. I feel like I'm going to be sick."

"You can't be sick. It's your birthday."

"I don't think my stomach knows that. I think it might have been the wine."

"That was two nights ago."

"Maybe it's car sickness. Can you pull over?"

"We're almost there. It's another two blocks to the parking lot. I can't stop now."

"Okay, I'll hold it." Michelle let the seat back to the lowest level.

Michael pulled into the parking area. "Michelle, are you going to be okay? We're at the museum."

"I know. I'm so sick, Michael."

He felt her head. "You don't have a fever."

"I woke up sick."

"Why didn't you tell me? We could have postponed this."

"I thought it would pass, and it did for a while. And, you

took the day off. You know how long we've talked about this."

"So, you woke up sick?"

"Yes. Can you get me something for my stomach? I feel like I'm going to hurl, but my stomach is empty. And, I feel dizzy."

"Okay, we passed a place about a block away. Will you be all right? I'll walk over. Shouldn't take more than fifteen minutes. I'll lock the doors and crack the windows."

"Okay."

Michelle opened her eyes when she heard the lock on the driver's side making the clicking sound. "Here's some Pepto-Bismol. See if that helps."

Michelle drank from the bottle.

"Better?"

"I don't know. I think, some. I can't do this."

"What do you mean?"

"I need to go back home. I'm sorry, Michael."

"No, that's okay," he said, kissing her on the forehead. "You keep the seat down and sleep on the way home. We'll do it another day."

———

"MICHELLE, honey. Wake up. We're home."

"Hmm, what?" Michelle said, groggily.

"We're home. Do you need me to carry you into the house?"

"No, I can make it."

"Okay, but you're going to bed. I'll make some broth and bring it up to you. You need something in your stomach."

"Okay."

Michael stripped off his wife's clothes and put the covers over her.

"You're so good to me. I'm so sorry we drove all that way. I was so excited, and then we had to turn around and come back. I'm feeling better now. I don't know what happened. Maybe something I ate."

"Or maybe something else. After you have some broth, I'll run you a hot bath. In the meantime, I want you to do something for me." He pulled a box from the drugstore bag.

"A pregnancy test?"

———

"Here we are. Five years later," Michelle said to Michael.

"Yep, we finally made it," he said, getting out his credit card.

"Do you want the Rosa Parks experience? It's five dollars extra," the lady at the desk said.

Michael looked at Michelle. "Sure, we have to have the whole experience," she said.

"The next one starts in ten minutes. It's right up those stairs."

"Hi, are you here for Rosa Parks?" the man at the table asked.

"Yes," Michael said.

"This is Sally. Follow her. She'll explain it to you."

"Sally?" Michelle exclaimed.

"Yes, ma'am."

"There's that word again," Michelle whispered to Michael. "Sally?"

"No. *Ma'am*. That's what happens on your thirty-fifth birthday. I'm surprised they didn't offer us the senior discount," she said.

"Michelle, you look great." He kissed his wife on the cheek. They sat on a bench beside another couple.

"You'll be experiencing what Rosa Parks experienced on

the bus on December 1, 1955. You'll be experiencing virtual reality. It's in black and white, in keeping with the times. You need to put on the goggles and turn your head to the wall on the right," Sally explained.

They put on their goggles. "I have a feeling this is going to be disturbing," Michelle said.

It lasted about ten minutes. They removed their goggles, handing them to the Sally, and walked away hand-in-hand.

"That *was* disturbing. I am so sorry, Michael."

"You have nothing to be sorry about."

"The white part of me, and that would be the majority of me, does. I can only imagine what it was like, day in and day out, if your skin was black."

He hugged her. "Let's see the rest of this place. Where do you want to start?" he asked.

"I guess, at the beginning, when the slave ships first came over."

THEY WALKED out into the sunlight. "So, Mediterranean?" he asked.

"Yes, sounds great."

"I looked up some restaurants. There's one that had lots of good reviews within walking distance."

"Sounds good."

"We'll bring Alice when she's old enough," he said.

"The lady's name was Sally."

"What?"

"The lady that explained the Rosa Parks experience. Her name was Sally. It was a sign. I quit working on Sally when I found out I was pregnant. I have to start again. I don't want Alice one day to find a box of Grandma's journals and my own research in the attic."

"Alice will be starting school this fall. And, you'll be back in a couple of weeks, too. Do you think you'll have time?"

"I'll make time. I figure I can write at night. Alice goes to bed at eight. I can write each night until ten. Is that okay with you? And, I can work some on weekends."

"Honey, you know I support you in whatever you want to do. You're done with the research part, I hope?"

"Yes. I don't think I can find out anything more. Besides, I can elaborate on Grandma's journals, make it a work of fiction like you said. But I have to admit I will miss talking to all those elderly folks."

———

"Did everything go okay?" Michelle asked.

"Yes, we had a great time, didn't we, Alice?"

"Look, Mommy. Grandma bought me a new doll."

"She's pretty. Have you named her?"

"I named her Docia. Grandma said that was a good name for her."

"Yes, that is a good name." Michelle smiled at her mom.

"Look, Mommy, her hair is curly like mine."

"Yes, I see."

"Mom, you really have to stop buying her so much. And, I see she is wearing a new outfit."

"Nonsense, that's what grandmothers are for. Besides, she spilled ice cream on her other clothes. Did you have fun?"

"The restaurant was great. Michael even liked the hummus. The museum was fascinating *and* sobering."

"I'm glad you finally got to go."

"Thanks for looking after her for the day."

"You know you don't have to thank me. I love watching Alice."

"Mom, I plan on working again on that book I started. This time I plan on finishing it."

"The one about Sally?"

"Yes."

"I think you should."

"I wasn't sure how you felt about it."

"We're living in a new age. You have a daughter now. One day she will be so proud of her mama. I know I am. And, I think your grandmother would want you to finish what you started."

"You didn't call her Grandmother Alice."

"What?"

"Oh, nothing. Never mind. Bye, Mom." She leaned over and kissed her mom. "Thanks." She took Alice's hand. "Alice, kiss your grandma goodbye for now."

"$\mathcal{M}$r. Veach?"

"Yes."

"This is Michelle Gibson. We spoke on the phone several years ago. I was looking for information on Sally Barnes, and you told me about how she would come up to your father's store, walking, with her basket of eggs. You said even if your dad had plenty of eggs he would always take her eggs as trade and give her whatever she asked for."

"Oh, yes, I remember talking to you."

"Well, I'm finally writing a book about her. It will be fiction, but I want to get as many facts about her as possible. Also, I wanted to make sure I had your name spelled correctly. I'll put you in the acknowledgments when the book is finished."

"It's V-E-A-C-H. But, there's a fellow here visiting. He knows all about Sally."

"Really?"

"Yes. Do you want to talk to him?"

"Sure."

"Okay, he's a little hard of hearing." Michelle smiled, thinking, *like old times.* "Just a moment."

"Hello," said the voice of the man on the other end. Wind chimes rang in the background. Mr. Veach must have carried the phone outside.

"Hello," Michelle said in a loud clear voice. "I'm Michelle Gibson, and I'm writing a book about Sally Barnes. Mr. Veach said you could tell me about her."

"My wife and I used to go up to the Bonzos for dinner once a week. She lived with them."

"When was that? I mean, about what time period did you used to go there for dinner?"

"When my wife and I were first married. Early fifties."

"Mr.?" Michelle hesitated.

"Farris."

"Okay, how do you spell that?"

"F-A-R-R-I-S. Truman Farris. Truman, like the president."

"Okay, thanks. Do you remember anything Sally talked about?"

"No. My wife talked to her a lot. She passed away in June."

"Oh, I'm sorry," Michelle said, truly disappointed. "Mr. Farris, do you know anything about Sally's child?"

"No, no, I don't know anything about a child," he said.

"She did have one." Michelle went into a short version of the second Sally.

"My wife did say there was a kid."

"Do you know if it was a boy or girl?" Michelle asked.

"No. But I have a picture of her."

"You do?" Michelle felt her heart speed up. "Could I possibly borrow it? I'll copy it and return it? Do you know when it was taken?"

"Do you know when Sally died?" he asked.

"She died on March 31, 1969. I have her death certificate," Michelle replied.

"Well, that's when it was taken," Mr. Farris said. "It's of her in the casket."

Michelle paused. The wind chimes in the background were deafening. The wind must have picked up.

"Oh, that's kind of creepy."

"It's up in the attic. I'm eighty-one. There's a ton of stuff up there. I don't want to go up there."

"That's okay. I really don't think I would want that particular picture."

"I can't hear. These damn wind chimes."

"Well, thank you, Mr. Farris. Bye."

"MOMMY, ARE YOU OFF THE PHONE?"

"Yes, honey."

"Daddy said we could get some ice cream."

"Yeah, that will be fine."

"ALICE, be careful. Don't let it spill." She tucked the napkin inside her daughter's shirt.

"Find out anything new this morning?" Michael asked, taking a lick of his cone.

"I called the man that gave me the egg story. There just happened to be a man visiting with him when I called, who knew Sally. He has a picture."

"Will he lend it to you?"

"I don't think so. It's up in his attic somewhere. I'm not sure if I want it."

"Why?"

"It's of Sally in her casket."

Michael grimaced.

"Yeah, exactly what I thought. But, he used to go to dinner at the Bonzos once a week. I didn't think about it at the time, but I bet he could identify the people in the group photo I have."

"It's a shame the lady who sent the picture didn't know who was in it," Michael said.

"She knew Martha and Sally. When she heard I was doing this research, she thought *I* might know who's in it."

"Well, you are getting to be the expert on this family. I'm just glad she was of the generation who had a computer and could email it to you. Where did you say she lived?"

"Michigan."

"I know you would have had us take a family vacation to Michigan to get that picture."

"Yeah, probably."

"Where does Mr. Farris live?" Michael asked.

"Quincy, near where Sally used to live."

"You aren't suggesting we drive to his house today, are you?"

"No, we promised to take Alice to the movie."

"Yay!" Alice exclaimed.

"Besides I don't have any classes on Tuesday. Maybe I'll take a road trip."

MICHELLE RAPPED ON THE DOOR. A truck was parked in the driveway, but no one came to the door, and it looked dark inside. Maybe she should have called, but she felt the element of surprise might be better. More so, she was afraid he wouldn't see her. She saw a lady, outside, a few houses up, working in her garden. "Ma'am?"

"Yes," she asked, placing her rake against the shed.

"Do you know the man who lives in that house?" Michelle pointed across the street, a couple of houses down.

"Mr. Farris."

"Yes, I'm doing some genealogy work and was hoping I could find him. I was hoping he might be able to identify some people in an old photograph."

"He drives a white car, and it's not in the driveway. His son lives down the road. But, he would be at work now."

"Would you know an Elmo Veach?"

"Yes, he lives down the road." The woman gave Michelle directions.

Michelle turned into a long drive. She got out of her car and walked up to two men sitting outside—one older, one younger. The older one had to be Mr. Veach.

"Mr. Veach?"

"Yes?"

"Hi, I'm Michelle Gibson. I talked with you on Saturday. I'm the one doing research on Sally Barnes."

"Yeah, I remember."

"I have an old photo." Michelle showed him the picture on her iPad.

"No, I don't remember the Bonzos enough to tell you who's who in the picture."

"Oh, well, I went to Mr. Farris's house, but he wasn't home."

He looked over at the young guy. "Have you seen Truman, today?"

"No. But he could be up at the cemetery," he replied.

"It's just up the next road to your right. He goes up there a lot," Mr. Veach said. Michelle remembered Mr. Farris saying his wife had died recently.

"Okay. I'll try there."

She drove up a steep hill. It was a small cemetery with a

circular turn area. Not seeing anyone, Michelle descended the hill. Just as she stopped, before entering the main road, a white car with a man who looked to be in his eighties drove by. She watched as he turned onto the road leading to Mr. Farris's house.

"Thank you, God," she muttered to herself.

Once again, she knocked on the door. "Mr. Farris? Hi, I'm Michelle Gibson. We talked on Saturday."

"Yeah."

"I was thinking after we hung up that you might be able to identify a group picture I have of the Bonzos." Michelle whipped her iPad open to the picture. "Do you care if I come inside? It's hard to see the picture outside."

"Sure, sure, come in." He eyed over the picture. "No, no, it's been a long time ago. I can't really say who's in the picture for sure."

"Oh, okay," Michelle said, disappointed.

"My sister-in-law would know more than me. She spent a whole summer with them."

"Really?" Michelle asked, her anticipation building.

He stood silent.

"Do you think I could have her number? Does she live around here?"

"Yeah, not too far. I'll see if I can get her on the phone." After a bit, he handed the phone to Michelle.

"Hi, I'm Michelle Gibson, and I'm writing about Sally Barnes. My grandma knew her. And, I'm trying to find out anything more I can about her, other than what my grandma said. I would really love to talk to you. Do you care if I come to see you?"

"That would be fine."

"Okay, I'm on my way."

"MRS. PARSON?"

"Patty," she said.

"Hi Patty."

"Come in, come in. Have a seat."

"Thank you. Mr. Farris was telling me about you staying with Sally. Do you mind if I ask questions and take some notes?"

"No, not at all."

"So, you stayed with Sally for an entire summer?"

"Yes, I stayed with her when I was a girl. I loved Sally."

"I think a lot of people did. How old were you when you stayed with her?"

"Eight. Uncle Ben asked my dad if I could stay and help Sally for the summer. Said if I did, they would pay for my school supplies and new school clothes when school started. We were dirt poor, and that sounded like a good deal to my parents.

"I stayed in Sally's room, slept with her. I helped her with breakfast. We got up real early. And then, we fixed a big lunch. All the farm workers came in and ate. And, for supper, we usually had leftovers. Seemed like all we did was prepare meals."

"Did Sally talk much?"

"She talked all the time."

"Hmm, I was under the impression she didn't talk much."

"No, she liked to talk. And, was always busy. Didn't sit still for too long."

"Maybe that was her secret for living so long."

Patty laughed. "Maybe so."

"Do you remember what she talked about?"

"Oh, this and that. I guess we talked about what we were fixing for meals, things like that. Then, she would take her break and smoke her corncob pipe. Always had to sit for a spell and take a few puffs on her pipe."

"I didn't know that she smoked."

"Oh, yeah, she loved to smoke that corn cob pipe. Uncle Ben would go to the barn and get her some tobacco, and she would stuff it down the pipe and sit and smoke for a while. She always asked me if I wanted to smoke some, too."

"When you were eight?"

"Yeah. I always said no. But then, one time I tried it. Only once."

"That's fascinating. I had no idea she smoked. This is something new."

"Oh, yes. She loved that pipe."

"Do you think the Bonzos were good to her?"

"Yeah, Uncle Ben was. They built onto the house to give her her own room."

"Did she have things?"

"Things?"

"Yes, like what she needed?"

"Oh, yeah. Uncle Ben gave her money whenever she needed it. But, she had her own, too. She got an old age pension. Yeah," she continued, "she had some nice things. If she wanted a dress, Uncle Ben would see that she had money to buy it. And the church women gave her a lot of things. They were always giving her something."

"I heard she couldn't count."

"No, she didn't even know the difference between a penny, nickel, dime or quarter. She used to hide her money in her room."

"Why would she hide it? Was she afraid someone would steal it?"

"I don't know. I just know she hid it. Sort of like a squirrel hiding nuts. She would come to the doorway of her room and whisper for me to come in. She would get some money out from under the rug or from wherever she had it and ask me if she had enough to buy something. I would tell her how much she had and if it was enough or not. Then my other aunt and uncle, Uncle Ben's brother and his wife, would take us to town. And, she would get me candy with whatever was left over.

"Yes, I remember her standing in that doorway, saying, *psst, psst.* And, she would motion me to come in like it was a big secret. And, she would pull her money out and I would say, this is a quarter, this is a dollar, well whatever she had. Of course, things didn't cost so much back then. Sometimes we would just walk down to the local store and get some baking powder and whatever was left, she'd say now, you pick out some candy for yourself. No matter where we went, she always bought me candy."

"Sounds like all this was an excuse to get you candy."

"Might have been. Sally was generous to a fault, always giving people little gifts. I saved a cup she gave me. It's an old tin cup she used to drink out of. Do you want to see it?"

"Sure," Michelle said.

Patty returned with the cup. It looked thin from years of use. "Do you care if I take a picture?"

"Go ahead."

Michelle snapped a photo with her iPhone.

"Do you remember anything else?"

"I remember everyone sat around and watched television in the dark. And at eight o'clock sharp, it was turned off, and we all went to bed."

"Okay, so Sally was treated well by Ben and Ted."

"Oh, Uncle Ben treated her well, but now Ted was a different story."

"What do you mean?"

"Oh, he was hateful. Or, at least I thought so. I think part of it was he had come back from the army and was so strict. But then, I was a child."

"You said you are seventy-one, now?" Michelle got out

her iPhone and opened her calculator app. "I'm sorry. It is so sad I have to use this instead of doing it in my head. I guess it's like Sally not knowing how to count." Michelle tapped some numbers in. "So, you would have been eight years old around 1954."

"I reckon that's right."

"I'm trying to get the time frame in my mind. Ted was born in 1905. So, he would be around forty-nine when you were there. Could do that one in my head. But, not this one." Michelle tapped more numbers in. "Okay, so Ben was born in 1882 according to census reports. He would have been seventy-two. I don't know why, but I was thinking they were closer in age until now."

"Ben was Ted's uncle. Sally raised him from a baby."

"She did? Yes, I remember that being in my grandma's journal, now."

"Yes. His mama left him on the doorstep in nothing but a diaper."

"Actually, Sally did say something about this to my grandma."

"Yeah, she left him and took off to Massachusetts, I think. I think it was Massachusetts. Somewhere up north. His mother wrote. I would read her letters to Sally."

"She was writing to Sally?"

"Yes. And, I would write back what Sally wanted to say. She sent me a small cross for reading them to her. I still have it, somewhere back in my jewelry box."

"You say Ted was hateful to Sally?"

"It was that woman."

"The one he was having an affair with?"

"Yes. You know about that?"

"Yes. I visited a Bonzo woman who told me. This was several years back. Was this the woman, the one he was having an affair with, the one who told Ted that Sally should be put in the nursing home?"

"Yeah. Ben would have never had stood for it if he had lived. It was greed. She wanted the land. As soon as Sally moved into the nursing home, she practically shoveled her room out. Threw everything away. Even Sally's doll."

"Her doll?"

"Yes, Sally had a doll she really loved. The woman moved in with Ted. Wasn't long until she moved Ted out. He died broke from what I understand."

"He died in Tennessee in a veteran's home, I think. I have it written down somewhere," Michelle said.

"My mommy went to see Sally in the nursing home. Said Sally begged her to take her back home."

"I'm sure a lot do."

"Oh," Mrs. Parson covered her mouth with her hand. "I didn't mean. I'm sorry. When we talked on the phone you said your grandma took care of Sally in the nursing home."

"Yes, my grandma loved Sally. She is the reason I'm doing this. But then, Grandma didn't really get to know Sally until the last months of her life. She retired from the nursing home but kept going back to visit her. And then, she couldn't visit her much after my grandpa got ill. I think she regretted not getting to go to her funeral."

"I'm sure Sally loved her. I think she loved most people."

"What about segregation?"

"At the time I was too young to know anything about it."

"Do you think Sally sat anywhere she wanted at church?"

"Oh, yeah. I'm sure she did. Like I said, the people there were really good to her."

"Do you think she ever voted?"

"Oh, no," Patty said, shaking her head. "I doubt it. Sally didn't go out that much. I doubt if she was even interested in voting."

"My grandma said in her journals that Sally refused to be segregated in the nursing home."

"Oh, she rode right up front on the bus. My mommy told me that. The bus driver told her to move to the back and she refused, claiming she was as white as they were."

Michelle's mouth dropped. "Seriously?"

"Oh, yeah. She sat right up front."

"And the bus driver didn't do anything?"

"No, I guess because she was old. Well, he told her to move to the back, but she flat out refused. Wouldn't budge. She rode the bus quite a bit. After a while I guess he didn't mess with her. No, my mommy said she always sat wherever she wanted."

"Mrs. Parson, Patty, thank you so much." Michelle got up and shook Patty's hand. "I will make sure you have a copy of this when it's finished."

"I look forward to it."

Michelle drove back, ecstatic with this new information about Sally.

"Mom, can you imagine? I mean Rosa Parks sat in the black section. She was asked to move further back to give her seat to a white person. Sally plopped herself right down in the white section and refused to move. What if that bus driver had called the police? We might be celebrating Sally's life now instead of Rosa Parks' life?"

Michelle's mom smiled. "This is quite a project that you and Grandma took on."

"Yeah, I feel as if she is watching over the whole show."

"I think she is. You're like her, you know."

"Like Sally or like Grandma?"

"Maybe a little of both, since we're all related, but I meant like Grandmother Alice. When she took something on, she didn't want to let it go. And, she cared so much for people. I couldn't have done what she did, caring for all those old people." Her mom smiled. "How are you coming with the writing?" her mom asked.

"I was basically finished before I stumbled across this new

information. But, I wrote way past my allotted time last night. I'm so close."

"And Michael doesn't mind?"

"No, he is as enthusiastic as I am. And, he wants me to get finished." Michelle smiled. "He has been fantastic about this whole thing. And, I've been reading parts to Alice before her bedtime."

Her mother raised her eyebrows. "Are you sure you should be reading this to Alice? Some of the things you told me are not something for young ears."

"I only read the most G rated parts. And, I've made up little stories about Sally. I call them Sally Shorts. There is one about her trading the eggs. And, I tell her Sally was one of her ancestors. She really likes hearing the stories. We've been putting them in a notebook, and Alice has been drawing pictures to go along with the stories."

"You have made this into a family project."

"Yes. But, what I wanted to ask you about is the nursing home where Grandma worked. What was it like? I don't know why I never thought to ask about it before. I looked it up online and couldn't find anything."

"It's not in operation anymore, or at least not like that. It was called Carrigan Benevolent Care Center when your Grandmother Alice worked there. There was an infirmary. That was probably where Sally was. That was the part Grandmother Alice worked in. The people who were there couldn't afford to pay. And your Grandmother Alice practically worked for nothing, but then Grandfather John was a lawyer, and they didn't need the money, which was a good thing. There was the main building. It connected to a cafeteria. There were other buildings that surrounded it. That's where the poor people stayed."

"Poor people?"

"Yes, they called it a poor house. They went there to stay

and learn a trade. And, they helped at the center. It was more than two hundred acres at one time. The ones who were able raised all the food and took care of the livestock."

"Could some have been orderlies?"

"More than likely. If you were able-bodied and lived there, you worked in some capacity."

"I wondered because Grandma mentioned a good-looking orderly named Max. I think it was Max. Or Mac. I'll have to look it up when I get back home. I wrote briefly about him. And, I think he was Latino."

"He probably stayed in one of the buildings. We have a little time before Alice gets out of school. Do you want me to show you where it is?"

"It's still standing? This is so strange. I don't know why I didn't think to ask about this before?"

"You weren't born yet for one thing—when your Grand-mother Alice worked there. And, you were off at school and then not living here, and you had your daughter. Life gets in the way. But it's a community center now and senior citizen apartments. It's out past the cemetery and the animal shelter."

"I know the building you're talking about. I just thought it was a senior citizen's home."

"It is. But, it was also once the Carrigan Benevolent Care Center, and it was where you Grandmother Alice worked for thirty years."

"I'll drive. My camera's in the car. I'll take some pictures. And then, we'll swing by the school and pick up Alice."

"This is Sally's grave?" Alice asked.

"Yes, sweetheart. Do you want to put the book on her grave?"

"Yes, Mommy."

"No. Don't take it out of the plastic. We don't want it to get wet. That's a good girl. Now, we'll go visit your great grandma's grave and do the same thing."

"The one I was named after?"

"Yes."

"Okay, Mommy. And then ice cream?"

"And then ice cream."

"Mommy, can they read the books if they are on their graves?"

Michelle bent down and hugged Alice. "I think they've already read them from up in heaven."

AFTERWORD

This journey started when I was eight. It was my aunt who first mentioned Sally. A slave? What connection did my family have to slaves? I didn't even know slavery had existed on my small piece of earth. I begged my aunt to tell me about Sally and Nell, the two women she called Nigger Sal and Nigger Nell, sisters. Or, could I have heard it wrong? I found out many years later that calling the two, *sisters,* was a polite way to avoid acknowledging some shameful happening—a way of protecting young ears.

It was the summer of 1961. I sat in the backseat of a car with the windows rolled down—no air conditioning. My father and uncle sat up front, complaining about the heat. When they weren't talking about the weather, their conversation drifted to farming, the Bonzos, or Bunzos, as they referred to them, and Sally. I never understood why old people cared so much about the weather until now. I thought them old at the time. At the time of the trip, my dad was in his late thirties, and my uncle, somewhere in his forties.

We were on our way to the Bonzo's house, where Sally lived. Maybe my many questions about Sally, to the point of nagging, was what prompted them to take this road trip with me in the back seat.

After more than an hour on the country back roads, a good deal of them gravel, we turned onto the dirt driveway of the Bonzo's house. It was a modest, white clapboard house with a wagon load of watermelons sitting under a tree on the front lawn.

We emerged from the car to be greeted by two men in denim overalls. I, the invisible small child, tagged behind the four men. It seemed like eons as they wandered around outside, talking farm stuff, pointing to this or that. All I cared about was seeing Sally. Finally, we meandered over to a set of steps on the side of the house. My dad asked while climbing the steps, "How old is Sally?"

Ben turned and said, "We don't know for sure, but she was a grown woman rocking me when I was a baby. We figure her to be one-hundred-three."

Butterflies were in my stomach as we entered through a screen door leading into a kitchen. The four men in front of me parted, like Moses parting the Red Sea.

There she was, a piece of history. Meeting her was like getting to go back in time in *Mr. Peabody's Way Back Machine*, one of my favorite cartoons. Time froze in that instant. The scene was a reversal of *The Wizard of Oz*. I came from outside from bright sunlight and rich hues of color into a dim kitchen where the only light that shone was the figure of Sally, a small, frail woman stooped over, emanating a glow that cast all that surrounded her in shadow.

She wore a cotton, blue-checked dress, coming well below her knees, almost meeting her thick rolled white socks. She wore pink, battered house shoes. In the midst of summer, in the hot weather, the other adults in the room were all so keen on complaining about, she wore an off white sweater, unbuttoned, with the sleeves pushed up to just below her elbows. And there was the white apron, something that was always a part of her, except on Sundays, something I was told later.

A metal bucket of sudsy water sat on the floor beside her. Bent over, she pushed a mop along the floor. She stopped and raised her head to look at us. Strands of white, partly curled, partly frizzed hair fell to the side of her ashen face as she smiled and acknowledged us. Time was suspended as our eyes met, and our souls touched. She lowered her head once again and went on with her work.

This touching of souls, although pushed aside for a good part of my life, was to remain with me. It was one of those moments of divine seed planting that would lay dormant, but because of its divine nature, blossom in later years.

Her wrinkled face possessed a tired beauty. This small wisp of a woman, chiseled down by time, held the mystery of the ages for me. Others content to relish in the logical and pragmatic side of life would not be blinded by the same aura that reached out to me that day. Sally was an anomaly to me, a pivotal point in my life. Yet, I had no idea as to why at the time. I was only eight. How could I have known?

So, I had met Sally, or rather saw Sally at close range, and life went on. It was several years later that Sally struck a chord with me again. The news came that Sally was put in a rest home. I heard my family talking about how she refused to sit in the back with the black people. She claimed she was white. I thought this meant she refused to sit in the back of the rest home with the blacks. It wasn't until I talked to Patty Carver Parson in 2017 that I realized it was the back of the bus she refused to move to. Sat right up front with the white people, saying she, herself, was white. Patty stayed with Sally one whole summer when she was eight years old. She told me Sally liked to smoke a corncob pipe and always asked her if she wanted to smoke with her.

In 1969, I remember hearing that Sally died. It resonated with me; however, I was sixteen. A lot is happening in your life at sixteen. Boys, mainly.

The memory of Sally faded once again. It wasn't until 2008 that the memory re-emerged. I was at a crossroads in life, retiring from one job, and doing mostly volunteer work. I wanted to do something that was totally mine but didn't know what. We were cleaning out a bookshelf and my husband discovered some poems I had written in high school. He said, "Why don't you write?"

I replied, "What do I have to write about?" It was later while strolling out in nature, more than likely on some of the same paths that Sally walked, the scene that had lain dormant so long in my mind became unlocked. "I'll write about Sally," I said out loud, to the squirrels, to the trees, to my dog Barney, walking alongside me.

Easier said than done. As far as writing went, other than college term papers, those poems written back in high school were the last thing I had written. And, I was to find that getting information on Sally was no easy matter. By this time, everyone who had told me about Sally in the past, other than my father, were all dead.

After several strokes, my father's memory wasn't as sharp as it used to be. He did remember Martha, saying everyone called her Aunt Marthie. He was also the one who told me Sally was afraid of black people and related the story that Ben repeated so often about the black man coming to the farm and asking in front of Sally where he might find a wife, to which Ben replied, "I don't know, but you might ask this lady here." My dad laughed as he told how Sally dropped her hoe and ran.

I made phone call after phone call. Some calls panned out. Others didn't. I was told she was a midwife. The same person told me there were slave graves and even the remains of slave cabins on some property near ours. We couldn't find any trace of them. I knocked on doors. I was like Columbo, following leads. My husband was my faithful sidekick in a lot of instances as well as my driver. It reminded me of the movie, *Driving Miss Daisy,* except my husband's not black and I sat up front.

I started out not even knowing what Sally's last name was. No one seemed to know. She was called Bunzo, Bonzo, and Erwin, as well as Nigger Sal.

I knew Sally was connected to the Erwins and the Bonzos. Someone gave me a copy of the Erwin family history. The Erwin family history began in Carter County with John Leander Erwin and Elizabeth Dickenson Erwin, who came from Virginia, probably in 1836. Sally was mentioned briefly in it.

Although most people were happy to talk about her, a few weren't. They couldn't understand why I was researching her. People that I knew, who I never dreamed of being prejudiced, clearly were.

I found a family of Bonzos who knew of Sally. We made an appointment to visit them on the weekend. My aunt and uncle knew of them and took us. These were a different branch although they stemmed from the same line. I went with anticipation that all my questions would be answered. I learned things from them I possibly shouldn't have. Some of it was denied later. I was thankful that my aunt and uncle were there. They verified my notes were correct.

I discovered that people open up much more in person than over the phone. Sometimes, they regret it later. This would be the case in another instance. One thing that wasn't denied was that there was a child out of wedlock and that there was a lot of speculation that one of the Bonzos was the father. One of the Bonzos told me this. Later, I would find other people thought it might have been one of the Erwins or the Burchetts who fathered the child. Some even told me Ben was Sally's son. I think that was idle gossip.

I visited one man right before his hundredth birthday. Someone was sick in Martha's family. Sally was purchased to help out. Purchased? After slavery was abolished? How could this be? He assured me money changed hands.

I later found out through a man in his nineties, called *Blink*, this was indeed the case. Martha rode on a horse into Boone Furnace when it closed to purchase Sally. Boone Furnace had a blowout on March 31, 1871 and closed shortly after. Ironically, March 31st was also the day on which Sally died. *Blink* told me there was a picture of Sally on the back of the horse with Martha. Oh, how I tried to find that picture or any picture of Sally. I had no luck with the horseback picture, but I did get lucky later on, as far as pictures went. Clarence Jones, aka Blink, also told me about Ben making moonshine.

My later research told me that Martha was married to Campbell Musick, who died young. They had traveled to Oklahoma for land, coming back disappointed. Martha's son, at age twelve, went back there with an uncle, and eventually became a sheriff. A descendant of the Musick family, a lady who was one hundred years old, told me, through her daughter, about the time the Oklahoma branch of the family came back to see Martha. She was only a child of seven but remembered it. It was 1922. Sally took her and all the other children to church at night.

On one day, my husband and I celebrated with champagne, when I found a Bonzo from the Ben and Ted line that said he knew Sally. He was a young boy at the time but remembered Sally fixing collard greens and churning butter. He said he had pictures. My hopes were so high. My husband and I were to travel for three hours to see him. He reneged. The rest of the champagne helped with the disappointment. I was later told by another relative he wasn't to be relied on. Maybe he had pictures. I'll never know.

My husband and I went to the Kentucky Gateway Center in Maysville. It was there we found Sally's obituary. I was elated at first. But, this is where the mystery began. This is where the two Sallys came into play.

It was in March of 2008 that we visited the infamous Erwin plantation where John Leander and Elizabeth Dickenson Erwin started their Kentucky farm. A lady who rented the house came to the door. She told us it had burned at one time. The fireplace was original. A gated cemetery was off to the side. It was there we saw the rocks marking slave graves. There were several. Two of them were more than likely the graves of Ib and Nell. And, like in the Erwin history report, the graves of John Leander and Elizabeth were not marked. One Erwin descendant later would deny they even existed, and that the family history began with Thomas Erwin. Not even the Knisley report or their names appearing on census reports could convince her they existed.

On my birthday, my husband took me to the Kentucky History Museum in Frankfort, Kentucky where I found the Jane Knisely report which held the bulk of information on the Dickensons and Erwins. There was a bad photocopy of a picture of an Erwin woman and a woman who was supposed to be Sally. Ironically, the lady who helped me at the museum was named Sally.

Jane Knisely wrote about the four slaves of Ib, Nell, Jacob, and Henry, saying that Nell had six fingers on each hand and six toes on each foot. In her report was a copy of the letter from John Brandon Erwin to his wife Susan during the Civil War. I included it—misspellings and all. The parts of the Knisley report and obituaries I've included in the book are also copied as is.

Most said Sally was demure—quiet. Some knew her from

church. One man worked in his father's store. Sally brought eggs to trade for other things. Even if they had plenty of eggs, they always took them and gave her what she needed. One woman remembered Sally outside over a fire, canning. Another remembered she did laundry on the back porch. Another one said she didn't think she wore shoes that fit, thinking what she wore was hand-me-downs.

I came across Karl Combs who knew Sally from church when he was a young man. He thought so much of her that he included her in a passage in a book he wrote, *Isle of Regret*, which he was kind enough to send to me along with a copy of Sally's death certificate. I tracked down the doctor who signed the death certificate. He was a young doctor at the time. Unfortunately, he didn't remember Sally.

We hiked around our own area, crossing creeks, finding Erwin cemeteries. I was fortunate in that my neighbor, Jewell Holbrook, eighty-two, at the time, knew where the original Charles and Martha Bonzo house stood. We saw the ruins of a foundation and cellar. How could a big family occupy this small space? We have no idea of how the average family lived back then.

I was also told the Bonzo's were dirt poor before moving from Carter County. And more than likely they didn't even own a horse. Few people who lived in this area back then did. After seeing their land, I believed it. And, what kind of crops could they raise on this small crevice of land between two hills that almost went straight up?

It was April that I found someone on an ancestry site looking for information regarding her grandmother, Sally Barnes. I answered her query. She was looking for the Sallie Barnes born in 1878. But, she gave me information that led me to believe that there was a connection between her Sally and my Sally. Her own mother was named Nell. Another coincidence? This Nell had recently died leaving questions.

She never wanted to talk about the past according to her daughter.

After tying pieces of information together like Columbo would do, I gave her my theory. This was after talking to several other people and visiting the Lewis County Historical Society in Vanceburg. The people there were extremely helpful. I found the obituary for the Sallie Barnes who was born in 1878, according to the census. She had lived in Vanceburg and worked at the St. Charles Hotel. Was this Sally's daughter? At least that is what I concluded. However, her descendants claimed otherwise, even though I found circumstantial evidence linking them as mother/daughter. The great granddaughter, if indeed she was Sally's great granddaughter, didn't want to buy it. Still, we talked by phone on several occasions and became online friends. I will never know for sure.

One thing that came up over and over again was the silver mine. I would have never expected this to enter into Sally's story. There was talk that the Bonzos found silver, and that was how they had the money to leave and buy fertile farmland near the river. I was told by one Bonzo that Sally would always be well taken care of. You can see from this how I wove Sally finding the silver into the story. I asked my husband after leaving the Bonzo man's house if he got the impression that Sally was the one who found the silver. My husband replied that it sure sounded that way. There have even been people digging for silver in recent times of what would once have been Erwin land and the surrounding area. One person was particularly interested in looking for it around where the slave cabins had once stood. And, one of the Bonzo descendants came back to Carter County looking for it after hearing whispers about it in his family all his life.

When asking one lady about Sally, I was told the story about the black baby being thrown into the pig sty. Also, the story of the black man falling into the furnace was true. Was he pushed? It was widely rumored he was. As for it being Sally's father? Probably not, just some imaginative writing. I only knew that Sally was orphaned at a young age. I learned some truly horrible things as well as some truly lovely things.

One of those champagne moments was finding that a girl (well, none of us are girls now) I went to school with had a picture of Sally. She also had a photographic memory. The picture she had is the one I use on the front cover of the book.

Later, another lady, who found I was researching Sally, sent me a group picture of Sally with the Bonzos at an earlier family reunion.

I was to find out about the Carrigan Rest Home only in 2017. Its proper name was the Carrigan Benevolent Care Center. It took in poor people, young and old, with nowhere else to go. Most worked on the farm that was a part of the center. There was also an infirmary. This was more than likely where Sally was. It exists now under a different name and is housing for senior citizens. I was told there was no segregation at the center, but in my fictional account I write that there was.

I talked to so many helpful people, most of them in their eighties and nineties. I laid the research aside for nearly a decade. Of course, most of them had died by the time I came back to it in 2016. It was a fantastic experience getting to talk to them, and I miss it.

I would encourage everyone to listen to the stories their elders have to tell, write them down and record them before it's too late.

End note: My husband finished reading my first draft and asked me if I knew what his brother's middle name was? I had forgotten it was Dickenson. I had never connected the dots, but it turns out my husband's mother's line comes from the Dickensons who came from England. That branch ended up in Texas. So, in essence, when I wrote about Elizabeth Dickenson Erwin, I may have been writing about some of my husband's family. Also, it is so serendipitous that they settled in the area only a few miles from me, and that my husband moved here to be with me on my own family's farm. But then, life is full of synchronicity if we only pay attention.

PICTURES AND DOCUMENTS

It's with regret I can't include more pictures, but doing so makes the Kindle and ePub files enormous and printing costs larger, and I didn't want to pass that along to the reader, not to mention the downloading times for people like myself with slow internet service. For that reason I will be putting more pictures on my website for those interested in the research that went into Sally.

Perhaps I might hear from people who can share their own pictures of historical significance that relate to the book. It would be fantastic if more pictures of Sally would turn up, especially the picture of Sally on the back of the horse on that day she rode out of Boone Furnace with Martha. As for the picture of her in her coffin—I will pass on that one.

Some pictures that will be on my website are: Boone Furnace (including the rock that contains the remains of the black man that may or may not have been pushed into the furnace), Carrigan Benevolent Care Center, Campbell Musick, slave graves, Sally's last residence (the house I visited when I was young), and various grave photos of the Bonzos and Erwin, to name a few.

https://www.jschlenker.com/

Bonzo Group Picture - Martha, sitting, center, Sally in background

Boone Furnace

Group Picture of Bonzos and Sally. The last three on the top row are Ted, Ben and Bill Bonzo. Martha seated in front next to Sally. circa unknown

Sally's Grave, Greene Cemetery, St. Paul, Kentucky

BIBLIOGRAPHY

- Carter County Bicentennial Committee, Carter County History 1838 - 1976
- George Wolfford, Carter County, A Pictorial History, 1985, WWWCompany, Ashland, Kentucky Publishers
- Lewis County Herald, Vanceburg, Kentucky
- Knisely Report, The Kentucky Historical Society, Frankfort, KY

ACKNOWLEDGMENTS

Firstly, I thank my husband Chris who supports me whole-heartedly in this writing endeavor. He took me to see people, to historical research centers and libraries, hiked out in the woods with me looking for remnants of house foundations, and took over on my phone calls when my soft voice wasn't loud enough for those on the other end who were hard of hearing.

There are so many people, that honestly, I won't be able to remember or name them all.

Mary Martha Littleton was a great inspiration in writing this. She let me use her ancestry account and provided Erwin information.

Karl Combs provided Sally's death certificate and was greatly encouraging in this project.

Neal Salyers, a local historian and author, shared his research with me. We even visited Boone Furnace together and were enlightened about the history of Boone Furnace by Don Underwood. Many thanks to him.

Ernie and Mildred Bonzo welcomed us into their home and offered what they knew of Sally.

Rebecca Wells Parker provided a champagne moment when she gave me her picture of Sally, the one used on the cover, and confirmed there were two Sallys. That was an *aha* moment.

I visited Clarence "Blink" Jones, in his nineties, in a nursing home. He was the one who told me Martha rode in on a horse to get Sally from Boone Furnace. I changed the horse to a mule in the story.

I'm especially thankful to Mary Jane Knisley for her tireless research on the Erwins. I'm thankful to the Kentucky Historical Society in Frankfort, Kentucky, where I retrieved the report.

I'm thankful to The Gateway Museum in Maysville, Kentucky. It was there I obtained Sally's obituary.

The Lewis County Historical Society in Vanceburg, Kentucky was more than helpful in aiding me in my research on Sally. I especially thank Karen Killen and Janey Clark. They both spent time looking up articles for me, and we exchanged several emails. I paid them several visits.

A special thanks to Patty Carver Parson, the lady who stayed with Sally one summer. So many others—Truman Farris, Elmo Veach, Patricia Temple, James Gannon (provided the group picture of Bonzos and Sally), Jewell Holbrook, Dewight Ruark, James Buddy Galenstein, and Grace and Gene Knipp. This doesn't even begin to name all the people I talked to both on the phone and in person.

And, I want to thank my faithful beta readers. Brenda Ricker, Kim Daniels, and Barbara Chambers. Brenda always goes far beyond the call of duty for me. For *Sally*, I added four more, Elissa Strati, Vicki Goodwin, Kenneth Morris and Kelsey Agunmadu. And, thank you to my editor, Emerald Barnes. They have all been instrumental in guiding me and helping me to shape my rough draft into, hopefully, a finished product.

ABOUT THE AUTHOR

J. Schlenker, a late blooming author, lives with her husband, Chris, out in the splendid center of nowhere in the foothills of Appalachia in Kentucky where the only thing to disturb her writing is croaking frogs and the occasional sounds of hay being cut in the fields. Her first novel, *Jessica Lost Her Wobble*, published in December 2015, was selected as a finalist in the William Faulkner - William Wisdom Creative Writing Competition and won a Five Star Readers' Choice Award. It also was chosen as a Novel Tea Book Club selection. *The Color of Cold and Ice* is her second novel.

One of her short stories, *The Missing Butler*, the lead story in her third book, *The Missing Butler and Other Life Mysteries (A Collection of Short Stories)*, received honorable mention in the first round of the NYC Competition. This book also received a Five Stars Readers' Choice Award.

For more information:
https://www.jschlenker.com/
jschlenkerauthor@gmail.com

Made in the USA
Lexington, KY
08 November 2017